THE
UPPER WORLD

THE
UPPER WORLD

FEMI FADUGBA

HARPER TEEN
An Imprint of HarperCollinsPublishers

HarperTeen is an imprint of HarperCollins Publishers.

The Upper World
Copyright © 2021 by Femi Fadugba
www.epicreads.com

ISBN 978-0-06-307859-8

Typography by Sarah Nichole Kaufman
21 22 23 24 25   PC/LSCH   10 9 8 7 6 5 4 3 2 1
❖
First Edition

For Cam

Part I:

DISTANCE

To Esso,

Once upon a time, a group of prisoners lived in a cave.

For their whole lives, they'd knelt in cold dirt, facing stone, with chains wrapped around their necks so tightly they couldn't even turn around to see where the amber light in the cave was coming from.

So each day they watched shadows flicker and dance on the stone wall, lit up by that hidden light behind them. They studied the shadows, named them, prayed to them.

Then, one morning, one of the prisoners broke free. He turned toward that bright light shining at the far end of the cave and he stared at it in wonder, desperate to know where it came from, where it led.

His friends, still chained, warned him: "Stay, you fool! You don't know where you're going. You'll die if you roam too far!"

But he ignored them.

When he stepped outside the cave, nothing he saw—not the trees, lakes, animals, nor the sun—made sense to him. Energy flowed so freely out there, it almost felt . . . wrong. But over time, he got to grips with his new reality, finally realizing that his entire life, and all he'd ever known in the cave, had been a mere shadow of this bigger place.

A place he named the Upper World.

He sprinted back into the cave, excited to share the good news with his friends. But when he explained what he had seen in the Upper World, they mocked him, calling him insane. And when he offered to break them free from their chains, they threatened to kill him.

A real man named Socrates told that story over 2,300 years ago in Athens. Most people who heard it interpreted it as a whimsical fairy tale, a metaphor about how lonely it can feel to venture into the unknown. But what people overlook, my child, is that Socrates really believed in the Upper World. And that when he told people what he'd seen up there, he was executed.

1

ESSO

IT TAKES AN impressive mix of stupidity and bad luck to not be in a gang but still find yourself in the middle of a gang war. I'd managed it in less than a week. And that was before the time travel.

I knelt down, resting my elbows on the one corner of the mattress where the sheet hadn't peeled off. Tired and alone in my bedroom, I was desperate for heavenly backup. But I couldn't make the call between Jesus, his mum, Thor, Prophet Mohammed (and the big man he works for), that bald Asian dude in orange robes, Jesus's dad, Emperor Haile Selassie, my granddad's voodoo sculpture, Morgan Freeman, or that metal slab on the moon in the olden-day film *2001*. So, to be safe, I prayed to the whole team.

"Dear Holy Avengers," I pleaded into my interlaced fingers. "First off, please forgive me for being a prick on Monday. And for lying to Mum about what happened."

MONDAY (FOUR DAYS AGO)

Before Monday went off the rails, I actually learned something in class. (Was that how school was meant to feel all the time?)

Penny Hill Secondary sat on the border between Peckham and Brixton. That wasn't an issue in the forties, when they built it, but it became one once the mandem arrived. Now you had kids from two rival ends forced to spend seven hours a day with each other, and the rest of us expected to learn with that cross-borough beef stewing in the background.

Our classroom was arranged in four rows of eight desks. The ceiling hung a foot too low, making you feel like a chicken in a battery cage if you sat near the middle like me. Miss Purdy was head of PE and doubled as a maths teacher. She could teach, though, as in, she actually knew what she was talking about and actually gave a shit. Her class had the fewest fights and highest marks because of it. Even *my* assignments were coming back with the odd B these days. Maths had always held some appeal with me. The naïve part of me clung to the idea that one day I'd have a boatload of money and maths would have helped me get it.

I'd always just respected the fact that 2 + 2 = 4. I spent most days switching between my African home voice, my semi-roadman voice, my reading-out-loud-in-English-Lit-class voice, and the telephone voice I put on when I needed someone to come fix the router. I liked that all that stuff mattered less in maths class. The teacher could think I was a dickhead all she wanted, but 2 + 2 was still gonna equal 4.

What I couldn't have known sitting there that Monday morning was that the 3-sided shapes Miss Purdy was drawing on the whiteboard would end up opening my eyes to all 4 dimensions. In fact, if anyone had tried to warn me I'd be moving like a superhero psychic by the end of the week, I'd have told them they were on crack, then shown them the abandoned flat in Lewisham where they could meet some like-minded people.

"Today, we're revising the Pythagorean theorem," Purdy said, circling an equation she'd just written on the board. "And we'll be using it to figure out the length of the longest side of the triangle."

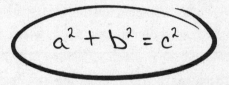

$$a^2 + b^2 = c^2$$

Purdy waited, arms folded, for the class to quiet down.

"Shhhhhhhhh!" Nadia said, whipping her neck round to glare at two girls chatting behind her.

Nadia wasn't a teacher's pet by any stretch, and she didn't always care *that* much about class. But we had our GCSE mocks coming up—the biggest exams of our teenage lives so far—and she clearly wasn't about to get dragged down by kids who didn't care at all.

Meanwhile, I was staring off in the distance, doing the pouted-lip serious stare I'd practiced in the mirror that morning. Nadia's eyes had to swing past me on their way back to the whiteboard, and I wanted to leave the best impression possible.

No cap: it was straight-up *embarrassing* how often I did stuff like that for her. I probably spent 60 to 70% of each class either: a) staring creepily at the back of her head; b) glancing at her in my periphery; or c) pouting and hoping she'd pay attention to me, which I never got to confirm either way since I'd always be staring off into the distance like an aftershave model.

Purdy turned to the board with two different-colored markers in hand. "To make this feel a bit real, I'll use a practical example. Let's say you're walking through Burgess Park. You start all the way down here at the south gate and need to get up to the top by Old Kent Road. There are basically two different paths you can take: the first path, up the side and along the top, is what you cool kids might call a 'long-ting.'"

She waited for someone to laugh . . . *Anyone*. After a long, cold dose of silence, she moved on. "Tough Monday. So, taking the long path means staying on the pavement and going *all* the way up one side, then *all* the way across the top. But the alternative, shorter route just cuts diagonally across the grass."

After she stepped away from the board, we could see that she'd written numbers next to two sides of a triangle, but left a question mark next to the longest edge. A collective sigh went around the room as we realized she was going to strip-search one of us for the answer.

"Let's start with the shortest edge of the triangle. Can anyone tell me what number I get when I take the number 3 and square it?"

Nadia's hand went up, the only needle you could spot in

the haystack. Purdy ignored it—she had to give the rest of us a chance once in a while, after all—and turned to someone paying much less attention.

"Rob, what is 3 squared?"

You'd have thought Miss Purdy was made of glass by how Rob looked straight through her.

Please tell me he knows that 3 x 3 = 9, I said to myself. Along with Kato, Rob was my best friend, and I knew maths wasn't really his thing. To be honest, not much at school was Rob's thing. But ask him the difference between UK drill, NY drill, and Chicago drill, and he turned into Einstein. Or tell him about a story you heard on the evening news and watch him find an ingenious way to connect it back to the Illuminati and their plot to take down Blacks, Browns, and Eastern Europeans. He was Polish as well. But knowing that didn't really tell you much about him.

Kato, sitting on Rob's other side, whispered to him, "Afghanistan! The answer's Afghanistan—trust me."

"Afghanistan," Rob repeated, showing his proudest face to Purdy.

She must have blinked three or four times in confusion. His response was so off it robbed her of words, and she had no choice but to shut her jaw and look away.

Kato was in pieces, using his sleeves to wipe at the tears of joy collecting on the ledges of his eyes. Everything in life was hilarious to that boy. Probably because everything in life came so easily to him.

Rob glared at him, kissing his teeth till the spit ran out. I sometimes worried that if I ever had to leave school for more than a week, I'd come back and find our fragile friendship cracked into three pieces. But ask anyone else at Penny Hill, and they'd swear we were unbreakable—the happy package known as "Kato, Esso, and Rob." Even when only one of us fucked up, all three of us got in trouble for it. "Kato, Esso, and Rob did it!" As if those were the three names printed on my passport.

"Esso?" Purdy turned to me with desperation in her eyes.

"You just take the number and multiply it by itself, innit?" I replied. I didn't mean for my answer to come out sounding like a question but couldn't help my voice squeaking at the end. She tilted her head forward, waiting for me to land. "So, it's just 3 times 3, which is 9," I added.

She made me go through each step, releasing me only once I'd given her equation the TLC she felt it deserved. "So, c—the long edge—is equal to 5," I finally answered.

I'd calculated the final number in my head a few seconds early, and while she wrote it all out on the board, I debated whether to ask my follow-up question.

Miss Purdy had told us at the start of the class that Pythagoras came up with his famous equation 2,500 years ago. *2,500 years ago!* I'm pretty sure that was before paper was even invented. *But how?*

Problem was, regardless of what adults said, there *was* such a thing as a rubbish question. In fact, most questions I asked earned me that what-a-rubbish-question look from them. At school, a teacher could cuss me for bringing up a topic that wasn't on the curriculum. And at home, I'd get the same harsh treatment from my mum for asking a question about Dad. Any sentence starting with "why" or "how" is scary to *someone*.

But once a question took shape in my head I had trouble leaving the hole empty. It helped that Miss Purdy was still smiling at me, and that she usually took it well when the mid-rowers raised their hands. *Fuck it*, I thought silently, clearing my throat in preparation. *What's the worst that could happen?*

"How did Pythagoras come up with that equation in the first place?" I did my best to sound detached when, in fact, the missing answer was a crater that doubled in size every second.

Then came a flick to my ear. Fast and crisp, but light. *Was that ... a ball of paper?*

"Neeeeeeeeek!" Kato hollered. I turned to see him circling his fingers over his eyes like glasses.

Rob laughed as well, followed by the back half of the class. *I need new mates*, I decided. But then Nadia turned to me with an expression that was equal bits surprised and impressed—a look that made all the embarrassment dissolve. I put my R&B pout back on just in time.

Miss Purdy spent the next five minutes showing us how Pythagoras had turned his hunch about triangles into a mathematical law that would have to be obeyed for the rest of eternity, everywhere in the universe.

The second Purdy finished explaining, I felt like a rusty padlock sprang open in my head.[1] And for only the second or

---

[1] *See Appendix I on p. 355.*

third time in my life, I felt like maybe—just *maybe*—I might live in a world where things made sense.

When she turned her back, I punched "Pythagoras" into Google on my phone. Turns out, like most of the sharp ones, my man was a nutter. According to the internets, he ran some cult where everyone swore never to eat black beans or piss in the direction of the sun. Oh, and they all worshipped the number 10 and believed that if you lifted the bonnet off what we all see as reality, you'd find nothing but maths under the hood— the language the gods wrote the universe in. Apparently.

There were also "related" links to a few of his stans—one guy called Plato, another Socrates—that I didn't bother clicking. It was all getting a bit too trippy, so I put my phone away, knowing I was lucky I hadn't been spotted by Purdy. I was in her good books and had no intention of leaving them.

And then Gideon Ahenkroh walked in.

Even with his cap pulled down, you could just about make out Gideon's eyes as they traced the floor on the walk to his seat. Like every other boy at Penny Hill, he hung his trousers as low around his thighs as he could. Most girls did the same with their skirts, just pulled in the opposite direction.

Rob, Kato, and I exchanged looks. Looks that said, *I feel it too. Something's off. Something hilarious is about to happen.* We turned back to make sure we didn't miss out.

"Gideon, you're late. Again," Miss Purdy said. "Also, no hats in class. Take it off and sit down unless you want to go to the headmaster's office. *Again.*"

When Gideon lifted his cap, all thirty-one of us flared up in laughter. There were penny-sized patches of hair missing all over his scalp, each one glistening like he'd dabbed glitter into his hair oil. D, who sat behind Gideon, had the best view of the zigzags coastlining the back of his neck.

If the phrase "still waters run deep" could be embodied in a single roadman, that roadman was D. D didn't chase clout, clout chased him. The few times he spoke up, people either laughed, nodded in agreement, or ran for safety. Everyone in South London generally agreed that D and his little brother, Bloodshed—both part of a Brixton gang called T.A.S.—were the least *light-skinned* light-skinned brothers ever made. It was like someone had convinced Young M.A to have babies with Fredo, then got a scientist to delete any traces of Chris Brown from their DNA. D was the stockier of the two brothers, but still clipped six foot and could fill any room sitting down.

"Blood, that haircut is *poor*," D said. "Just holla at man if you want me to send the mandem to your barber's house. No one gets to boy you like that, except me." He sank in his chair, his gold tooth glistening as he laughed at his own joke. After a short pause, we all laughed as well—it was less trouble that way.

An idea for a follow-up joke popped into my head. Part of me thought, *No, Esso. Don't be a prick. Gideon's already having a bad morning. Just allow him and move on.* I was staring at the back of Nadia's head, knowing she'd be telling me the same. But the remaining 99% of me was shouting, *Go on, son. Give the people what they want. This is God's plan.*

"His mum cut it, innit," I said. "She knows she's not getting any, so she wants to make sure Gideon doesn't either." A much louder rumble of laughter went around the classroom. I was pushing my luck with that joke, considering how rusty my fade and twists were looking, but even D nodded in appreciation. *Mission accomplished.*

Until year nine, I'd never appreciated how much funnier having power made you. I was only a few feet down from the top of the pole at Penny Hill, which meant people were supposed to laugh at my jokes now, *especially* if they were funny.

Nadia, meanwhile, wasn't laughing at all. I should have copped some of her disapproval, but instead, she aimed it all at D, staring at him with eyes that could break vibranium. He blew a kiss back with a smile.

It always cracked me up how much those two hated each other. I remembered the day D's phone was going off in class and Nadia, seeing Miss Purdy couldn't do anything about it, walked over to D's desk, snatched his iPhone, and chucked it out of the first-floor window. She even stood by to watch it skip across the concrete like a pebble on water. D felt like he had something over everyone, and Nadia felt like she owed nothing to no one. So yeah—milk and orange juice.

It turned out Nadia wasn't the only one not amused. Miss Purdy's arms were crossed, and Gideon's head was still sunk into his chest. *Poor lad*, I thought, surprised at how much I was regretting the joke.

But Gideon Ahenkroh had different plans for how things were going to end. He shot up from his seat, and a split second later, I felt a hard *thump* against my forehead. I looked down to see a white-and-orange glue stick rolling on the floor.

Did Gideon really just chuck a glue stick at my head?

I hopped out my seat and chased him three whole laps around the classroom. Gideon faked a left, then stepped off in the other direction. By the time I pivoted back, he was out the door.

"It's on sight, fam!" I shouted into the corridor after him. For some reason, my tough talk always came out high-pitched and weirdly kinda American in the heat of the moment. "What you running for? Come and let's do this, bro!"

I could hear Rob and Kato cackling behind me. They knew better than anyone that I wouldn't do shit to Gideon. I was built like a pencil; half the year sevens at Penny Hill could've mashed me up.

I turned back to Miss Purdy, whose face was neon pink.

"Get back in here and *sit* down, Esso! Right now!"

That's how I got my first demerit.

That's how the maddest week of my life began.

WEDNESDAY (TWO DAYS AGO)

Penny Hill was too cheap to buy anything but second-class stamps. So the minute I got my demerit on Monday, I knew the letter wasn't getting home till Wednesday morning, earliest.

When Wednesday morning finally came, I watched the envelope slide through the flap in our front door and snatched it before it even scraped the floor. I didn't bother opening it, just wedged it in the bottom of the garbage skip outside and kept moving. *Mission accomplished.*

Well, sort of. The postman had arrived an hour late, which meant I was an hour late for school.

That's how I got my second demerit.

I wasn't shook this time either, though. I had a system: Penny Hill would send the demerit letter on Wednesday afternoon, and it would arrive home on Friday morning. Hopefully, the postman would be on point next time and arrive *before* I had to leave for school. Even if he didn't, Mum worked nights that end of the week, so I could run home during lunch break and snatch it before she was up.

Mum and I were getting on quite well these days. She'd started opening up about the pranks she pulled when she was my age, and it was cool to see her goofier side. Better still, she trusted me to keep the flat tidy during the day, and double-locked at night, and had stopped asking questions when I came home late on weekends. Why mess that up? Especially since I'd already done the maths on the delivery timing and calculated there was zero risk of her finding out.

When Wednesday evening swung round, I decided to celebrate my newfound invincibility by going shopping in West End with Spark. His new Air Maxes were *sick*. Come to think of it, I couldn't remember the last time I'd seen Spark in an old

pair of Nikes or wearing anything but a full-body black tracksuit—all-year road uniform.

Spark was handing the size-eight trainers he'd just tried on
to the cashier at NikeTown, who promptly rang up his 160-
quid bill. Spark produced a card from his bottoms, which, even
after he pulled them up, were still too baggy for his short legs.

After the fifth card and eighth attempt, the card reader
gave up. It couldn't have been easy for Spark to keep all those
PINs in his head, especially since most of them weren't his.

The cashier chuckled while turning to me. "It looks like
you might have to bail out your little mate here."

As soon as he said the word "little," my jaw dropped.

Then my heart sped up.

Spark was my guy. And a nice guy, at least to me. He and I
had lived on the same block since we were six, so I knew him
well. Well enough that if Mum hadn't banned me from hanging out with him so many times, we'd be cousins by now. I'd
heard this saying once, about how we all carry around a bucket
on our heads, and every day, the people around us, whether
they know it or not, pile their shit into it. Most of us are born
with deep, wide buckets, which means even when we do lose
our tempers, things don't ever get too messy. But then you had
a kid like Kyle "Spark" Redmond, who, instead of a bucket, was
born with a teaspoon.

I only hung out with him once every couple months, and
never this far from our ends, and now I remembered why.

Spark grabbed the open box out of the cashier's hands and

hurled it to the far end of the shop. I moved in quickly, knowing I had to wrestle him away from the counter and out of
there before he ruined the night for both of us.

By the time we reached Tottenham Court Road, 15 of Spark's
mates had joined us, each wrapped head to toe in black, clog-
ging up the already crowded pavement. Spark had told me
before we went into NikeTown that he had a "few friends" coming, but he hadn't told me he'd ordered the whole batch. And
they were all Peckham yutes—East Peckham, to be precise,
an even rowdier group than the T.A.S. guys D rolled with. I'd
nodded heads at a few of them over the years but clearly hadn't
left a strong enough impression for any of them to remember
my name. The one with crossed eyes and a plaster on his chin
wouldn't stop staring at me, like *I* was the one who'd crashed
the party. I nudged Spark, who whispered a few words to him
and got him to go back to ignoring me like the rest of them.

People who aren't from ends tend to view it in one of two
ways. On one side, you have the exaggerators. The ones who
make it seem like every time you step out of Brixton station,
you're dodging machine-gun fire. But I knew plenty of people
who'd lived in South London their whole life and never seen a
crime happen. In fact, you were more likely to find guys holding Bibles, diplomas, or bags of plantains than weapons—the
main reason Mum had moved here in the first place. But at
the other extreme, you have the people who see UK gang-
sters as way less serious than the guys they see in American

rap videos. Maybe it's because the guys doing the killing here are 15-year-old boys in trackies (as if muscles and maturity stop bullets and blades). Or maybe it's because kids here prefer using knives over guns (and people forget what it takes to get within hugging distance of a kid and then slice his life away). Or maybe they just fall into that trap of believing that no one born with an English accent could move vicious (despite everything British history should've taught us).

Regardless of who was right, the rules for survival were simple: don't hang with roadman. Or, if you were like me and had to, since you grew up with them and occasionally found yourself on a high street with them: know exactly what qualifies as a violation and don't violate.

I couldn't decide where I stood on Spark and his boys. Part of me only saw wasted potential. But the other part saw precious gemstones with histories so rare and raw that any time one of them posted a song online, thousands of kids in Lancashire logged on to listen. Most of the kids walking the streets that night had unpopped spots on their foreheads and inches still to grow. And yet between them, they'd probably sold more hard stuff in Peckham that week than Superdrug managed in a year. They weren't boys; they weren't even men. They were road legends.

Each one had a story that walked with him: a detention order they just beat; a traphouse they just robbed; a shout-out on the evening news. The world had sent them to the scrapyard years ago, not realizing that with all that rusted metal around, someone would eventually figure out how to make a spear, then a cannon, then a fortress. And I had to admit, being in the fort with that group of soldiers, some of the hardest in London, felt good. Safe and dangerous at the same damn time.

Still, I should have come up with an excuse to leave right there and then. I should have paused and thought about all the ways sticking around could mash up my night, my week, my life. I should have jumped on the number 12 bus rolling past and rid it all the way home.

But I didn't. Because walking down that road with all that smoke, all I could think about, all I cared about, was Spark not thinking I was a neek. Even when we were young—kicking his deflated football against the car park wall—nothing had mattered more. And like every other guy out that night, I knew Spark would die for me, not needing a please or a thank-you. It didn't matter that he was the shortest and softest-faced out of the lot of us; I stayed because Spark, for all his faults, was the kind of guy you wanted to stay for.

"Bro, once Finn learns how to use the Force, my man is turning straight to the dark side. No long ting." The voice came from the front of the mob.

The kid next to him hollered: "Man like Boyega wanted to go full road on *Star Wars*."

"Blood, imagine that?" the first one replied, a smile beaming on his face. "Man using the Force to pull chicken wings off people's plates at Cantor's."

Half the crowd started giggling, and the next kid jumped

in, "Jedi-mind-trickin' girls into giving out their numbers."

Then the next. "Using his lightsaber to splash man from the whip."

"That film would be a mad one, still. Man would queue up for that one," said the one who'd kicked off the conversation. His smile faded as he came to a hard stop, whipping his arm across the chest of the kid next to him. "I seen that bredda before, you know." He squinted a few seconds longer, pointing in the distance. "That's Bloodshed—the T.A.S. yute. Him and that paigon boy Vex did up my young G the other day."

The kid blasting music through his mini-speaker turned it down as a tall figure swung through the rotating doors at McDonald's. Skinny. Light-skinned.

Please don't let that be Bloodshed, I prayed.

Bloodshed: the kind of nickname you laughed at—until you found out how he'd got it.

As we walked closer, the unmistakable tats on his fingers came into view. We all watched Bloodshed's eyes widen in panic.

Eeesh, I thought. *Think, Esso. Think!* I scrolled through the options in my head. I could run away. But then I'd have to live with the whispers and disgusted looks that would follow me every time I stepped outside. Or I could drift to the back of the crowd, crouch, and pray that logic, compassion, or some miracle would stop these guys from doing whatever they were about to do.

Or I could lie, was my final, desperate thought.

"Nah, I don't think that's him, you know," I said, dropping my voice a couple levels. "We should go back toward Leicester Square."

But they all pressed forward like my words were nothing more than a pat on the back. It was easy for them. They wouldn't have to face D in class the next morning and explain why we'd rushed his little brother. They were built for this. I wasn't. I had no war scars, no gang stripes, and no interest in trappin' at the speed of light for the rest of my life.

"What!" the first person in our group shouted when he reached Bloodshed. Then everyone else in the group started barking the same thing.

"What!"

"What!!"

"What!!!"

The kid on my right shaped his fingers into a logo he knew Bloodshed would recognize. And Bloodshed, who stood half a foot above us, looked like a greyhound trapped in a kennel of starved pit bulls. He was the kind of kid who was mad enough to run into a fight one-up against five. But not fifteen.

Spark was at the back and had missed the start of the action. I could see the FOMO on his face. He sprinted full speed at the huddle and, when he reached the edge of it, instead of slowing down, dug his foot in and leapt off the ground, soaring over our heads with his arm stretched out toward Bloodshed.

The echo of the slap vibrated in my bones. A moment of silence then followed, as everyone nearby paid tribute to the level of disrespect Spark had just inflicted on his victim.

"What you sayin' now, pussio?" was Spark's first taunt.

"Pusssssssio!" someone else shouted, and threw a quick jab at Bloodshed's temple. Then another fist came crashing down on his body, which at this point was balled up on the ground. And another. Whatever circulation had been flowing in Bloodshed's face raced to the edge of the knuckle marks on his forehead, making the rest of his skin turn a sandy shade of green.

Spark's mate with the long dreads reached into his Gucci pouch. He smiled like a man who'd already made his decision, was happy with it, but out of courtesy was giving the universe a few seconds to come up with a reason Bloodshed shouldn't be wed in eternal matrimony with his cutter.

Thankfully, that reason came when three *stupidly* peng girls sauntered past. Their skin was glowing and showing, and you could tell they were from East by how hard they gelled down their edges.

"Cheeeeeeeeeez!" two boys shouted at the same time, which set off a chain reaction in the rest of the group. The taller two had bored faces on, but the shorter girl couldn't quite hide her toothy smile. Everyone turned their attention away from Bloodshed and toward them.

Everyone but me.

Which meant that when Bloodshed's eyes started darting around for an exit, they locked on mine. *Crap!*

I whipped my face away, praying he hadn't recognized me,

but knowing he had. How could he not? I'd literally been there when D first taught him how to ride a pedal bike. It dawned on me that there was nothing I could now do or say to make Bloodshed believe I was innocent. There was no special ID I could pull out to prove I was just a harmless bystander. No website I could share that showed I wasn't a registered gangster and that on every other day, I lived a moist, anonymous life. To Bloodshed, I was *there*, so I was now an opp as well. That's how it works: stay on the roads too long, or get seen with a roadman at the wrong time, and the scent never wears off.

Before I could process another thought, I heard the cracking of Bloodshed's knuckles against Spark's jaw, then watched as Bloodshed barged past the wall of yutes in front of him. His strides got longer and faster and longer again, wiping away any hopes the group had of chasing him. Spark had the most motivation out of all of us to run after him, but he was crouched on the concrete cradling his chin, mumbling about how Bloodshed and his guys were all dead men.

And soon Bloodshed would be saying the same thing about me.

2

I STEPPED FORWARD for the free kick, glancing at the keeper's muddy boots one last time, eyes low. She was fanning her gloves toward the far corner of the goal, her way of warning me she was prepared to dive the whole width of it if she needed to. But her feet told a different story: the true story. They were flat and spread wide apart, which meant the only plan she had was standing her ground.

It's easy to catch a crap liar. All you have to do is sit back and wait for them to fall into the traps they set for themselves. Catching a second-division liar takes a bit more skill, though. The key there is checking to see if they move differently when you pose (what should be) a perfectly innocent question. But the only way to catch a truly *great* liar (and I mean Champions League standard, the kind of liar who's so wedded to their lie that they've even convinced themselves) is by looking at their feet. Feet don't lie. On or off the pitch, it's one of those laws of nature that can't be lawyered around. No one bothers training their feet for deception because no one else is looking down there.

When I told my foster sister, Olivia, all this, she thought I was nonsense-ing her. But the next morning in class, she crouched to grab her stylus off the floor and noticed something curious: everyone's feet were aimed at the door. She said it was like their shoes were compass needles pointing to where they all secretly wanted to be. Then, on her walk home, she saw a police officer questioning some yute on Rye Lane, and realized the officer was standing with the same outstretched feet feds always stand with . . . which must be, she realized, how *all* feds stand, even plainclothes ones. Not the worst knowledge to have on ends. And to really drive it home, before bed that same night, a rerun of *Who Wants to Be a Billionaire* was on and, according to Olivia, whenever a contestant got a question right, they got Happy Feet. Not Dancing Feet, mind you (you have to think to dance), but Happy Feet: the messy kicks that come out of you without your permission.

"Twenty seconds, Rhia," Coach Gibbsy shouted, her violet whistle hanging limp on her lip.

The arctic wind blew the rain flat across the pitch, each drop stinging as it hit. Like at most training sessions, the stands were empty, but the pitch itself was overflowing with anticipation. Everyone was staring at me, wondering if I'd screw it up, hoping I would.

I was used to playing competitive games in training, just not used to them mattering. In a few short weeks, I'd know if

I'd made the squad for the knockout stages of the Academy Cup or not, which turned every remaining second of training into a chance to either impress or implode. And the free kick I was lining up to take? Possibly the difference between redemption and rotting with the reserves.

The spot was just outside the box, but at a horrid angle out to the left.

"Heat map," I said, scanning the graphics that popped up on my contact lenses. Visual analytics were a massive part of our training. Cantor's (the company that invented 3D-printed chicken, then somehow got a monopoly on the entire tech landscape) made the best AR simulators around and had just released a 32K update, which was looking scarily crisp. But the only area of the goal that the simulator had colored green was a speck in the top-left corner. With the wind stalking and ready to veer the ball off course, my strike would have to be beyond perfect. The lenses gave me so much more to analyze: the keeper's save percentages, wind vectors, strike gradients. But I knew they could only tell me so much.

"10 seconds left," Gibbsy said. She was in charge of both the girls' and boys' academy teams. She managed every training drill, dictated every play, ruled over every blade of grass. Most important, she alone would make the call on which five out of us 25 girls would enter the kingdom of SE Donnettes Seniors at the end of the year. Just *thinking* about the day I'd get to peel open a signed letter with *DONS F.C.* printed at the top—and the salary figure written below—was enough for me to grow another foot. A full-time contract meant not having to worry about uni, or exam results, or my extra weekly tutorials, the first one of which was happening in half an hour.

"Play me a precedent shot," I commanded. "Triple speed."

A video of a tall blonde with *Kennedy* on her jersey scrolled across my contact lenses. The footage was from an American league match a couple decades back and showed her taking a kick from the same spot as me. Watching her slot the goal that smoothly was comforting; the computer having to dig that far back in the archives to find an example—less so.

"Five seconds."

I knew what the team psychologist would be whispering in my ear right now if she could, some version of the self-help-faux-ga bollocks she always spouted: "Forget the pitch, Rhia. Forget the grass, the ball, everything. The bull's-eye is inside of you—if you manage to hit that, the ball has no other choice but to follow."

Bun dat, I thought. I needed to know *exactly* what was around me. Then strip it all apart and use it to my advantage. I took a last look at the defensive line.

"Three!"

The floodlights were suddenly blinding, my heart thumping so hard I swore I could hear the swoosh of blood from the vessels inside my ears. *This could be my last free kick*, I realized. *The last time Gibbsy ever plays me. My last week in this club.* My attention split across the thousand futures where this kick went wrong and everything came falling down. If I missed this shot, would my foster dad, Tony, keep me around? What about Poppy? Would she fight for me? Or like everyone else, would they just—

"Two."

In went a deep breath. I dipped my head, molded my concentration around the ball. I could see the sweet spot and knew hitting it could change everything.

"One."

I took the first step forward and then let myself roll into a jog before lowering to strike. An instant later, my toe kissed the ball, and I watched it sail away.

Judging from how all six defenders swiveled their heads, they'd clearly prepared for a power kick. But the ball whipped left, floating inches above the ponytail of our captain, Maria Marciel. It hit the joint where the post meets the crossbar before deflecting to the back of the net with a *swoosh*.

Goal!

Top bins.

"You fucking beauty," I whispered to myself. The keeper was still watching, wide-legged. As predicted, she hadn't even gotten a chance to move.

Gibbsy blew the melodic whistle for full-time, breaking the silence on the pitch. "Two goals to one. Great day at the office, ladies," she added. And I couldn't have agreed more.

What the raas was up with the silence on the pitch, though? Even the girls on my own team, the ones who were meant to be going nuts after our late comeback, had barely reacted—well, assuming I didn't count the shoulder shrugs and eye rolls.

I thought back to last year, when I'd been playing for my old school team, before the school got shut down and I got shipped to a "better" school with no sports program for girls and had to look for local clubs. Back then, if I'd scored a goal *half* this good, I'd have been buried under a pile of girls celebrating. But as everyone kept reminding me, SE Dons was a "professional academy," not a school team. Here, only vets like Maria were meant to take free kicks, let alone score them.

Not the girl who'd joined a couple months ago and had never played club footie before in her life.

Gibbsy, at least, tipped her beanie at me on her way to the sideline—the closest thing to approval I'd ever seen from the woman. I nodded back, with a keen smile, and as the field emptied, I collected the few limp hand slaps I got with grace. I had no time to gloat or moan. There was a busy night ahead.

The rain had that annoying texture where you couldn't tell if it was dying down or might continue drizzling forever. I flicked my hood up and wiped a dry streak into the pitch-side bench before sitting on it. One girl after the next exited the changing rooms and joined the huddle gathered in the car park. Everyone was heading to tonight's weekly social—a sold-out concert we'd be watching from a wedding hall in Deptford, using the same contact lenses that had just helped me score a goal.

I hadn't been to a social since the very first one. That night, I'd stayed a safe distance behind the mini–mosh pit on the dance floor, and managed to have a few decent one-on-one convos with the girls who weren't high on neon. But groups were where my awkwardness shined brightest, and where those same friendly girls turned into monsters. Another law of nature: wherever two or more youths gathered in the name of competitive sport, astonishing levels of sweat and cruelty gathered with them.

I'd skipped every social since, which earned me the reputation of "not being a team player." After two months of that, I noticed the midfielders were passing to me that little bit less ...

So I started scoring that little bit less, too.

Once the goals dried up, the coaches stopped playing me. And just like that, despite initially leading the squad in goals, I was dropped to the reserve team.

Even the rare match-winner I'd scored tonight just added one more reason for everyone to hope I stayed there.

Clearly, I had to fix it, so I was enthusiastically attending tonight's social. In fact, I'd signed up to help set up the event. I just had an hour-long maths and physics tutorial to get through first.

But when the last floodlight had dimmed to black, 20 minutes into our scheduled lesson time, my new tutor was still nowhere in sight.

Just as I reached for my phone, ready to share my million and one frustrations with Olivia, Maria jogged in, already changed. I'd heard that she and the girls were planning to hang out on the grounds till they were ready to leave for the social, and it wouldn't be long till they started making their way out.

"Hey, some guy's at the gate waiting for you." She pointed at a figure in the distance.

"Finally," I muttered.

If my tutor had arrived on time, I'd have been rushed, but I'd have probably got to the social just as it was starting. My new calculations put me a whole half hour behind.

"Oh, and by the way," I said, biting my nail. It was smarter to let Maria know now than after. "I'm gonna be a *teeny* bit late tonight."

"Oh," she said, a little off balance. "I mean, no worries at all. I get it. It's completely your call." She'd started walking off, when she turned back with a bright look suddenly on her face. "But obviously, if you think you're gonna be more than 15 minutes late, lemme know so I can replace you."

It was hard to miss the extra emphasis on the word "replace." *Go play in traffic* was what I wanted to tell her. But instead, I served a smile, and replied: "I won't. Thanks, though."

My walk to the gate was a vexed one. I wasn't angry about my foster mum, Poppy, signing me up for extra tutoring; we fosties were used to having catch-up lessons forced down our throats. Plus, failing my GCSEs would mean losing my chance at an SE Dons contract, and probably a whole lot more. But of course my new tutor had to show up late today. For our very first lesson. Even after I'd written *7pm SHARP* in my message to him. I'd meant it!

I took a second to steady myself. My social worker had told

me my new tutor was blind. I'd assured her that I was ready to be *very* grown-up about it, and that "I don't see blindness" . . . which was a pretty tasteless comment in hindsight.

He had a fresh cut and boyish smile; early to midthirties was my guess. His jacket had *A V I R E X* slapped across the front in the same black patent leather as his retro Air Max trainers. I could picture the moment (probably a decade prior) when he'd gotten a compliment on the outfit, and had decided to keep rocking it since. He turned to me as my steps got noisier.

"Hi," I said, waiting till I was closer before finally adding: "I'm Rhia."

It wasn't till I shut up that I noticed them: his *feet*, looking all sorts of dodgy.

Olivia reckoned my whole feet-don't-lie thing went back to the photo of Mum in my sock drawer. My real mum, that is. In it, Mum looked around my age and was sitting alone on a park bench, smiling at the camera in a pretty dress. But it was everything happening below her knees that I'd spent so long trying to decode. Her right heel was off the ground and blurry as if she'd been midtap when the shutter closed. And her toes, which you could see poking out of her white slip-ons, were pointing as far away from the lens as possible. I'd spent ages staring at the bottom of that photo, wondering what she'd been so anxious about. I'd looked through every public park in London hoping to spot that crosshatch bench. And after a paid darknet search confirmed that she was gone forever, like everyone had warned—swiped from the earth a month after she'd given birth to me—I was closer than ever to giving up on learning more about her.

As my new tutor stood frozen and focused on me, a growing group of girls were giggling with Maria in the car park as they watched us. Even from there, they could taste the awkwardness.

As much as I was suspicious of the man myself, I also felt kinda bad for him. Somewhere between foster homes seven and nine, I'd gotten acquainted with the fear that came with a first impression. I knew how it hijacked the body. And how being laughed at generally didn't help.

I turned my full attention back to him. "And you must be . . ." I asked in my gentlest voice.

"My bad," he said, extending his hand with a smile. "It's nice to meet you, Rhia. You can call me Dr. Esso."

3

ESSO

THURSDAY (ONE DAY AGO)

With my shirt cuff covering my thumb, I pressed the *4* on the elevator panel, then spent the journey up blocking out the smells and the groans the wiring made as it pulled me up. A blue door and the number *469* came into view after the short walk across the fourth-floor landing. I sighed, almost drowning in my own relief. The only thing greeting me this evening was the gingery scent of Mum's tilapia. Not the mandem or the stress of having to think about them.

D hadn't turned up for school, but the silence of his absence had only raised the volume on the questions swirling in my head.

Had Bloodshed recognized me? Or was I overthinking that half second of eye contact between us? Surely they'd know it was Spark's boys who'd done the G-checking and not me. *He'll give me the benefit of the doubt. Right?*

Or maybe the T.A.S. boys had spent all of last night plotting when and how they were gonna rush me. *It was only a slap and a couple punches*, I'd been reminding myself all morning and afternoon. But I knew as well as anyone how sensitive a roadman's ego was, and that if any footage made it online, social media would make that ego a million times tenderer.

I'd also resorted to reminding myself that me and D had always been cool; our mums even went to church together when we were young. His family lived on Rio Ferdinand's old block, and I remembered visiting D's flat and always being shocked at how much of a pushover his mum was. Whether D got caught picking on his little brother or in a full-blown fight downstairs, she'd take one look at his baby picture hanging above the TV and go back to hugging and kissing him like he was the thirteenth apostle.

When I first met D he was 13, and the only dangerous thing on him was his mouth. You'd see him in the hallway between classes telling hood stories about how some Brixton yutes robbed a grown man at knifepoint at the bus stop, or how a clash near his house involving all kinds of weapons got broken up by police. He gossiped about Liam the Yardy getting stabbed. Rachel getting stabbed. His cousin getting stabbed. How some other kid down the road got stabbed, died, and then shat himself right there on the street. Hearing that story was the first time I learned that people shit themselves when they die. And D laughed after every punch line, as if the more violence he saw, the funnier it got. So it goes.

Rob's theory was that something savage happened to D one summer, because when he came back to Penny Hill that September, all the joking and smiling had stopped. So had the hood chronicling. He'd somehow gone from telling those stories to living them. And since then, pretty much every free-style video coming out his ends had him and Bloodshed in it: D posted up in the background, throwing up gang signs behind smoke; Bloodshed, ad-libbing the outro with, "Free Tugz, Free Bounce, Free Maxxy" and name-dropping a dozen other yutes locked up in Feltham. Guys whose names still rang bells on the roads and maybe didn't have to be freed *just* yet. All the driller stuff never seemed to fit as well on D as it had on Bloodshed, though. It was like D had been dropped into it, and instead of trying to swim to shore, he'd just stopped struggling and let himself drift farther out.

I ruffled my key out my pocket, and just as I slid the tip into the keyhole, the door swung back on its own, almost taking my arm with it. On the other side was Mum, looking more furious than I'd seen her in months.

I straightened up. Whatever she was about to say or do would not be good. In fact, it would almost definitely be terri-ble. I looked down and saw in one hand she held a letter with Penny Hill's crest on it. I guessed they could afford first-class stamps after all.

"'Dear Mrs. Angelique Adenon,'" she read out loud. "'This note is to inform you of your child's recurring misconduct, having earned his second demerit this week . . .'"

She repeated the two key words in the paragraph—"second demerit"—rolling the *r* for extra sting. My nan would have turned in her grave if she could've seen how bad an impression Mum was doing of her. Whenever Mum cussed me, she went from South London girl to African tyrant, but never quite nailed it. It didn't help that the French influence in her birth country of Bénin meant words like "the" and "this" came out as "zee" and "zis" and had also given her the habit of shrugging before each sentence—hard to take seriously.

"Esso Adenon, I'm only asking you this once: where've you been hiding my letters?"

She stood her ground, refusing to let me inside. I was going to take this bollocking standing in the cold—her way of letting me know my residency wasn't guaranteed. I stared down at the faux-wood floor on her side of the doorway, focusing on a grain of broken rice by her slipper. Mum's eyes were too experienced, too knowing—just looking at them meant *some* kind of information would leak. How was I meant to explain what I'd done in a way that meant I got to keep my innocence, and she kept her temper?

Instead, I kept my mouth shut and head bowed, hoping shyness would save me.

"I'm going to smack you if you don't speak up." Her apron rocked side to side from the force of each word. I'd outgrown that runaround a few years ago; now, at 16, I had a solid foot on her. She continued anyway. "You think you're so grown, don't you? I swear I'll put you on a plane to Cotonou first flight tomorrow morning. By the time the council remembers to check on you, you'll be at your uncle's house in the village, sweeping the floor."

The girls next door giggled at that last one. I could see them watching through a slit in their kitchen curtains. One day, Mum would describe her homeland as a paradise of palm trees and angels; the next day, Bénin was Alcatraz, and if I didn't behave, I'd be on the next boat out there. But there was something about her voice this time, a new gullyness, that made me think she might actually do it. She had more grays in her hair now than anyone else I knew under 40, and we both knew who'd put them there.

"Mum, it wasn't even my fault, you know. It's the stupid teachers at school. They're always tryna get us in trouble."

Since my voice had broken and hair had started showing up willy-nilly on my body, I'd picked up this wrong habit, where when I was meant to be thinking about something serious, my mind would sometimes veer into filth.

So, while I was trying to take in Mum's scolding, an old Nadia fantasy was playing in my head. The one where she's holding two giant ice cubes and wearing a skimpy bunny outfit with pointy ears and night-vision goggles and—

"Esso!" Mum looked even more livid now. "First you have the audacity to steal my post, and now you're not even paying attention when I talk to you?" Once she started using big English words like "audacity," things were about to escalate.

She took a moment to find the paragraph where she'd left

off. The lenses on her glasses were thick enough for a tele-scope, and her GP had been begging her for years to see a specialist about her fading eyes, but what did he know, right?

Mum brought the paper closer to her right eye, then started listing all the offenses that qualified students at Penny Hill for demerits, about half of which I'd done at some point that term, but not gotten caught for.

"Esso," she sighed. "I thought we were past this."

She was telling no lies. We'd had this exact same argument near the end of last year, when I'd gotten suspended. And I made the same promises to her then. To stay out of trouble. To get better grades. To be better.

But every time I tried to stay out of trouble, every time I promised Mum from the trench of my soul to be good, trouble still found its way back to me—like a fox waiting outside my bedroom door with a rat in its jaws. Still, if Mum knew half the crud my friends got up to at school, she'd be congratulating me. It wasn't possible to be what she wanted me to be. And in the jungle I walked into every morning, no one's advice was more useless, more dangerous than Mum's.

Her interrogation stayed on course. "I never got the letter for your first demerit. I'm guessing you stole it, just like you were planning to steal the one that arrived this morning."

Lie. Straight-up lie. There was no way she could have dug to the bottom of the skip downstairs to find Monday's demerit letter. Plus, post goes missing all the time in London. *No face, no case.*

"Mum, I genuinely don't know where that letter is. I can look around the house to see if it maybe dropped between the—"

"I wasn't born bloody yesterday." She let the letter drop to her side. "You realize if you get expelled, they'll send you to Centre with those lowlifes on the second floor? You want your mug shot in the *South London Press*?" She took in another deep breath. "I just wish you knew the kind of sacrifices I made so you could have it better than that. So that you could have it better than me. And yet you keep throwing your life away."

Throwing *my* life away. That was rich. Suddenly, I wondered why I was still standing there, with a life-or-death situation coming for me in the background.

"I can't be bothered with this, Mum—it's not like you get it, or even want to get it. I'll probably die before I ever win an argument with you."

She covered her mouth, and her eyes multiplied in size. I knew what I'd said was crossing some line, but only after watching her face implode did I realize how far I'd long-jumped over it. It was like she was staring at a ghost that happened to be standing in my spot.

"You're turning into him," she said, shaking her head in disbelief. "I can't believe I let this happen."

My heart was hammering. "Turning into who?"

"You know who," she said with a tone that had anger and pity in it. "And if you don't find a way to break the cycle you're in, I can't promise things will turn out better for you."

The dead dad card?

The walls got blurry and I almost lost my balance. That was a new low, even for her. My dad had died before I was born, and whenever I'd asked Mum about him, she either lied, changed the subject, or didn't answer at all. And now she had the *audacity* to use him as a warning that she could wave in my face. Did she really think that was what I needed to hear? Did what I needed even matter to her?

"Fuck off." The words came out on their own, surprising me as much they did her. Whether on TV or on ends, I'd always laughed when I saw how white kids swore at their parents. And yet here I was, dropping the f-word on my own mother.

"What did you say to me?" She didn't wait for a response; she didn't need to. Her palm went up and struck me flush on the cheek. *K-TCH!*

The slap echoed down the walkway, probably touching the floor below as well. Mum was heaving while staring up at my bald chin.

I refused to look down, and the next time she tried slapping me, I parried it away. "Nah, I'm not taking this from you any-more," I shouted, hawking down on her. "You're always on my back. Always telling me what I'm doing wrong. Always making me feel like I'm dirt. Nothing I've done in my whole fucking life has *ever* been good enough for you."

"Esso." She cleared her throat, trying to add strength to it. "Esso, I won't let you talk to me like—"

"I don't care!" I snapped back. "Have you ever looked at

yourself in the mirror? What the hell have you done with *your* life? You say I'm getting bad grades and I'm not serious, but *you're* the one who dropped out of uni, *you're* the one who can't hold down a job. You complain about me hanging around thugs, but it's *your* fault we live in this hellhole!" Tears were crashing down in pairs now, and I didn't care if the girls next door could see.

"I didn't know Dad. And I have no clue what he did to make you hate him so much. Since you never bloody told me. But what I do know is that I *never* want to end up like you."

She put her hand on her chest, blinking at triple pace. Whatever was stirring in her made her take a step back, and once she got her balance, her hand went in her chest pocket and came out with a cigarette and a see-through lighter. A spark later and the stick on her lips was on fire—she even blew the first cloud into the corridor behind her. Unheard-of. She never smoked in front of me. She never smoked in the house. And she'd never looked as disappointed and hurt as she did in that moment.

So disappointed that she couldn't even look me in the eye. So hurt that, for once, she didn't care about having the last word.

She shifted to the side. I didn't know if her motivation was getting me out of the cold, or making room so she could finish her cig in peace. But the fact I didn't hear her hair beads rattling after me, or feel her loading up another slap after my comments, meant we weren't in normal territory anymore.

And we were both too proud to take back our words.

I stormed past the open door of the front room on my way to my bedroom. Mum must have had the news on when I'd gotten home, because the TV volume was close to max, just the way she liked it: "That's right: *minus* 5° Celsius tomorrow, with a massive hailstorm expected from 8 p.m."

I was too focused on getting to my room—where I could be sulky and angry without dragging Mum further down with me—to properly reflect on the forecast. Not till I lay down did I remember that we'd had the hottest summer on record, plus flood warnings across London the past week. And now another hailstorm? Assuming Rob was wrong, and this global warming ting was real, it needed a rebrand. Something like: *Global . . . Surprise, Bitches!* would have done a better job.

The first couple hours under my covers I spent in that weird space where I wasn't really sure if I was awake or asleep. If I was asleep, there was no way my body was counting these hours as rest. If I was awake, I wasn't *quite* awake enough to react when my bedroom door creaked open in the middle of the night.

In came a gliding silhouette darker than the unlit hallway behind it.

Mum, I thought, keeping still. She placed something on my bed that was just heavy enough that the depression in the duvet tugged on my ankles. On her way out, she twisted the door handle slowly so it wouldn't latch too loud.

More awake now, I reached for the spot where she'd dropped

the thing and felt around with my fingertips. *A Bible?* I thought.

Nah—it was too thin. Maybe my biology notebook? I'd promised my teacher all week I'd remember to bring it to class, even though I was 99% sure I'd left it on the bus along with my earphones. More likely it was whichever self-help manual Pastor Rupert was forcing down the congregation's throats this month. Maybe one with a "relevant" message for "today's youth." Sure, I was hollowed out, but that didn't mean I was ready to be filled with that garbage.

Lying back and closing my eyes, I decided that no book could change what I was going to have to face at school the next day. It was just a book. A book could wait till morning.

4

RHIA · (15 YEARS LATER)

IT HAD BEEN my idea to have the tutorials on the Dons grounds—that way they wouldn't eat into my training time. Clearly, I hadn't thought it through. The light in the kit room on the top floor of the stadium was an eye-stabbing shade of white, and the little free floor space left for us—after you subtracted the broken hardware and gear that smelled like wet socks—was the size of a confessional. The makeshift desk we'd just wiggled into place was the only thing separating me from my ghetto-looking sensei.

"Again, I'm sorry, but we've gotta do the full hour," Dr. Esso said, shrugging. "And we've got a lot of stuff to get through." Instead of remorseful, he almost sounded excited. Even though he'd rocked up a half hour late and even though I'd told him I *had* to leave on time. It was infuriating.

I could already feel the girls' stares sniping at me when I inevitably arrived late and excuseless to the venue. I could picture Maria—ringleader and captain—pretending not to gloat.

I wouldn't go back on my word and lose even more points. Whether I had to go around my new tutor, or through him, I was going.

Something was definitely off about this guy. He'd mostly dusted off that initial nervousness and had grown into his smile and small talk. But the sight of his feet freezing up when we'd first met was still alive in my mind. Maybe he was just a bit odd? Or shy? Or maybe he was hiding something.

"So, how'd you do in your last physics exam?" he asked, unwrapping the man bag from his neck and hanging it on the desk corner.

I'd decided to keep my responses brief—partly because that was how I jived in class, but also because I didn't want to give away my suspicions.

"B," I replied.

"And in maths?"

"C-minus," I said, telling the truth on the second go.

I'd always had a decent grasp on most of the topics that came up in maths. But still, whenever I saw an equation for the first time, I turned into six-year-old Rhia, who had to raise her legs above her mattress so the bed goblins wouldn't pull her underneath. It was amazing how doodles on paper could do that to you, so easily triggering that human reflex to fear first and understand later.

"Makes sense," he said, biting the butt of his pen. "People who find maths hard don't usually dig physics either, since it requires a lot of maths. Get me?"

"Sure, Dr. Esso."

My social worker had referred to him as "Dr. Adenon" in her email, but he was clearly one of those teachers who thought going by his first name would make him look "hip."

"Personally, I think the *real* reason people find both physics and maths difficult"—he held a breath—"is that they both require *imagination*."

As if he'd heard me mocking him in my mind, he carried on explaining. "Physics asks you to believe that just by looking at a few lines of maths scribbled down on a piece of paper, you can see a fuller version of the world—of *other* worlds, even. Things you would have sworn couldn't exist. Physics asks you to believe in miracles." He chewed on his bottom lip for a second. "This probably all sounds a bit mad, but like my old man used to say, maybe it's one of those things you have to believe to see."

I was pretty sure he'd gotten the phrase backward. I waited just long enough to give the impression I was soaking in his nonsense about physics and his dad and other worlds. Then, in my most sincere voice, I asked: "Do you wax your eyebrows?"

He tilted his head back. "Whhh . . . what's that gotta do with anything I just said?"

"Nuttin'. I just felt like giving your arches the credit they deserve. I mean, your attention to detail is impeccable."

He was pretty annoyed when he responded. "No, Rhia. I don't wax my eyebrows."

In truth, the only thing I'd noticed about them was that

they were bushier than my armpits in winter. This was my way of serving revenge cold and passive-aggressively. He'd doubly earned it by wasting even more of my time with this pre-tutorial philosophizing.

He took his time straightening his chair before resuming. "You know what? I think we both got a bit sidetracked there." Still rattled, he asked, "Why don't you tell me what you lot are learning in physics at the moment in school?"

"Ummm," I responded, thinking back to Mrs. White's class that morning. "Electricity and magnetism."

"Safe," he said. "Let's start with electricity, then."

Who the hell said "safe" anymore? He was probably still using words like "lit" and "sick" as well.

For the next 20 minutes, he forced me to read out every line of maths I wrote down, before having me summarize *why* each equation mattered. As if they mattered! The worst part was that whenever I gave a vague response, he forced me to reword it into a sentence that a "10-year-old chimpanzee" could understand.

"When you pass electricity through a wire," I dictated, "a magnetic field forms around the electricity."

"Safe," he said. "And . . . ?"

Given we'd gone through it minutes ago, it was taking me an embarrassingly long time to remember. I really did need this tutoring. The other crap part of switching schools mid-year (besides losing my old football team and all my mates) had been keeping up with a reordered curriculum and kids who brought in apples for their teachers. Full-on, tree-fresh apples. Unbelievable.

"And the reverse is true as well," I added, recalling the clip we'd watched in class that week on how power stations worked. "When you pass a magnet by a wire that's coiled up the right way, you generate electricity in the wire."

"Okay, so electricity generates magnetism and magnetism generates electricity. What's the *speed* that one thing creates the other?"

"How the hell am I supposed to know?" I shot back.

"Rhia," he said, a little sterner than I'd expected. "You've got all the numbers you need in the back of your textbook, innit. So please go ahead and calculate the speed of this electromagnetic effect. It's the same speed in both directions, so I only need one answer."

"Fine." Into my phone's calculator went the figures I'd jotted down. Out came the answer: "Two hundred ninety—"

"Just round it up."

"Umm . . . so, *around* 300,000 kilometers per second."

"Yes, blood," he said, weirdly animated. "Now go on and punch that number into the search engine on your phone."

I did. None of the results had either electricity or magnetism in their titles. Instead, they all featured the same word: *light*. It felt out of place, like asking for rice and peas and getting jollof instead.

"The Man is tellin' me this is the speed *light* travels at."

He sat back in his chair, grinning. "Ain't that a coincidence?"

"I don't get it. Weren't we learning about magnets a second ago? What's all this light malarkey?"

It was an innocent question, but the grin that appeared on his face made me think, *Oh no, what have I done?* A minute-by-minute countdown to the end of class was already sounding in my head; my question was one more hurdle between me and the last train that would get me to the social on time. The maths that *actually* mattered to me unrolled in my head: if I wanted to get to the venue within 10 minutes of the start time, train and bus wouldn't cut it anymore. Getting a Zuber was my only remaining option. But my debit card had precisely 18 pence on it, meaning I'd have to hope that: a) the driver was cool with doing a cash deal off-app; and b) the coins I had in my pocket could carry me at least halfway.

As he peeled back the next textbook page, his phone started vibrating, a song I didn't recognize humming from the back speaker.

"Apologies," he said, angling the screen away from me while double tapping it. The ringing stopped and he resumed the lecture.

"At the most basic level, physics is a simple dance between storytelling and equation writing. It's just metaphors plus maths."

He pulled a silver gadget the shape of a Coke can out of his bag, then placed it on the desk. I'd seen adverts for it on the Tube: a Caster-5. It looked clunkier in the flesh.

"We've patterned all the maths already." He pressed a

glowing button on the side of the device. "So now we've just gotta come up with the right metaphor: a good *story* to help us see it and make sense of it."

"Sure," I responded at bullet speed, hoping he'd get the hint and talk faster as well. It was ten minutes to eight. *Max* five minutes before I had to head out.

"Imagine Millwall is playing SE Dons right here at Dangote Stadium," he said. The device shot up a blue cone of light, which, after a few seconds, condensed into a 3D projection of the stadium we were sitting in. "Now picture the two sets of fans sitting in small, alternating blocks around the stands. There's only a few minutes of the match left and it's been a dry one, so one bored Dons fan starts a Mexican wave." The projection morphed as he described the scene, providing matching visuals with zero lag. "If my Caster-5 is doing its job right, you should be seeing a group of dark-skinned yutes springing up and sitting down; then, as the wave hits the next section, a bunch of white Millwall fans doing the same. And it just keeps going, round and round the stands, in perfect, zebra harmony.

"It turns out," he continued, "that's what an electromagnetic wave looks like." He leaned closer to the device. "What *light* looks like."

A final hologram appeared—a diagram.

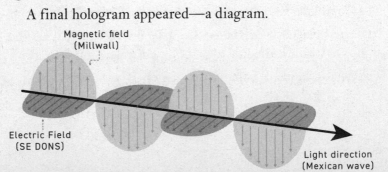

Magnetic field
(Millwall)

Electric Field
(SE DONS)

Light direction
(Mexican wave)

"Light is just a series of electrical and magnetic waves, each ripple creating the next ripple, then the next, and moving the whole beam of light forward in the process."

"Just fascinating," I responded flatly. To be fair, his comparison wasn't that awful, and neither were his gadget's pyrotechnics. Any other night, I'd have even complimented him. But not with two minutes left before I had to dust or potentially face lifelong consequences.

As if the gods were hell-bent on seeing me wait and suffer, his phone rang again.

"My bad," he said, facing me. "I'm gonna answer this proper quick in the corridor. I'll be back in two minutes. Promise."

Before I could protest, or renegotiate for my early exit, he was out the door. Whatever he was discussing was dodgy enough for him to take the call a full 20 meters down the corridor. I sat in the room, alone, bored, frustrated. *Angry*. It was the perfect storm of emotions to lead to the most brazen of ideas. "Criminal" was actually the closer word.

As I got up and moved toward his man bag, I wondered what the odds were of him having cash in there. *Decent*, was the answer for anyone born that near to the millennium.

It's only a tenner, I assured myself, while sliding the zip down, hands shaking slightly. *I'll 1,000% pay him back this time next week. In fact, when you think about it . . . he basically owes me this money. It's his fault I'm late, so it makes sense that he's subsidizing part of the fare.*

I couldn't remember the last time I'd stolen anything from anyone, let alone a complete stranger. It was wrong, and I knew it. I felt like shit. A fly-covered, steaming pile of shit. And the only thing sleazier than coming up with the twisted moral logic I'd used to justify my actions was forcing myself to believe it.

The first item I saw was a tattered brown notebook. I'd not seen anything like it before, not in any stationery shop I'd ever walked into. It looked even older than Dr. Esso; one corner was scorched black and the other split apart by time, with writing on the cover so smudged I could barely make it out.

"Blaise Adenon?" I mumbled. *Same surname as Dr. Esso.*

I got some small comfort from knowing I'd hear the tutor's footsteps before he walked in. But the time I'd spent fiddling about with his diary had probably used up some cushion.

Farther in, I found a wallet. And tucked in the main fold—a crisp set of bills.

I pulled out the 20-pound note and stared at it. It was like King George, printed in purple on the front, was looking back at me. Like he was peering into my soul and damning me to hell.

This ain't you, Rhia, I imagined him telling me with a royal shake of the head. And he was right.

I couldn't go through with it. I refused to. Whatever consequences were gonna come from me arriving late, I'd just have to ride it.

It's just one social, I thought while stuffing the cash back into the wallet. Another convenient lie I was forcing myself to believe.

I heard trainer soles squeaking on the polished floor outside. I had just seconds.

My fingers were clasped around the zip, ready to pull it shut and sprint back to my seat.

Then I saw it.

"It" was a photo—scratched up and tucked into a side flap—of four kids at a lunch table. One was a skinnier, fresher-faced version of Dr. Esso, and to his right sat a girl the same age.

A girl I knew instantly—because there was a photo of her tucked away in my drawer at home.

"Thanks for your patience," Dr. Esso said as he opened the door and strolled back to his seat mere milliseconds after I'd shut the bag.

What! The! Fuck! I wanted to shout. How was I meant to act normal with my eyes burning from what I'd just seen? I gripped the pen in my hand so hard it snapped in two, and Dr. Esso, none the wiser, picked up where we'd left off.

"The sickest part is that the guy who figured out that light is an electromagnetic wave did it the same way we just did: with some quick maths. He then had to wait two decades till someone finally did an experiment proving he'd been right all along. Can you imagine how insane he must have felt?"

I could. I was feeling pretty fucking insane. *This man knew my mum.* And well enough that he apparently carried a photo of her wherever he went, which he couldn't see. My hands were shaking even harder now under the table, my ankles wobbling at the same speed on the ground.

"I guess you've gotta go now, innit," he said after a moment of silence. "Since it was my fault we started late, I'll sort you a taxi so you can hopefully get there on time."

Yes, I do need to go. I wasn't even thinking about the social anymore. I just needed to get out of this room. Get myself back under control.

My whole life I'd wondered who my birth mum was, and the faded Polaroid under the sports bras in my drawer was all I'd ever gotten in response. No matter how often she appeared in my dreams, in the real world she only existed as a three-by-three print on a long-dead leaf of time. I thought back to an ancient memory—I must have been four or five, sitting on a gum-pink stool and gazing up at the first foster carer I remembered having. "Where's my mum?" I would ask her, followed by, "Well, then where'd she go?" Sitting in that claustrophobic room a decade on, I had the same questions. Only now, an answer was sitting opposite me in a tracksuit.

I sat, dazed, studying the shifting contours of his face and wondering who this guy was. I'd known something was off about him from the beginning but could never have guessed it would be *this*. And I still didn't know where, when, or how he'd gotten hold of a photo of my mum, Nadia Black.

"Yeah," I responded, sending a loud gulp down. "I'll definitely take you up on that taxi."

FRIDAY (TODAY)

When I woke up on this fateful morning, my first thought was the argument I'd had with Mum last night. I still felt proper shit. I couldn't unsee her outline at the door, pulling on a cigarette while the hem of her nightgown chased the wind outside. I also couldn't forget how fragile she'd looked when I'd left her—a life's worth of burnout in her baggy eyes. With everything going on with D and Bloodshed, I wondered when we'd get a chance to fix things . . . *if* we'd ever get a chance. The violent finality of that "if" sent a shiver up my spine.

And to make things extra awkward, tonight was Friday: *Fish & Chips & Film Night!* I was still chuffed with my seven-year-old self for coming up with that tagline. Once 8 p.m. swung around, me and Mum were on for two hours of solo time.

But today it would be two hours of chewing silently and avoiding eye contact on our tiny couch, instead of our usual laughing while shouting, "Run, you idiots!" at the telly.

I sat up, and a slim tan leather notebook sitting on the corner of my bed shook loose a memory from the night before—Mum coming in and placing it there. The name, written in felt-tip on the front, sat me up extra straight:

BLAISE M. ADENON

My dad's full name.

I wondered what had prompted Mum to give it to me now—the harsh words I'd spat at her the night before, or something else? Something deeper? If this really was his notebook, it meant she'd been hiding it from me my whole life. And yet I was too excited to even care.

In fact, in that moment I felt grateful. The only other testimonies we had of him were a pile of tax forms she kept in her bedroom and an unpaired sock of his that I kept in mine.

Seeing the surname—*ADENON*—written in block print got me the most gassed, though. It wasn't just his name; it was *ours*. It was a portal to my past, my roots spelled out in ink. The man responsible for the other half of my DNA was just sitting there on my duvet. He was finally in arm's reach. Here was my chance to know the kind of man he was, maybe even catch a glimpse of the man I could become.

I reached for it hungrily. A part of me genuinely believed that after reading the first page, I'd be zapped with a magical link to him. Failing that, I'd at least get some closure before a new day started. And the two first words I read only amplified those hopes:

To Esso.

But in the end, instead of magic, all I got were the shivers.

Once upon a time, a group of prisoners lived in a cave . . .

It got even weirder from there. Flickering shadows on a wall, the Upper World, a guy named Socrates getting executed . . .

Never in my life had words taken me so high, then so low, so quickly. The next few letters, all addressed to me, had notes on everything from time travel to atomic bombs to dimensions you could only see through maths. It was all in there, and half reminded me of the Pythagoras stuff I'd dug up in Purdy's class on Monday—just more cultish. The kind of stuff I'd sooner see in the sci-fi novels Nadia devoured most weekends.

"Disappointed" was too weak a word to describe how I felt. "Alarmed" was close, but still fell short. The most obvious verdict was that I'd just read the ranting of a three-quid lunatic who, if he were still alive, would be preaching about the endtimes from a megaphone in Trafalgar Square. His words were so serious, like he *actually* believed what he was writing. Maybe Dad wasn't all there in the head, and that was why Mum had kept it from me. What Mum had said about him the night before—about her not wanting me to turn into him—still stung like chili pepper on a cracked lip. And I was feeling much less forgiving now about how long she'd kept this from me.

I really can't get into this right now, I decided. My daddy issues and questions would have to wait till the evening. To get out of here on time, I'd have to figure out how to take a crap, shower, brush my teeth, and eat cereal all at the same time. I'd have to accept my dad had probably been mad, and think about the day in front of me.

Before I left my room, I slid the notebook under my pillow.

As I walked toward the stairs, my first sniff of the morning came cold and wrapped in jollof rice. The scent must have escaped from that flat downstairs, where the Ghanaians lived. The rice was at the stage where each tomato-soaked grain at the bottom of the pot was starting to char, and after skipping breakfast, I wanted to kill the lucky bastard who would get to scrape it up.

Back-to-back texts from Nadia paused my scheming thoughts.

Nadia: Yo E. Heard some mad shit about u and Ds brother.

Nadia: Everything OK? How come you never told me?

Nadia: Anyway text me yeah? xxxx

I was surprised she'd been paying such close attention. Kinda touched, actually. My thumb hovered over the screen, waiting for the right words to arrive. I waited. Then I waited some more. And then I gave up.

No, everything's not OK was the obvious response, but also the one requiring most explanation. I would have to tell her about how, by accident, I'd parachuted myself into the middle of a live road beef. And how I was now one demerit away from getting kicked out of school. I thought about all the work I'd put in over the last few months to project the perfect blend of mysterious-yet-fun to her. I didn't want to give up the illusion I was too cool for fear. As much as I was dying to share my fears with someone who cared, it just felt too soon.

A part of me wondered whether I'd ever stop thinking it was "too soon." I'd had a golden opportunity the week before, when we'd gone to watch another sci-fi film Nadia had insisted on seeing. I could have gone full romantic—opening doors, paying for overpriced popcorn, then coming clean about how I'd obsessed about her every day since she'd transferred to Penny Hill . . . or I could have taken Rob's typically useless advice to "just be myself." I hadn't even risked asking Kato. In the end, I picked something halfway between the two terrible options I had in front of me: I did nothing. I genuinely wished I didn't fancy her as much as I did. I even fancied the bits of her I was meant to find ugly. That snort when she laughed too hard. The oversized birthmark on the darker side of her wrist. The steel braces framing her smile . . .

By the time I got down to the second floor, my phone was back in my pocket, and I'd boiled my focus down to two words: *survive today*. Once Friday was over, we'd have the weekend, then half term—a whole week to lie low at home and figure out how to smooth things out with D, Bloodshed, and any other Brixton yutes who had me on their hit lists. I just needed to stay out their way over the school day. That was all.

Generally, the faster my mind raced, the slower my legs

tended to move. It was like I'd been born with a maximum amount of speed that I had to ration between my brain and lower limbs. And my watch was now telling me that because of that rationing, I was on track to miss the next 36 bus by at least a couple minutes.

I skipped down the last few sets of stairs, jumping off the third-to-bottom steps to shave off a second each time. With every stride, the jollof scent weakened, and as I raced past Homeless Dave, he lifted his glass bottle and howled, "Ahhwooooo!" Twenty yards on, I could still hear him cough-laughing like he had gravel in his lungs.

My route to the bus stop was flanked by council flats just like ours on both sides. They were the same ones you saw in every ends in London. Each tower was wrapped in a scarf of white-and-blue plastic, their brick faces pimpled with idle TV dishes. People from every corner of the planet had their prayers planted under those blocks, waiting for their dreams to bloom out of the concrete once the never-ending British rain let up. Those blocks were all I knew. The Narm—Peckham— was all I knew.

A clumsy sidestep was all that stopped me from smashing into a half-familiar little girl as I rounded the final corner onto the road where the 36 was scheduled to stop in less than a minute. She was holding her dad's hand, and her puffy pink jacket was zipped up so far that only a tiny oval was left open for her eyes to track me as I skimmed past. Only on seeing how warm she looked did I realize I'd forgotten my own jacket at home. At the same time, I noticed the oniony smell seeping from inside my shirt. "Shit," I muttered. I'd remembered to spray deodorant all over my balls that morning but had somehow forgotten my armpits. I thought about going back but instead flapped my shirt a few times to let the nastiness out. The bus was slowing down at the stop across the road, meaning I had 10 seconds, max, before it pulled away again.

Just ahead, a slender woman in a light-gray jacket and matching pencil skirt was crossing the street, holding hands with two kids who flanked each hip. A dozen more kids in matching primary school uniforms strolled just behind. I started a diagonal jay-sprint across the road, hoping to cheat space and time, and when I looked back for oncoming cars, I saw a matte-black Range Rover with matching black rims speeding toward the crossing. A multiethnic-looking dude with a long, wispy beard was driving, but he had his eyes locked on the phone in his lap, maybe assuming the pedestrians were watching the road for him.

Meanwhile, the last kid in the group crossing the street, a primary school version of Benedict Wong with a 360-degree bowl cut, was still inching across the road like he had nowhere safer to be.

The chaperone lady turned back to the boy. "Hurry along." When he didn't respond, she shouted, "I said, move it! We haven't got all day." But her calm pose told me she clearly hadn't seen the car and genuinely believed the biggest danger the child was facing was being late for registration.

The tire screeches came first, followed by a muffled yell from inside the Range Rover. The boy stopped cold in the middle of the road, and his eyes widened, finally matching the enormity of the moment, the biggest moment that might ever happen in his tiny life.

A million thoughts crawled through my head, each climbing on top of the next until only one was left standing: *Get him before the car does.*

I didn't make the choice because I wanted to be a hero. It wasn't really a choice at all—more a mindless reflex that I let take over because the terror waiting for me at school meant it didn't really matter what happened right now.

Looking back, I probably should've kept running for the bus.

Part II:

TIME

FROM BLAISE ADENON'S NOTEBOOK

To Esso,

Little has been written about the Upper World—mostly because of how little we know. We do not know if all people can access it, or whether there are differences across individuals, cultures, or even species. No one has ever seen where the Upper World starts and ends, assuming it ends at all. The only thing scarier than the thought of you going up there alone is the tragedy of you not knowing it exists. And so the little I know, my child, I will tell you.

First you have to speak it to see it.

Language influences what we see. In Greek, for instance, there is no such word as "blue." Either something is "galazio" (a lighter shade of blue), or "ble" (a darker shade). Any Greek settling on this cloudy island will swiftly find their color vocabulary cut in half; two vibrant colors tucked into a single English word, "blue."

But as one curious study showed, Greeks who abandon their mother tongue also stop being able to **distinguish** *between galazio- and ble-colored objects. They literally see half of what they used to—because of language.*

Just like the shades of blue, time itself is relative. It passes at one pace here and a slower pace over there, all depending on where you are and what you understand. And since time, light, and everything else in the universe can only be properly described through the language of the gods, even a few lessons of childhood maths can provide a brief glimpse of the Upper World. But until you are fluent in the sacred language, do not expect to see much more.

Last, you must look through your WINDOW.

Our brothers and sisters in the East say that each snap of your finger contains 65 unique moments. Using pen and paper, physicists today can prove that the number is even greater. Now imagine the vast multiplicity of moments contained in one breath. One smile. One dream. How does the mind continually hold the near-infinite granules spanning an entire **lifetime***?*

It can't.

To ensure our survival, nature decided long ago to restrict our view of time to a single moment: a solitary and ever-changing canvas on which the immediate concerns of shelter, sustenance, and procreation could be projected. The now. Our view of the past was therefore relegated to a fuzzy blur, and the existential distractions of the future blacked out completely. And yet our ability to tap into chronosthesia (mental time travel) was not destroyed. Only unplugged. Locked inside a crevice of our minds called the WINDOW.

The WINDOW is a memory from the past or the future. A memory unique to each individual, often so severe or traumatic that our minds force us to forget it. Due to the WINDOW being the lens through which we perceive true time, it is common to hear people claim that time "slowed down" or even "completely stopped" in these buried memories. It has been suggested that an acute or repeated concussion can temporarily "yank" open one's

WINDOW. But all we know for sure is that the only safe path to the Upper World is through an elder guiding you to your WINDOW, once you possess the language to see what's on the other side.

In a few months, you will leave your world and be born into ours, my child. You will be told that what you see with your physical eyes is final, and that men like me who claim otherwise are fools. But know that just beyond the tug of our chains and the warmth of this cave, a clearer, more terrifying world awaits us.

6

RHIA · (15 YEARS LATER)

MY OLD ENGLISH teacher once said that the "-cide" in the word "decide" is the same as the one in "homicide." "To choose one future is to murder all the rest," she warned. "Deciding is a ruthless act." As I sat on the carpet between Olivia's knees, debating what to do next about my Dr. Esso situation, trying not to flinch each time Olivia tugged a new strand into a new braid, I understood just how right my old English teacher had been.

I'd told Olivia (pretty much) everything. How I ran out the kit room the second Dr. Esso ordered my Zuber because I'd thought if I stayed any longer, I'd spontaneously combust. I'd told her that my mum looked happier in his photo than in the one I had in my drawer, although she wasn't even smiling in his. I'd also told her about the social, which I'd arrived only five minutes late to in the end thanks to a super-fast Zuber ride. Looking back, it was laughable how stressed I'd been about that. With bigger things on my mind, I spent the entire night swaying back and forth—desperate to submit to the onslaught of emotions, but afraid of being consumed by them. My teammates were probably still debating what was wrong with me—so much for my plan to restore my reputation.

Olivia was also the only person who knew about my recurring dream (which she rightly called a nightmare). The one where my mum had blacked-out eyes and was reaching out to me, crying. Honestly, Olivia's dreams were even weirder. Every foster kid I knew dreamed about their real parents. Even the ones with messed-up ones. *Especially* the ones with messed-up ones. She understood full well why I was so fixated on getting answers.

"I just can't believe this is happening to me," I said over my shoulder. Somewhere inside me was the child who'd always believed she'd find her way back to her mum. It was scary and exciting and amazing that it might finally come true.

But when all I got was a forced "I know" from Olivia, I remembered to rein it in, to stop sounding so bloody happy about it all. She'd spent the past four days matching my excitement revelation by revelation, smile for smile. But she couldn't quite hide (not from me, anyway) the somber gazes in between, the moments when I could see the sorrow she was holding back. That was the toughest part about growing up in struggle—your gains shone a light on the loss around you. Wins never fully got to feel like wins. I'd even considered not telling her at all, knowing she'd have given up everything to be where I was now.

But we were tied to each other, and sworn to transparency. Literally weeks after first meeting three years earlier, we'd pinkie-sworn to never let 24 hours pass without sharing big news. And it didn't get bigger than this.

The state of our bedroom didn't make it easy to think through the options. The outfits Olivia had tried on over the weekend were dotted in a trail from her wardrobe to the bottom bunk. The only things made up in there were our beds, and even that was thanks to the self-laying Blankoos that Poppy had bought us earlier in the year.

I had exactly three days until my next tutorial, so I needed a decent plan fast. Specifically, I needed to find out everything Dr. Esso knew about my mum, and that meant digging up information on *him* first.

"Tilt your head forward a bit, sis." Olivia brushed through a kink before twisting the strand into a finished braid that she let fall to my collarbone.

I'd been sitting cross-legged in the same spot for so long my right bum cheek had gone tingly. It was well past bedtime, and we hadn't reached the back of my hair yet, let alone a good answer. I'd offered to braid Olivia's as well, but she was already booked in for an appointment tomorrow and committed to shaving her locs down to a level three.

"I still think you should just confront him," she insisted.

Neither of us could tell how or why Dr. Esso had found me, but we both agreed it wasn't a coincidence. His overall sketchy behavior . . . the photo. I was willing to bet everything he'd been in my mum's life. And now—somehow—he'd snuck into mine.

"What if he attacks me during the lesson?" I replied. "Pulls out a knife or suttin'?"

"Just keep doing them at the stadium. There's security guards everywhere, aren't there?"

"Fair," I said. Maybe the idea that he'd pull a slicer on me had been a tad extreme. "But what if I confront him and he bails? Or just straight-up lies?"

I'd found surprisingly little about him online. The Open University had his profile on their website since he was a virtual teaching assistant there, and his bio mentioned he'd gotten his PhD in physics from the same department. What I didn't find were any social media profiles, avatars, or news articles on him. Nothing in the wedding or parent registries, no trace of him socializing with other non-university humans. I still didn't know him from a tin of beans. But the photo in his pouch had proven he was capable of keeping secrets. One careless step by me, and he could easily disappear, along with the answers about my mum.

"And even if he *did* tell me the truth," I continued, "I'd have no way of knowing if he was lying or not. He could just report me to Care for trying to nick money off him and then—"

"I get it, sis," Olivia interjected, sighing. We had to toss that idea along with all the other rubbish ones we'd come up with, including telling Tony and Poppy. "Back to the drawing board we go."

The moment my foster dad's name crossed my mind, our bedroom door creaked open, and he slid his large head through it.

"Rhia," Tony whispered, pushing his face an inch farther in. I used to joke with Olivia that you could use his chin to tell the time of day: white and smooth in the mornings; shadow by lunch; stubble before supper; and bristle right after it. "Could you do us a favor and grab a Christmas gift for Mum this weekend?"

He'd made the same request the last three years, but never this early in December. *Good for him,* I thought. To be fair to Tony, Poppy was by far the hardest person to buy gifts for. And that meant a lot coming from me. Olivia was big on these things called love languages and was convinced my preferred dialect for expressing love was giving gifts. I did enjoy that shit. But even with my natural enthusiasm, it was impossible to figure out what to get our foster mum. We all knew what she hated: night shifts, dishes in the sink, any activist with a marketing deal. In terms of what she (mildly) liked: fried Mars Bars, being a mum, Tony about six days of the week. But what she *loved*? It certainly wasn't the 3D-printer cartridge I'd gotten her last Christmas that came preloaded with a synthetic cashmere scarf (I thought that was pretty manic). It wasn't the paisley-patterned flower vase that Olivia had gotten her either.

"I'll send you the cash in the morning. Just make sure it's nice and unique. And under 120 quid, ideally. Oh, and we need a Christmas tree as well, so I'll throw in another 30 for that."

"That all?" I replied, secretly fired up for the challenge of nailing the holidays this year.

He reflected a cheeky grin back at me. "Thanks, Rhia. Now, don't be up long, you two. Night, Liv."

Almost any sound made it through the leaf-thin walls of our two-bedroom flat, so to be safe, Olivia waited a while before relighting the conversation in a whisper.

"So." She put the comb down on the bed. "Have you thought about *why* he has your mum's photo in his wallet?"

"I think they probably went to school together," I said. "But not sure. Still tryna figure it all out."

"Right, but you don't think he might be . . ." She went quiet for a second. ". . . your dad?"

It was a fair question; I just hadn't worked up the courage to ask it myself. He seemed old enough, and the photo of my mum in his wallet was another potential hint. My dad, whoever he was, had never really been in the picture. Maybe because he *literally* wasn't in that picture in my drawer. And ignoring how awkward Dr. Esso had been in our first meeting, there was something faintly appealing about the idea. He was smart and knew how to have a laugh, and I'd have gone as far as calling him considerate, if he'd not gone full CPT on the worst possible night. But for now, I had to resist reaching for too much in one go. I wasn't sure I could survive double disappointment. Finding out more about Mum, even if only a sniff of her, would be enough. Whatever else came out of my information dig, I'd judge when I saw it.

"I just think there's more to this guy than . . ." She probably noticed how tightly my shoulders had clumped in the last few seconds. And so she caught herself, sighed, and moved on. "Lean forward again, please."

"My bad," I replied, grateful she'd eased off the topic.

After hearing our exchange, the carpet decided to tell us off via the speaker in the floorboards. "You have spent sixty . . . three . . . minutes . . . in a suboptimal sitting posture," came the automated message. "It is advised that you take a walking break and when you return, retain a flat—"

"Shut up, carpet!" I said, aiming my voice down at my lap. And then it dawned on me. The answer to how I could get the information about my mum that I needed . . . I was literally sitting on top of it.

Specs lived in the exact same flat as us, same maroon-painted door, same front room facing the landing—just one floor down. His parents had moved into the flats a year ago, and since their arrival, opinion on the block was angrily split on whether Specs was a looker or just a geek with a deep voice. For reasons beyond my intellect, Olivia was convinced he was perfect for me. She tended to have much stronger opinions on my love life than I did, especially when it came to my last and only ex, who she positively loathed. I maintained (even a year later) that he was a decent guy. Strange, yes. Acquired taste, sure. But decent overall.

Specs was an inch taller than me (five foot ten-ish on air

bubbles) but towered over Olivia as they negotiated back and forth.

"By the way, what happened to your glasses?" she asked him.

She'd read online about this negotiation tactic called a "snow job." To me, it sounded like something a call girl in the Alps could charge for, but apparently, it meant drowning your bargaining opponent with confusing questions to get the upper hand. Ultimately, what we wanted from Specs were the keys to Dr. Esso's digital life. We needed the answers to how he knew my mum, what he knew about her, and what he might want from me. And with the right access, there wasn't much you couldn't find on the dark web, including his government data and any articles about him that might have gotten archived.

"I don't wear them no more," Specs replied.

"Did you get holo-lenses put in? Stem cells?" Loudly popping bubble gum must have been part of her act as well.

"Nah, I just don't wear them anymore."

Given everything that was at stake for me, I had the shortest patience imaginable for this eye banter. "What's your final price, bruv?" I butted in.

"80."

"And once we bring his iris scan back, how long will it take you to pull his deets from the dark web?"

Specs stared at Olivia, equal parts surprised and annoyed. "As I already told your sister three times"—he gripped the door handle, as if he might shut it at any second—"you need to get someone else to pull this guy's data. The price I quoted is *just* for the iris scanner."

Olivia gave me a reassuring look before fighting back. "Specs, ain't you going to Cambridge or suttin' next year? Why you being so tight, you little posh boy?"

"Yes, I am going to Cambridge," Specs replied. "No, I am not posh. And the reason I'm being tight is because tuition is 23 bags a year and I don't get to earn proper money until *after* I graduate. And getting nicked for hacking someone's private data is a sure way to guarantee I don't graduate."

I could feel my stomach lifting, as if it could also sense the ground rapidly disappearing from beneath me. I'd felt *so* close to getting answers.

What use is half a key? I wanted to shout. *What am I meant to do with just his iris scan?!*

Specs must have seen the life fleeing my face, because he turned to me with a softer look. "I'm sorry, Rhia. I really wish I could help you with the data pull." He cleared his throat. "Honestly, I just happen to have this illegal piece of tech. I'm not a proper trapper. And I'm definitely not a scammer."

"It's lax, bruv," I said, shielding my sad eyes from him.

"Well," Olivia declared. "I guess we should just take our money somewhere else, then. Come on, sis."

She grabbed my hand and started down the landing, winking at me once she knew he couldn't see. *Principle number three*, I could imagine her reciting in her head, *always be willing to walk.*

And that was exactly the problem. I *wasn't* willing to walk.

I couldn't unsee what I'd found in Dr. Esso's wallet even if I wanted to. And how was I meant to live out my life knowing I'd reversed at the first pothole? Maybe half of the key wasn't nothing. For all I knew, getting his iris scan might be the hardest part.

One foot in front of the other, I told myself. *Get the scanner . . . then figure out how to get the data pull . . . then you'll have your answers.*

I snatched my hand out of Olivia's, turned back, and shoved my trainer into the crack just before Specs managed to close the door.

"The scanner. You said I have to hold it how close to his eyes?" I asked, forcing a brave face while pain skipped across my wedged toes.

Thankfully, he opened the door again, asking a hundred times if I was all right.

"How close, Specs?" I repeated, ignoring him.

"Five inches," he said. "Max." He dangled the disc-shaped device in the air between us. It was built like a slice off the fat end of a carrot. "Just hold it steady in front of his right eye until this red light on the back goes green."

"Deal." I held out four sparkling notes.

Just before he could take the money, I lifted it above his head. "Best know—if your ting don't work, I'm coming back and collecting 120 off you." I paused. "For wasting my time."

"Say no more," he replied, raising his hand to take the cash. His expression turned more serious. "Be careful, though, yeah. This guy is a ghost online. And there are lots of good reasons to be scared of ghosts."

I thought about Specs's words while scaling the stairs back to our flat. I thought about my old English teacher's warning, too.

We all make decisions every day, never knowing which one will destroy us.

7

ESSO

AFTER THE COLLISION, I expect to turn and see a carrot-colored bench stuffed with people waiting for the 78, 381, 63, or 363. And on the other side of the road, I expect a barbershop, followed by a Western Union, then a pub, then a corner shop selling fufu and Oyster card top-ups—the same rota of shops that repeats itself across Narm, interrupted only by the odd £1 store or chain café . . . I expect to see a Range Rover with a dent in its front end and I'm ready to go ballistic on the driver, threaten to sue him, punch him, both. I expect—no, I *hope*—to see a little boy, sitting safely on the pavement, in roughly the same shape and condition I'd met him.

Instead, I can barely see my own hands. Darkness has swallowed them. And inside the darkness are echoes: half-familiar screams and hushed voices, each one loud enough for me to hear, but not clear enough to make out the words. My mind draws its own imaginary lines in the dark, filling it with demonic creatures with jagged teeth and talons.

Scenario A, I think, *this is a dream, and I'm alive.*

Scenario B: I'm dead, and this is either heaven or hell.

A bead of sweat tumbles down my forehead. Above the echoes, I can hear my heart pounding and my breaths getting shorter. In all the Sunday-school lessons I remember, not one mentioned heaven looking like a barren wasteland filled with screams. Not to mention the scorching heat. *Please let this be scenario A.*

A bolt of lightning strikes a hundred meters or so in front of me with a flash so bright I have to turn away. The light hangs in the air for a few seconds after landing, and I take the chance to look around.

I put my hand to the ashy ground as the light slowly fades. It's blacker than volcano skin and filled with cracks as wide as rope. Staring up, I sense a frantic *busy*-ness to the place, even though it's empty and flat in every direction. Well, almost every direction. I haven't looked behind me. I haven't wanted to. Because from the moment I entered this place, I've known something was there.

Tensed up, I ball my hands into fists before turning around.

I've never been to Victoria Falls or the Burj Khalifa or the Great Wall of China, but none of them could fill me with any-where near the sense of insignificance this . . . *thing* . . . does. It's like nothing man or nature could have built. I can only describe it as a kind of massive thread floating above the ground and stretching farther than I can see. It weaves back and forth and around itself, starting from ground level and stacking up so high the top is scraping space. And even though the flash of light is long gone, I can still see all of it clearly, like it's supplying its own faint glow.

I'm urged on by the same why-the-hell-not curiosity that pushes us forward in dreams. Because my first instinct isn't to run or panic but to walk toward it. I think back to the first time I put my eye to a TV and realized that the Power Rangers I'd just spent 20 minutes drooling over were just a line of pixels changing color on the screen. In a similar way, this *thing* isn't a single thread at all. Close-up, I see it's made up of objects hanging near enough together that they *look* connected, but they aren't.

Things get even weirder as I eat up the meters and realize the object closest to me looks almost like . . . *a person?* Whatever it is, it has on the same checkered boxers I wore to bed last night.

I stop dead, hoping that when I reopen my eyes, I'll be seeing and thinking straight again. But the next three objects I see are all wearing my favorite charcoal tracksuit. And each one has the same dark skin and height: *my* dark skin and height.

"That. Is. Mad," I whisper as my eyes widen. "It's *me.*"

Floating above me is another row of objects, one hanging low enough that I could probably touch the heel with a running jump. I squint to get a better look at the features. He has crow's-feet around his eyes, but there's enough resemblance to think this could be me 15 or 20 years on—at least, what I *imagine* I might look like then. Wrapped around the ears of older me is a pair of headphones straight out of *Star Trek*, and the logo on the side seems to say . . . Cantor's? As in the chicken restaurant? *This* has *to be a dream*, I think.

Either way, playing it safe won't get me out. Everyone knows the only way to escape a nightmare is to get so close to the boogie monster that your mind has no choice but wake you up.

Another ground-level shape catches my eye. It—*he? I?*—is wearing my Penny Hill blazer and the same mismatched socks as me. He's hunched over and, for some reason, has a tent-shaped bulge at the zip. I start giggling, then laughing. Soon, I have tears in my eyes and I'm holding my knees for support.

I extend a finger toward my clone's crotch, slowly enough that I can pull back if anything weird happens. But instead of feeling four and a half inches of hot steel, my hand passes through thin air. It's a *projection*: a high-definition, self-illuminating, sick projection. The light pulsing inside it is dim and grainy, like a hologram living on low battery.

But where's the energy coming from? Where's this whole *thing* coming from?

There's only one way to find out.

I angle my front foot into the same spot it's placed in the projection and immediately feel a tingling in my toes. What I'm doing feels risky, but no one's here to save me from myself.

I slide my legs and arms into place and feel the tingling get tighter, almost like the projection is winding itself around me. Finally, I inch my head forward, gasping for whatever surprise is coming.

Sparkling red light fills my vision, then—

I hear cheering and laughing from behind classroom doors. I'm standing in the school hallway, and it reeks of Dettol disinfectant, like it always does.

I can't see if anyone else is nearby because I'm too busy staring down into Nadia's big brown eyes, one arm cradled around her back, my free hand forming a cup around her right bum cheek. As if I've just caught her.

"I see you got a nice handful there, E," she says.

I grin back at her and —

The projection kicks me out after a handful of seconds, and I find myself on the dirt again, scorching wind brushing ash into my eyes and whipping my back.

I guess that explains the boner. Another lightning bolt crackles on the horizon as I stand, smiling. It feels a lot less like a nightmare now. My first dip in the bag was a sweet one, and I wonder if all the projections are the same.

There are at least a thousand projections around me, and those are only the ones close enough to see. I jog to one a few meters along, hoping it'll let me skip to the steamy ending of the scene I just left.

It's night. This time the air comes with a light scent of . . . *fried chicken?*

Filling one corner of my vision is the orange surfboard that sits on top of Peckham Library. I'm in a narrow alleyway—it feels weirdly familiar, but I can't place it; it's too dark.

A hailstone bounces off my cheek and cracks in two on the concrete, and I look up to a sky brimming with them. Bigger ones crash down, faster by the second.

Through the white mess, I make out a face: D's.

He's got a plaster across his cheekbone. He's pressing forward. He looks destroyed, ready to destroy. I catch Bloodshed jogging in behind him.

They're cornering me.

After falling out of this hologram, I land hard on my back. *Okay, that one definitely felt more like a nightmare.*

While lying in the dirt, I struggle to fit together the pieces. The BBC weather lady *did* mention a "massive hailstorm" would be hitting London on Friday. That, at least, explains why my subconscious dropped hail into my dreams. And my ongoing beef with D and Bloodshed obviously explains why they've shown up. But why here? Why now?

Staring at the shimmering Essos floating around me, I'm not sure I even want to see more.

But I have to. How could anyone resist? Plus, while dunked in the last projection, I noticed something—the milky coating that usually helps me tell a dream from reality was missing. I could feel everything that was happening with my whole body, like I was actually there and then.

I start to walk forward. However itchy the next experience might get, it will feel safer and more familiar than the bleak and blazing-hot desert I'm standing in.

Black.

Weird. But I step into another projection right after and it's the same.

In the end, I try eight more projections, counting how long the trip lasts on the final two runs. Each one gives the same result: seven seconds of pure black. A few had faint sounds in the background, but there was nothing to stare at but darkness.

I jog back toward the projection with Nadia, and notice a figure behind it. It's me on my feet, but curled up in a ball with that ugly flinch face I make when I'm shook.

"The car crash," I whisper, trying to figure out what role the order of the holograms might play.

Then I step in.

I'm staring at thick zebra markings on the concrete. Then someone—a woman?—who I can't see screams.

"Preston! No!!!!!"

Tendons snap, bones crunch. The sounds make me nauseous and my mouth fills with bile. When I look up to see where the screams came from, I see the chaperone lady frozen on the roadside—her face and blouse covered with specks of blood.

I run out of that projection so fast, I have to sidestep the next one to make sure I don't fall straight into another nightmare. A shiver prickles up my spine. I *thought* I didn't dodge the car in time, and if the vision I've just seen is true, now I know the little boy didn't either.

It's not real, I remind myself. *It's definitely not real.* But I can't stop replaying the moments before the crash, seeing that ghostly look on his face before impact.

Suddenly it feels like the heat's been cranked up two notches, to the point where I wonder if I might suffocate in the hot air. If death exists in this place, it's on its way. I notice I'm thinking about everyone I left behind. Rob, Kato, Nadia. Mum. Even with the whole D situation waiting for me at school, it's enough to make me miss the warm familiarity of a place like Penny Hill.

"It's just a dream; it has to be," I shout while sprinting as far away from this impossible thing as I can. My legs struggle to keep up as I imagine some giant bat sweeping in to claw me back.

"Remember," I say, panting, "it's just a dream." But inside, I'm screaming, praying I wake up soon.

8

RHIA · (15 YEARS LATER)

I WENT THROUGH the notes I'd jotted down before the tutorial in my head. First (and unlike what the new Daredevil comic would've had you believe), blind people didn't have enhanced smell or super hearing; they just listened to their other senses a bit more. Second, blind people did blink, which meant I'd have to time my scan just right. If at all possible, I'd try to take two. Finally, and most important, of all the people who were certified blind, the majority weren't actually *fully* blind. So only *after* I put the iris scanner to Dr. Esso's eyeball would I know whether he'd see it.

He came in wearing the 2033 editions of the Cantor's Kinetic headphones and, with a magician's finesse, slid them into the front compartment of his rucksack. I couldn't leave that kit room without his biometrics in my pocket. I had a plan, but the riskiest part of it was holding my nerve till it finally came time to execute it.

"I see you got your eyebrows done again." I laid on an

extra-casual tone. "Don't get me wrong, I trim mine pretty often. But, mate—you're dedicated."

Olivia and I had agreed I couldn't be any less snarky than I'd been in our first tutorial. I admit it brought me some comfort to know he couldn't diss me back based on my own looks. With the pea-sized pimple on my forehead and the girls at school crowning me president of the itty-bitty titty committee, I'd never seen myself as bulletproof.

"Thanks for the encouragement," he replied, deadpan. "Make sure you bring that same positive energy when you're cheering on your teammates from the bench this weekend."

Wow, he'd been keeping tabs. I had to force a gulp down my throat before I could answer. "If our midfield weren't a bunch of hoggers, I'd have *a lot* more goals by now."

"Right," he said. "And if my bank was a bit more generous, I'd be rocking a Rolex."

"Yeah, but . . . I mean . . . you know . . ."

After waiting for me to break the two-word barrier without success, he waved at the open chair opposite his, then said: "Shall we?"

Fifteen minutes left, and I still hadn't been able to segue into the discussion I needed to have. His face was a foot too far away for me to stretch over and take the scan from my seat. I had to get much closer, which meant I had to be smart. *Be patient*, I kept reminding myself. *You've got a plan, just be patient.*

My homework was open and, as usual, he made me read it

out loud. "'No matter how slow or fast you're going,'" I said, "'light will always be going 300,000 kilometers per second faster than you. No matter what. PLEASE DISCUSS.'"

I'd actually spent a decent amount of time on it the night before, but after an hour of staring at the sheet, I still hadn't come close to a satisfying answer. I also knew there was much less chance of Dr. Esso raising one of his scraggly eyebrows if I showed interest in his mid-lesson monologues. It worked in my favor to have him believe I gave half a shit. Showing any sort of curiosity about an adult's interests was the easiest way to have them eating from your palm.

"And?" He leaned in for my response.

"And it doesn't make any sense."

"Don't it?" he asked.

"I literally spent all night wondering why you'd put me through this torture."

He chuckled to himself. "I know it sounds crazy, but it's important you proper get this one." He started tapping his foot. "That way, you'll understand everything else I need to tell you."

I felt my chest tighten, my neck getting so tense that I couldn't move it. *Mum*, I thought, wondering if that was where he was leading me. Maybe Dr. Esso *had* found me on purpose. Maybe she *was* why he was here.

No. I had to focus. I couldn't afford to hold those hopes too long or let one shady comment dismantle the trap I'd planned.

After some time rummaging, he placed his Caster-5 on

the table, smiling like a rich kid on Christmas. I still couldn't understand why he was so fanatical about this physics stuff, but knew I had to pree everything he said, regardless of the topic.

"Okay." I took a quiet breath in, reminding myself to use the same kind of words he liked using. "So, I actually came up with my own 'thought experiment.' Just to prove how ridiculous the statement in your assignment is."

"Let's go," he said with the same overexcitement he'd had from the start.

"All right—so, imagine it's just me, you, and my sister, Olivia, in Dangote Stadium. Olivia's sitting up in the stands, while you and I are down at the halfway mark on the pitch. You've got a flashlight in your hand and decide to turn it on and point it at a goal. And, for some reason, I decide to chase after the light beam that comes out of it."

A hologram appeared above the table, a near-perfect rendering of the scene I'd been imagining.

"Safe," he added. "I'm following."

If he says the word "safe" one more time, I'm going to shoot myself in the face, I thought, but out loud, continued:

"Now, imagine Olivia has this device that can measure the speed of the light coming out your flashlight. There's no reason she wouldn't get the bog-standard speed for light when she measures it, right?"

"Right. So around 300,000 kilometers per second."

"Exactly," I confirmed. "All right, boom. Now, let's say I'm carrying my own light-speed measuring device as well. And I know it's stupidly far-fetched, but let's just say that by some miracle, maybe with a jet pack or something, I'm able to reach a superfast speed while I'm running after the light beam . . . as in, *almost* light-speed fast, so like 298,000 kilometers per second, instead of around 300,000."

"I'm digging it, still," he confirmed. "Keep going."

"Well, this is where it all goes pear-shaped: if I'm running fast enough to *almost* catch up with the light beam, I should measure the light beam as only going a *tiny* bit faster than me, right? 2,000 kilometers per hour faster?"

"Don't get me wrong," he replied. "Your logic makes sense for pretty much everything in the universe. Except light. Here, your gadget would say that the light beam is *still* going 300,000 kilometers faster than you. And it would be right."

He smirked. I should have been happy as well; I was executing my plan perfectly, convincing him physics was all I had on my mind. But I still felt like chucking my textbook at him.

"So, let me get this straight," I demanded. "On one hand, Olivia is sitting completely still, and she measures the light beam as going 300,000 kilometers per second faster than her toward the net. On the other hand, I'm running at a whopping 298,000 kilometers per second, and my device says the same thing? That the light beam is going 300,000 kilometers faster than me as well?"

"Correct."

"But that makes no bloody sense!"

"Like chasing after a sunset, innit," he added, grinning. "Or like tryna fill up a bucket with a hole in it. And the faster you dump water in it, the faster it leaks out." He stopped himself from coming up with a third comparison when he realized I wasn't laughing.

"I can't tell if you're just lying, or if you got your PhD from a pawnshop and don't actually know what you're on about."

"Well, let's do one more thought experiment to find out." He was rubbing his beard, probably thinking what he had to say next was *so* deep. "Imagine it's a decade in the future," he said. "And by some train smash of luck, you find yourself on the Henry Kyle talk show."

Bloody hell, I thought, realizing we only had five minutes of the lesson left. I just needed to find a subtle way of shutting down his story and redirecting the conversation to one that justified me standing next to him with a gadget in his face.

"Sorry, mate, but I'll pass on that story. I've got enough problems in my life without you jinxing that kind of energy into it. But I do have a question from school I needed to ask you—"

"Why do you hate fun so much?" His shoulders dropped and the sparkle left his eyes. "I feel like I've been proper trying . . . and nothing's working."

Maybe I'd taken my mean-girl act a step too far.

"I'm sorry, mate." It wasn't until the words came out that I realized I almost meant them. "I was just messing about."

"Is it cancer?" he asked, looking even more serious and concerned.

"Excuse me?"

"Cancer of your fun glands?"

"Jeez," I said, shaking my head. "That joke was terrible."

"Or is it fun-givitis?"

"Yep, that's the one, Doc," I responded. "You got me there."

"Or maybe you fractured your funny bone. I heard that injury ain't a joke."

"Okay, okay, I get it—you can carry on with your Henry Kyle story. Anything to end these bloody dad jokes." A weird, prickly feeling came up with the word "dad," which I managed to push aside. "Just *please* be quick."

He wasted no time accepting my thorny olive branch. "All right, let man set the scene," he said, wriggling his body into character. "A decade from now . . . you're sittin' on one of them red couches, center stage. Then out of nowhere—*bam!*—your old team captain Maria runs in from behind the curtains. She's smiling and shouting about how *your* husband—your buff, loving, faithful husband of four years—is actually the father of *her* brand-new baby boy."

"You're really taking it there."

"Mind you, you've had three yutes for them man there; you decided to give up your footy career and everything. Meanwhile, he's on his knees, pointing to the ring on your finger to remind you he would *never* cheat on you. The camera zooms in on your face, and the home audience wonders: Will she take what he's saying at face value? Will she allow him?"

"Are you mad?" I responded, sitting up. "First I'd scratch up Maria's face. Then I'd get the DNA tests off Henry, and even if they came back negative, I'd still *physically* choke the truth out of that waste lieutenant."

It wasn't clear who broke the silence first. But after a minute of imagining the most ratchet moment in daytime television history, we were both bent up in laughter.

"Your response proves my point perfectly, though," he said, still creasing. Then he took on an even, almost wary tone. "Everything we see is thanks to light. We rely on it so much that everything it shows us seems like the whole truth. And yet you don't know a damn thing about this partner of yours. You never thought it might be worth scrolling through his text messages when he left his phone on the table? You never wondered how many other chicks light says *I love you* to?"

"All right," I said, rubbing my neck. "No need to lay it on so thick. I get it: light is dodgy."

"Proper dodgy," he responded.

"And I guess what you're practically tryna tell me is that one of light's dodgy secrets is that no matter how fast you move alongside it, it will *always* be moving 300,000 kilometers per second faster than you."

"No. Matter. What." He hammered his finger into the table on each word. "I didn't make that up to piss you off. It's just a cold, hard fact. People have done hundreds of experiments to prove it's true. The Michelson-Morley experiment, the Kennedy-Thorndike tests, Ives-Stillwell. Look them up after this."

He paused, chewed on his lip. Under the table, I spotted his trainer caps pointing straight up, like he was getting ready to launch through the ceiling with his next words. "Let there be light. Light was there from the beginning, but it wasn't till Einstein came along that we bothered paying attention. He used maths to prove how dodgy light is, but even today, we're still finding out more, still scratching our heads at *why* it acts the way it does—"

"This is that quantum physics shit, innit?" It was a wild guess, but also the go-to explainer for everything in films these days.

"Nah, it's actually Einstein's theory of relativity," he said, being gentle so I wouldn't feel shot down. "It's all about space and time, and how they behave differently from different per-spectives. It's about the fact that everything's relative."

Amy, the weekday janitor, poked her head through the door. "Sorry to interrupt, you two." With two minutes of class left, this was the *worst* possible time. "I know you live in Peck-ham, Rhia—just wanted to warn you to be extra careful going home. There was some news on the radio about a shooting around there. Thirteen dead. Bloodshed affiliates, apparently."

"Again," I sighed once she'd shut the door behind her.

"D'you know him?" Dr. Esso asked with eager eyes. "Blood-shed?"

"Of course," I replied, baffled that he'd asked and wondering why he cared. Everyone in the country knew about Bloodshed and his guys. His face came up on *OppWatch* so often he was in the opening credits. Realizing I might have missed the point, I clarified: "I mean, I don't know him *personally*. Do you?"

"Yeah," he said, toes back down. "When we were kids, though. He was active back then, to be honest. But not like this. Nothing like this.

"Anyway," he said, in a lighter tone. "You're from ends, innit, so you know I can't say much more."

Another heart-racing comment I'd have to ignore. At least for now. I was gripping the sides of my seat, fearing how far above my head I might be. The same man whose feet had gone dodgy when we'd first met, who kept a photo of my mum in his pouch, was also childhood mates with Xavier "Bloodshed" Teno?

And apparently obsessed with physics. He talked about equations the way most people talked about family, curling his fingers into twin pistols as he spoke, like he was ready to defend them.

"Anyway, I guess that's it for today," he said.

Get in the zone, Rhia, I shouted in my head. I'd buttered him up more than enough—it was now or never.

"Before I forget." I cleared my throat, wiped my palms off on my trackie bottoms. "During our Brand Management class today, our teacher mentioned that back in the twenties, teenagers used to do this thing on social media. I think they were called *selfies?* Basically, when you stretch your arm out and take an awkward photo of yourself in a completely nonironic way."

"Yeah." He was smiling and shaking his head. "A selfie."

"Well, for my homework I have to take one with someone I know who was born before 2008."

"Cool," he said, taking a while to catch up. "Oh, shit—you want one with me, don't you? Sorry, I don't actually know how to use the camera well on most phones —"

Before he could finish, I'd scuttered round to his side of the table, phone in hand. "Use mine. Just hold it there and press any button when you're ready." I couldn't believe I was taking part in this bizarre tradition, but I knew it was for a greater cause. "I'll be throwing up a peace sign. You can do whatever your ting was in the olden days."

A couple seconds of open eyes were all I needed. I yanked the scanner from my pocket and held it just in front of his face as he squared up my camera. *One,* I counted silently, *two—*

"Which button was it again?" His eyes flicked away just as the light was due to turn green.

"Any button!" I replied, forgetting to rein myself in.

"All right . . . Jesus." This time he counted down: "Let's both say cheese in one . . ."

Please work, I was crying inside.

"Two . . ."

Please!

"Cheese!"

I barely registered the flash. Once the light on the scanner went green, I quickly slid the device back into my pocket and felt my entire body sigh in relief. I still had to find someone who could retrieve his records with it, but I'd accomplished part one of the job. Now I had to get the hell out of there.

"Before you go, Rhia." His voice made me jump as I was already twisting the doorknob. "I also had a bit of a random, somewhat theoretical, question for you."

I waited in silence, getting antsier with each passing second.

"We talked for a while about the future today," he continued. "But what about the past?"

"The past?" I checked, wondering where this could possibly be going.

"I guess my real question is: If you could go back in time—you know, to the past—and change things, would you?"

His question punched me with a force somehow bigger than the sum of his words. Maybe it was the fact it had arrived out of nowhere. Maybe it was his serious-as-death tone. Or maybe it was the question itself.

In what universe would I *not* want my mum alive and with me instead of dead and forgotten? My heart wanted to scream,

YES! in response. But my gut, which had sunk the moment he asked the question, knew it wasn't that simple. I had no idea what a happy family life with Mum would even look like. And most important, I still didn't know or trust this man.

"I'm not gonna lie," I lied. "I've never really thought about it." But he'd picked loose a thread of curiosity that was now dangling between us, waiting to be pulled. "But how exactly is that related to the speed of light?"

"Well . . ." He shoved in one of his painful silences, and that was when I noticed he was wearing the same face he'd worn when I'd met him, the time I'd looked down at his feet and seen them: shook. "Because light is the key to time travel," he continued. "And time travel is . . ."

He stopped before he could finish, before I could process what I was feeling, but well in time for his guard to slide right back up. "Let's chat about this next time," he said, zipping his coat to the top.

And yet I had a feeling I knew exactly what he'd wanted to say. I might only just be seeing it, but the message—in all its warped, delusional logic—had been written on his heart all along. He'd found me on purpose. He was *here* on purpose. And the reason he was pushing me through these lessons, forcing me to understand every line of maths, was that he wanted me to believe what he saw as fact.

That time travel could be real.

9

ESSO

"CHRIST! THANK *GOODNESS* you're alive."

I couldn't have put it better myself.

The voice came from an oval blur hovering above me. I crossed my fingers, hoping the air I was breathing was made with real, earthly oxygen. Once my eyes cleared, my prayers were answered: it was the chaperone lady, kneeling over me and smiling. Each one of her individual features was a smidgen off: her eyes looked almost *too* round; her nose was stick-thin at the base; and her lips, although nice and full, were chapped on every goddamn edge. But somehow it all came together in a peng package.

It *had* been just a dream.

As more detail came into view, I saw bodies of all shapes standing over me. On my back and spread across the tarmac, I felt like I was watching my own wake—paralyzed in an open coffin while strangers looked down, mourned, then walked on again.

"I saw your eyes turning this dark shade of gray—I was *seconds* away from giving you mouth-to-mouth!" the chaperone said, laughing, with her manicured fingers resting on her windpipe.

"You were?" I responded.

Seeing her cheeks redden, I wished I could go back in time and choose two slightly less thirsty words as my first ones.

Focus, Esso. My school shirt was drenched in sweat, reminding me how scorching it had been in that dreamworld. Despite it being below zero on the street, the juju energy of that place had somehow followed me, and the scream of *Preston! No!* still rang in my ears. I shook my head and searched for memories from just before the crash. Once the first one arrived, the rest flooded in all at once, fast, along with a minute's worth of heartbeats. It had only been a dream. Surely it had only been a dream.

"Where's Preston?" I asked the chaperone.

Her face tangled. "Who?"

I wasn't sure what to say next, how to explain. So, instead of trying and failing, I scanned the crowd myself in case there was anyone who looked remotely Asian in it—ideally a young boy under five feet. A group of children were standing at the entrance of an alleyway roughly 20 yards down the road. I squinted for a gap between their bodies and found what I'd been searching for.

He was at the center of the crowd, same bowl cut and corduroy trousers, though his tie had come loose into two strands down his chest. The same boy who'd almost gotten me killed was now jumping around, reenacting the car crash scene, starting with a slo-mo sprint on the spot, then a swan dive with arms fanned out like a keeper.

I saved him, I realized. *I actually saved him!* Plus, *I* was alive. Considering how badly things could have played out, no one could blame me for feeling as wavy as I was.

But my excitement disappeared the second I recognized where he was standing. Now, in the clear light of day, I could see it was the same narrow alleyway from that dream of D and Bloodshed coming for me in a hailstorm.

But if the vision of Preston getting splattered by an SUV hadn't come true, why would that one? Surely that scary dream of D and Bloodshed was just my subconscious trying to tell me that I still had serious danger in the real world to look forward to. In the real world, I'd just gotten hit by a Range Rover, and the ride to Guy's Hospital—only a short walk from the biggest T.A.S. block—could be my last. The real world needed me to get off my ass. And fast.

The chaperone lady was waving her hands in front of my eyes to steal back my attention. "I just have to say, what you did was incredibly brave. You saved his life." She scanned around to see if anyone was in earshot, then said, "You probably saved my job, as well."

"Can you help me up, please?" I asked her.

"Of course. Of course."

I grabbed her extended arm, and she wrapped her free one

around my shoulders. I could hear my polyester shirt peeling off the wet tarmac, and my back clicking as my spine curled its way up. A man in the crowd, seeing I was struggling, shuffled forward to help. He was bald, cheerful, and enormous, with a pair of stonewashed jeans and a matching jacket that he was rocking like Commercial Way was his catwalk.

"Why are you babying dis guy? Come on and gerr'up, my friend," he said, yanking me to my feet. He was definitely Ghanaian or Nigerian. He had that square-head and beefy-shoulders combo that Ghanaians kept on lock, but then again, he pronounced his "t"s like they were "r"s—just like this one fresh Nigerian kid at school. He was the smartest kid in our class by a hood mile but had us in stitches when he'd say stuff like, "We jus' wanna parry," and "We're jus' poppin' borrels."

Giant speech clouds condensed around the man's lips: "How are you feeling? Is your body hurr-ing? Your upper leg? Your lower leg?" He and the chaperone leaned in for the gruesome details.

"I'm all right, you know." My mind was already on the third and final demerit I was about to collect for being late to school. "My hip feels a bit sore, head's kinda light. But nothing serious."

The most English smile possible appeared on the chaperone's face. A smile that was polite and caring on the surface, but underneath said: *You do not have a say in this; you are an idiot.*

"An ambulance is on the way." She held her careful smile.

"Once it arrives, we'll call your parents, so they know which hospital you're headed to."

"Safe," I said, and while scanning for an easy exit, I happened to notice one paigon in the crowd ahead.

His leather jacket was zipped to his nose, so only the top of his face was visible. But it was a face I could never forget. Staring at him triggered a flashback to before the crash: him playing on his phone while me and junior ran for our little lives. At first, he froze, part of him clearly wanting to leg it. But after a long sigh, he waded through the mass of onlookers toward me.

"Bruv, sorry about that—I was trying to slow down, but I didn't see you till the last second." He kicked away the one-legged pigeon picking at his feet, but it came hopping right back. It was one of those intimidating pigeons that you only get in places like Peckham and Pakistan. The pigeons that make you walk around them like they have the right-of-way.

He continued talking down at me in the same shifty and surprisingly high-pitched tone he'd started with. "Honestly, mate, I'm just glad you're good. Going hospital would have been long, still." He looked at the divot in his car bonnet, then back at my leg, as if comparing the damage on each object. "Next time, just make sure you look both ways before crossing, innit."

I knew—from seeing everyone zoom in on my forehead at the same time—that the vein that ran across it was thumping. If I'd been hot before, I was doused in flames now.

Say something, Esso. Anything. You can't let this dickhead par you like that, I thought. *Don't let him just shirk the blame.*

The crowd had grown to fifteen, maybe twenty, the nearest ones standing by for my response. But as usual, I was too rattled to redeem myself—all my best comebacks tended to pop up in my head a week after they were needed. I closed my gaping mouth and stood quiet while my righteous anger melted into shame. And as the disappointed crowd started to disperse, I felt a tug at my sleeve that couldn't have come at a better time.

"Thanks," the tug said. I looked down, and it was him— the boy I'd saved. He spoke in a mellow whistle, sweet enough to soothe a serial killer. Even his bowl cut, which would have looked ridiculous on any other human being, just seemed to add to his glow.

"That's all right, man," I replied, bending down. "Lucky neither of us got too banged up, get me?"

Another paranoid thought popped into my head. And once it latched, it refused to make space for anything else. I had to ask him. I was already sure; I just needed to be *extra* sure.

"By the way, your name's not Preston, is it?"

The big man in denim—still standing between me and the chaperone lady—burst out laughing and cut in before the kid had a chance to respond. "What kind of nonsense name is Preston?" he asked, personally insulted for the boy. "My friend, look at his face. We both know they don't do such foolishness in China."

The chaperone lady stormed in, making herself a protective barrier in front of him. "He's barely nine years old. And you think it's acceptable to make such blatantly racist comments? You should be ashamed of yourself."

"Racist?" He drew the word out while jerking his head back like he'd been punched. "Me? *Racist?!* Is it not you who walked all these white children safely to the side of the road, where they could be singing and dancing nicely? And then you left this Chinese boy to die in the street?"

"My name's Tom, actually," the boy threw in calmly. "And I'm Vietnamese."

"Yes, yes, I know," the big man responded. "But my main point still stands."

The chaperone lady's mouth hung open. Her bag of comebacks must have had a hole in the bottom, because she had nothing to add.

What a damn mess, I thought. Of course his name wasn't Preston. Of course he was alive. Of course it was just a goddamn dream. The big man might have been wrong in every other way, but he'd been right to call me an idiot.

As we'd been debating the boy's name and what exactly qualifies as racism in modern Britain, the driver had been stumbling backward, almost tripping over the pavement ledge. "'Ow the hell d'you know that name?" His widened eyes traced me up and down like I was an alien. *Just* when I was ready to draw a line under all the spooky shit that had happened to me that morning.

"So, what—is *your* name Preston?" I asked, just in case.

He shook his head, before turning back to his Range Rover parked up the road. "This is long. I'm off."

"Good," the big man shouted after him. "Go back to tha' rubbish 2018 vehicle." He looked down at me and winked, and I couldn't stop myself cracking up inside.

The engine on the black tank roared to life, and before the window on the driver's side could reach the top lip, a fluffy terrier dog hopped out.

Right as an 18-wheeler was rolling past.

"Jesu!!" the big man in denim shouted. Everyone scrambled for safety on the side of the road—everyone but the dog.

I turned away, squeezing my body into the tightest ball possible. But that didn't stop me *hearing* everything that happened—starting with the man in the Range Rover yelling the two words that had been ringing in my ears ever since I'd left that heated dream.

"Preston! No!!!!!"

10

RHIA · (15 YEARS LATER)

EVEN ON WEEKNIGHTS, SE Dons matches felt like block parties. Olivia and I were in the stands and down to our last two nuggets when the referee blew for the start of second half, inspiring a fresh chant from the crowd. Smog might have roamed the streets outside, but mega-tycoon Dangote buying the club had brought a shiny layer to everything inside the grounds: leather dugout seats; a pair of eight-figure Chinese strikers; the newest Bugatti for Don Strapzy; and a silver-haired manager who looked like a Bond villain. With over 50,000 fans exchanging body heat, it wasn't the most ideal spot for our weekly debrief. But academy players got free tickets and Olivia had let me pick the venue for once—so I figured we might as well spend our time supporting the boys.

I'd finally found someone to pull the data from Dr. Esso's iris scanner. But I wasn't exactly rushing to tell Olivia, knowing how she'd react when she heard who was helping me.

Five days had passed since Dr. Esso made his comment

about light being the key to time travel. I couldn't stop thinking about it, and was more convinced than ever that when
he'd mentioned going back in time to *change* things, he'd been
talking about Mum.

I didn't have proof of anything yet, though. In fact, the only
solid thing for me to touch was the dirty napkin in my coat
pocket, which I'd scribbled on with equations on both sides.
Once I'd started my most recent extra-credit assignment, I
hadn't been able to get it off my mind. It was weird how much
time I'd spent on it; it was weird that it mattered to me. I'd gone
from refusing to see the point of Dr. Esso's questions to seeing
the answers rise off the page. I knew what Olivia would say if I
told her about my new obsession with homework: Dr. Esso was
selling me on a science-based cult and I should run a mile. I
should have been telling myself the same thing.

As she shared the gritty details of her latest date, I pushed
the napkin farther into my coat—*No need to go into that tonight.*

"I had on the Alonuko corset you got me—the one with
the aerographene mesh. And you know how excited I get on
my birthdays." She bumped my arm. "My expectations were
probably a bit too high, though."

I braced myself in my seat, knowing the story would turn
any second.

"In fact," Olivia continued, "I stepped out the house thinking, *Nothing can spoil this day.*"

"Wait, before you go on," I interrupted. "Red flags? You
gotta start with the red flags, sis. You know the rules."

"Nah, you're gonna laugh."

"I won't." It was a lie, but that was part of our routine.

"His name . . ." She paused, squeezing her face like it hurt all over. "His name was Ricky Christmas."

Whatever cool I'd held up to that point shattered to bits, and I turned away so she couldn't see how hard I was cracking up. Hearing his surname also reminded me of the plastic tree we were meant to set up in the living room that weekend.

"I know." To soothe herself, she patted the gelled ridges of her finger waves. "So, anyway, Ricky Christmas picks me up from our flat. And literally, within 30 seconds of leaving, he's already looking for parking. Now, we both know there ain't no nice restaurants between our yard and Queens Road station. But, I'm trying to be open-minded, telling myself: *Stop being so judgy; give the boy a chance.*" It wasn't lost on me that the voice she used to mimic her nagging conscience was the same one she used when she was mimicking me.

"So, then, Christmas leads me into the train station. The *train* station, Rhia. And we walk right past the ticket barriers, the shops, all dat, till we reach a section I ain't ever even seen before."

"Not gonna lie," I said, just to pinch her back, "this guy's getting 10 out of 10 for originality in my book so far."

She ignored my comment. "Then we walk into this dark, abandoned-looking restaurant—basically a graveyard that smells of pork. And no one else is there—it's *literally* just us two—and my G has the nerve to say to the waiter—wait for it"—she paused to gather her composure—"he says to the waiter, 'Table for two, under Sexy Santa,' then winks at me."

I was sliding off my seat again from laughing too hard.

"Oh, you reckon *that's* funny?" Olivia said, giggling. "Wait for the part when lover boy showed me the pine-tree tattoo on his bicep."

My phone rang in my pocket as she was talking. I snatched it up. *It's him.*

He'd promised me he could pull everything ever documented on Dr. Esso—social media, police reports, hospital and council records, taxes—and all for free. Which meant I'd have my answers. *The* answers: Who I am. Where I'm from. Where I'm going. Answers that most kids come built with and don't even know it.

"Is that . . ." Olivia snatched my phone as I was lifting it to answer.

"Give it back!" I reached across, very ready to wrestle her for it.

She grinned while stretching away from me, the guy next to her not too pleased about having his side of the armrest invaded. "Not until you tell me what on earth you're chatting to *him* about at 8 p.m."

The "him" she was referring to was my ex-boyfriend, Linford. His mum worked high up at CantorCorp, which housed all the government's civilian data, and according to him, there was a way to get in.

"Tell me why he's calling. Or I'm gonna pick up and tell him you hate Italian mopeds."

It wasn't till after I'd broken up with Linford that I found out how much he irritated Olivia. You could see her holding back vomit each time he mentioned that 16,000-quid Vespa he rode into school every day. Not that it ever stopped him. But most of Olivia's dislike came from her seeing how flaky and shifty he'd been in our three-month relationship last year. She kept telling me I deserved much better.

As my phone kept ringing, I imagined Linford's frustration on the other end, which only amplified mine. What if he got cold feet mid-ring and changed his mind? He'd only agreed to help because we'd shared saliva in the past and agreed to "stay friends" after. But what I had asked him to do was technically illegal. He'd have been smart to bail, especially if he thought I was ignoring his call.

Coming clean to Olivia ASAP was the only way to rescue the situation.

"Linford agreed to do the data pull for me," I shouted, still trying to retrieve my phone. "I'm going to his house tomorrow to get it. It's nothing."

"And I"—she wrapped my phone behind her back, pushing it even farther out of reach—"am coming with you."

I stopped and sat back to get a look at her. I'd expected a scorching, a long lecture where she scolded me for coming up with the idea, then for going through with it, and finally for keeping her in the dark.

"Sisters before misters, innit." She pressed the phone to her ear.

Her final comment made me a tad less nervous, but I was

still hanging on to my seat.

"Hey, it's Olivia," she grumbled into the phone. "Yeah, but she's not here right now."

I bit my nail down to the pink waiting for his response, praying she wouldn't scare him off.

"Tomorrow, 8 p.m. it is." She hung up and handed me back my mobile.

"Thank you," I sighed. I couldn't remember any other time I'd meant it so much.

"Instead of thanking me, why don't you tell me what else is going on here?"

Maybe the sight of me chewing off my fingers was what had made her ask. Or maybe it was just a guess. Either way, she was too smart for me to play dumb, and I'd been sitting on these secrets for the best part of a week.

Plus, deep down, I was dying to tell her. I *wanted* her to accept me obsessing over my physics homework the same way she'd gotten behind my Linford plan. Her scowl sank deeper the longer I kept her waiting. So I reached into my jacket pocket for the final secret.

"Wow," Olivia said, after grabbing the napkin. She spent a minute trying to make sense of it. "I'm gonna need you to explain why the hell you've got a Cantor's napkin with equations written all over it. And more important, why you're being so weird and secretive about it."

"I'm not being weird and secretive," I answered, hoping the less bothered I sounded, the less she'd bother me. "It's just some homework I was doing before you got here since I had no paper on me. It's to do with this weird time-travel thing called time dilation."

"D'you actually understand this stuff?" she said, handing the napkin back.

"Yeah." I paused to think on it further. "Well . . . maybe like 80%."

"Explain it to me, then."

I twisted to get a fresh look at her, make sure she wasn't ill.

"What, you think I haven't noticed the hours you're putting in on your homework? Look, I get it—you don't want your GCSEs to be the reason you don't get your Dons contract."

Phew. She still believed this was about football, which was a relief since my real reason for being so nerdy would have been a much tougher sell.

"Also, don't sleep on me," she added, probably spotting the doubt still on my face. "Just cos I'm buff and sociable doesn't mean I'm not up for a bit of time-travel maths."

"You used that line on Christmas, didn't you?" I passed off casually. "It's a lot classier than your hand-shandy joke, to be fair."

"Whatever," she responded. "All right. Time travel. Maths. Explain. Now."

"You asked for it." I took a fresh napkin from Olivia and unfolded it, pausing for just a few seconds to think through my explanation. Then I clicked my gel pen. "Imagine the ink in here is a source of light. So any line I draw on this napkin represents the path a beam of light can take."

I asked her to pull up the stopwatch on her phone. "I want you to press *start* on that once I start drawing. Then press *stop* once I reach the top. Cool?"

After I'd finished drawing, she read out the time stamp. "Around 4 seconds."

"Nice one. Now I'm gonna draw a second line, starting from the same place as before, but this time I'm making the light travel *vertically* up, rather than diagonally like the last one."

"2 seconds," she said the second time, watching me scribble her numbers on the napkin.

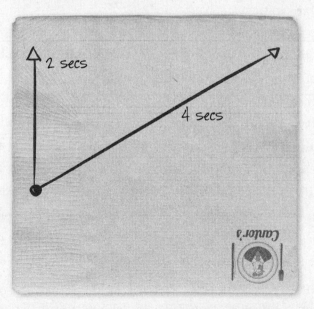

"As you can see—it took me twice as long to draw the diagonal light beam as it did the vertical one. Why?"

"Cos it's twice as long, innit?" She looked unimpressed so far. "The light had twice as far to go."

"Yes! And because I kept my writing speed—i.e., the speed of light—the same both times."

She opened her mouth to speak, but before she could get any cheek out, I reminded her, "You're the one who asked me to explain this to you. Gonna let me land or not?"

"Chill, fam—I was actually just thinking," she replied, leaning forward again. "Jesus."

"This final bit will only take a minute, anyway." I stole the last remaining napkin from her lap. "All right, boom. Now, I need you to imagine Tony driving his old Tesla out at night with Poppy in the passenger seat."

"So all I have to do is imagine a world where Tony has his license back," she said, giggling. "And hasn't chugged half a bottle of Famous Grouse before getting into a car."

It crossed my mind that—in a roundabout way—maybe Tony liked a drink because he was into time travel as well. A half bottle of spirit let Tony take all of today's problems and dump them into tomorrow. And with just a few more swigs, he could steal all of tomorrow's energy and squander it today.

Even if you never quite knew *when* he was, at least he was there. He and Poppy were the only ones who gave enough of a shit about kids like Olivia and me to put us up. Tony was also the one who'd pulled strings with Gibbsy—his old mate from when they were at secondary school together in Devon—and gotten me my trial at Dons. So we had Tony to thank for the heated seats we were sitting on and, assuming I kept impressing the head coach, for my soon-to-be full-time contract.

"Anywaysss," I hissed, trying to remember where she'd interrupted. "So, yeah—Tony's speeding along. Poppy's in the passenger seat, and by mistake, triggers the flashlight on her phone, making its bright white light shoot straight up into her eyes. Now, imagine *you*"—I lifted my pen at her—"are standing on the pavement when the Tesla goes by. Since the car is speeding past you from left to right at the same time that the light from Poppy's flashlight is shooting vertically up into her eyes inside the car, you basically see the light beam taking an overall *diagonal* path. Sort of like this."

"Now, if you're looking at the same event from *Tony's* perspective—i.e., watching this scene play out from *inside* the whip—the picture's quite different. Since everything inside the car is moving at the same speed as the car itself, the phone in Poppy's lap looks stationary to Tony. To him, the phone isn't moving backward or forward—it's resting in the same spot in Poppy's lap next to him the whole time. So when Tony turns to the side, he just sees the light beam shoot straight up into his wife's eyes—he sees it travel vertically." I sketched the final bit of the diagram for her.

"You see where this is going?"

She stayed quiet. The guy next to her shook his head for the umpteenth time, probably wondering why our analysis couldn't wait till after the match.

"Lemme summarize. You and Tony both saw the exact same event: a light beam going from Poppy's phone into her eyes. But the path you watched the light take was diagonal—and therefore *twice* as long as the vertical path that Tony saw from his seat."

I overlaid the second napkin on the first so she might catch the resemblance. "So if Tony claimed that the light took 2 seconds to get to her eyes, then you would say it took—"

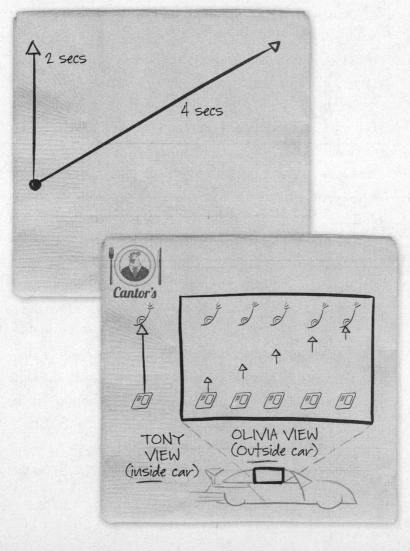

She put her hand up, so she could answer. "I would say it took 4 seconds. Twice the time."

"Yes, Olivia!" I held out my right fist, but she was too busy napkin-gazing to notice.

"So the time it takes the light beam to go from the phone to her eyes is different, depending on who you ask . . ." A corner kick later and she still looked spooked by her own answer. "*Shiiiit.*"

"I know," I replied, glad to see she was having the same reaction I'd had when I'd realized it.

"But who's right?" She was still absorbed in the diagram. "Did the light beam take 2 seconds to reach Poppy's eyes? Or 4 seconds?"

"That's the manic bit: you're *both* right!" I grabbed her shoulders, turning her to face me. "We grow up assuming there's some invisible, silent grandfather clock out there that sets the time that the universe marches to." I could feel my pulse rising, but I forced most of my excitement into hiding. "But that's all *completely* wrong. We actually all have our *own* clocks: some ticking at one pace over here, others ticking slower over there. And turns out, the faster you move, the slower your clock ticks compared to everyone else's." I pointed back to the napkin. "So, because Tony was in a speeding car, he saw the same event take half as much time as you did." I paused to let the next line really bang. "Fewer seconds passed in that car, which means time *literally* went slower for him and Poppy.

"When time stretches out like that," I continued, "it's called time dilation. It happens all the time in real life, and the effect is just too tiny for us to notice. But if you got near the speed of light, you'd notice it. You'd see time slow down to a fucking trickle."

"You've changed, Rhia," she said, only half joking. From the look on her face, she'd gone from curious to suspicious, and I'd missed the turning point.

"Nah," I replied, spinning to the pitch before she smelled the rest of my anxiety. "Just showing you cah you asked."

She'd taken the Linford thing quite well, and had breezed through the physics, and that would be enough. Asking her to believe the napkin in my lap had any connection whatsoever with my mum felt like a step too far. I was still working up the courage to say it to *myself* out loud. I knew how ridiculous it sounded. And I knew any possibility could die if you let it out too early.

I could feel her staring at me, analyzing me, judging me. But I kept my nerve. "These assignments have also been really helpful in getting Dr. Esso's trust."

And she kept hers. "Fair enough." After a long pause, she added, "But when he starts trying to lure you into a cult, just remember I warned you."

The ref blew the final whistle. Three–nil. A happy Dons crowd sent applause around the stands, while Olivia and I sprang to our feet to get to the aisle.

As we snaked through the masses and toward the stadium exit, she turned to me: "One last question, sis."

I tensed up, hoping she wouldn't notice the new bead of sweat dancing down my forehead.

"That time-slowing thing . . . time dilation, I think you called it."

I nodded, letting out a humongous sigh inside now that the personal interrogation was done. This kind of question, I could handle.

"Well, you mentioned that time dilation is only noticeable when you're almost at the speed of light. What happens when you actually *hit* the speed of light?" she asked. "What happens to time then?"

The only thing that traveled at the speed of light was light itself, and according to my textbook, it took eight minutes to get from the sun to Earth. But if time shortened at higher speeds, how long did that journey take from *light*'s perspective?

"I guess . . ." The first answer that came to me felt too odd, too extreme. *Nah. Can't be.*

But the harder I fought, the brighter the truth shined through: to light, that 90-million-mile journey across space happened in a single moment. To light, no seconds ever passed at all.

"I guess it stops, innit," I said to Olivia, scared of the words escaping my mouth. "I guess time stops."

11

ESSO

ALWAYS GO FOR the last or second-to-last shitter. That rule had served me well for as long as I could remember. Unfortunately, both bogs on the ground floor at Penny Hill were looking overly sloppy. Even if I went to the hassle of wiping the seats, there was still a fifty-fifty chance that once I sat down, I'd look up and see the sky filled with flying balls of wet toilet paper, each one a soggy arrow aimed at my face. And by the time I pulled up my trousers and opened the door to see who'd thrown them . . . crickets. The seniors would already be out the door.

Because of the slight delay caused by getting hit by a Range Rover, I'd arrived 20 minutes late to school. But thankfully Purdy, seeing me looking a bit dazed and roughed up, had let me off. I'd still had two hours till lunch, though, so I'd had to negotiate a leak break with my geography teacher, which I now planned to spend in a cubicle clearing my head. Thinking about that poor dog getting peeled off the road after I'd left had cast a long, furry shadow over my morning. Then there was that vision of D and Bloodshed cornering me, and worrying that it might come true as well. Although the finer details of the vision had already started fading, it wouldn't stop playing in my mind: I could still feel them creeping toward me, still hear the hailstones crashing down around all three of us with Peckham Library in the distance.

Not for the first time that morning, I felt like I was losing it. Maybe me and Dad had a lot in common, after all.

It was a throwaway thought, but made me pause. That place I'd dreamed up after the crash did have stuff in common with what he'd scribbled in his notebook. The "Upper World," I thought he'd called it. Hadn't he also written some shit about seeing time differently there? I was pretty sure he'd even used the words "Hidden Energy" on one line, which reminded me of that searing heat from nowhere that I'd felt throughout the dream. What if the impact from the crash had somehow jolted me out of that "cave" he'd described on the first page?

I patted the sore side of my head. My brain clearly had me imagining stuff, seeing my dad's words where they didn't belong.

But then again, a jumbled mind didn't explain the whole "Preston! No!" thing. It couldn't. Once that premonition had come true, everything else had no choice but to be more real as well.

Maybe, I thought, smiling while I inspected the next cubicle, *Dad wasn't that mad after all*. Maybe he'd known way back when that something like this might happen and had cared enough to tell me.

Even if I was wrong, it still made sense to be shit-scared of D and Bloodshed. In fact, on the bus ride over, I'd sent a just-in-case-this-shit-is-real text to Spark, and had breathed a sigh of relief when he'd responded a few seconds later:

Brixton yutes in Narm tonite? Say nuttin

"Say nuttin." Two teeny words. But look close enough, and you'd find a multiverse of hatred in the short gap between them. It was funny—whenever I told someone Spark was my guy, they'd respond with something like: *You don't mean Spark as in . . . the* gangster *Spark . . . ?* And after a careful pause: *Do you?* I remember one night at his house, he confessed to me that his sickle cell meant he spent about 6 out of 24 hours each day in excruciating pain. I wondered if that was part of what made him so ruthless—he was so used to being hurt it was nothing to make someone else feel the same. The fact I'd sent another message to Spark clarifying that my first text was "not worth telling anyone about" and "just a rumor" would have no effect—before the sun went down, he'd have a circle of shooters waiting for the word.

I ended up going for the urinal farthest from the door— more out of loyalty than logic. *Danny B* ❤ *batty crease* was scribbled on the wall, and a few inches to the right, in the same neat handwriting and ink, was a phone number.

I'd always wondered if one of Danny B's mates had written it to take the mick. Or if Danny had written it himself.

Corey Marciel walked in, smiling into his phone. My guy was clipping six foot four at 15. Not only was he the most chased-after boy in school, but he was also arguably the most talented midfielder in South London. Girls turned into stuttering messes when they were around him. Even guys got kinda neeky and beg-friendly when he was about. Lineup fresh, he bopped to the urinal next to me, pretended I wasn't there, then we both unzipped and let our streams loose.

"Whuuuuhaaaaaa…" I was stuck between the words "what," "oooh," and "ahhh," and that was how it all came out.

Instead of its usual solid lemon color, my urine was filled with red streaks.

In my confusion, I lost control of my line, and it scraped the edge of the urinal before I managed to swing it back to center. Thankfully, none of it splashed on Corey. He must have been wondering what the hell was going on, because his eye wandered down to where I was aiming, and I watched him snap upright like he'd been tased.

"I . . ."

That lonely, pathetic word was all I managed. But what words could I add to make the situation any less embarrassing, without also making it worse? *I promise, Corey, the next time you look over at my urinal, we'll both be better prepared for it?* Or maybe I could maturely acknowledge the situation: *I know exactly how this looks, Corey. But trust me, I'm just as concerned by the color of my piss as you are.*

I'd checked my whole body after I got hit by the Range,

and there hadn't been any blood anywhere. Plus, I wasn't in any serious pain, definitely not near my crotch. Was this what internal bleeding looked like? Maybe it was my lungs or my liver or something? *Fam*, I thought. *I really need to pay more attention in biology.*

While I was thinking things through, Corey was staring forward like his life depended on it. What I wanted more than anything in that moment was to cut my piss short, zip up, and duck out. But I couldn't. I'd never been able to. I still remembered when I was six or seven, and Mum's brother-in-law came to stay. At some point, he got sick of me watering the toilet seat like a houseplant and, knowing my old man wasn't alive to guide me, he decided to intervene. He'd stand behind me, holding my shoulders, telling me in his gentlest voice that peeing was like flying an airplane: "The hardest part is taking off and landing; the rest of it is smooth sailing, *see?*" Unfortunately, my uncle went back to Bénin before I got the lesson on how to stop a plane midflight.

I tapped my right foot a couple times. Corey did the same, but we both stopped once it got obvious we were mimicking each other out of nervousness.

I swayed to the left at the exact same time he swayed to the right, and our elbows touched. We sprang away in opposite directions, desperate to stretch out the space between us.

He turned away and stared at the front door—it was like he was trying to use his mind to pry it open or *will* someone else into walking in. But no one came, and he stared back at the wall in front of him in defeat. It was probably the longest piss of both of our lives. I remembered more things happening in that one minute next to Corey than I could recall happening in most weeks.

He stopped his flow abruptly and zipped up. *His* uncle must have stuck around. Then, without even glancing at the sink or soap dispenser to his side, he jogged out the door.

Thankfully, by the end of my run, my urine was mostly back to yellow. My shoulders dropped, and after flushing my panic down the drain, I yanked down the handle a couple more times just to be sure the evidence was destroyed.

Then I washed my hands.

When I stepped out into the hallway, I noticed the *CAU-TION: WET FLOOR* sign had been taken away, despite there being a brand-new puddle below the cracked ceiling tile. *Interesting*, I thought. But not that interesting. Seconds later, my phone was in my hand—a clinic visit would have to wait till the weekend, but I had to know ASAP what was good with my insides. Time for an incognito search: *What causes blood in urine?*

"C'mon, hurry up," I mumbled as the page loaded.

"Hey, Esso." The voice behind me was as luxurious as mink on silk. Nadia, I realized. *Shit!*

As the crush of my life made her way around to my front, I tried to tap the *X* button on the search window. But my normally delicate fingers had turned into blocks of cheese, prodding the whole corner of the screen while hitting nothing useful. I gave up and tried to swing the phone around to my back pocket, but it dropped instead, and we both watched it bounce, then land next to her heel.

Faceup.

I jumped on top of it, smothering it like it was a grenade about to pepper her in shrapnel.

"What on earth . . ." She looked almost nauseous as she stared down at me in confusion. "What exactly are you trying to hide?"

"Uhhh . . . nothing," I replied. But while getting back to my feet, I realized there was a get-out-of-jail-free card hidden in her question. "But it had boobs in it, and it's weird to be looking at boobs on your phone at 10 a.m. in the school hallway."

"Ummmm." She stretched out her face in surprise, and after a few seconds . . . "Fair enough, I guess."

I double-checked my hip was still in its socket and, once my phone was safely pocketed, even managed a fake smile.

"Anyway, I'm late for class, E." She chuckled. "Maybe you can reply to my text from this morning after you're done *browsing?*" She raised one cheeky eyebrow.

I knew I should have just texted her back earlier, I thought, kicking myself. Three years we'd known each other. Three years she'd sauntered through my maths classes and weirdest fantasies. *Three years!* And just one wrong move could crumble those well-laid foundations.

My mouth creaked open, ready to shower her with sorries, to make up some excuse about my texts not coming through all day or not having had a chance to check my messages all morning. But I'd been down that path before—a cold, winding road that wouldn't take me anywhere better than the lonely spot I was already standing in.

Nadia, meanwhile, tired of getting nothing but rubbish from me, announced, "Later, E," before dusting off. The clever people had their history lessons at the far end of the corridor, so she had a distance to cover. I'd have been lying if I said I wasn't staring at her the whole time she jogged away. *How on earth*, I wondered, *does she look that good even in school clothes?*

As I was mulling it over, the strangest pair of coincidences collided: a strong whiff of Dettol from beneath me, then a roar of laughter from room 4A—the exact two sensations I'd had after stepping into that first vision in the dreamworld.

Déjà vu, I thought.

Watching Nadia pick up her pace, I realized she'd probably not seen the puddle, nor the warning sign they'd taken away minutes earlier. And just as I feared—just as I'd basically *foreseen*—her foot scraped the edge of the spill, spinning her whole body backward, with her skull tracing a straight line to the unforgiving floor.

And I was there to catch her.

My left arm cradled the top of her back, the other arm a bit lower.

She was panting, dazed. She'd probably just watched her whole life flash before her eyes, then blinked and saw me.

After taking a few seconds to catch her breath, she smirked, "I see you got a nice handful there, E." Each syllable came out of her mouth right on cue.

That. Clarted. Dream. Was. Real, I mouthed in my head. It had predicted the future, not once, but twice with perfect precision. Had I not been supporting Nadia's weight, I'd have probably fainted right there.

She smiled up at me, and I stared back into her piercing eyes. Not only had I dreamed this exact moment after the car crash, I'd watched it in basically every rom-com ever made. *This is the moment the girl falls for the guy, the moment he shoots his shot.* Even if I had dreamworld problems to figure out, I also had real-world opportunities to nab.

But my sore leg was seconds away from buckling under the load. I could just about reach her lips with mine, but I'd drop right after. Plus, the BO sneaking out my armpit crevice smelled like a gremlin was taking a dump in there. It had hints of an old bag of spinach, and the worst part was, the more I smelled it, the more I sweated—a funky, rotten cycle. I'd hoped to keep my distance from any and all girl-kind till the day was done, but here I was.

"E . . ." she said, looking a little less comfortable now. "Help me up, please?"

"Yeah, I got you," I replied, then spent everything I had getting us upright again. *If only I'd started going to the gym like Kato*, I thought in regret, *we'd be lips-ing right now.*

"Hey," she said, calling me back to my senses. "I reckon it's safe for you to let go of my bum cheek now as well."

"Oh, my bad." I threw my guilty hand behind my back. "Was just holding it there for safety, innit."

Her full-toothed smile somewhat dampened the blow. I

fancied the pants off her; that much I'd always known. But now *she* definitely knew as well. Worse, she knew that *I* knew she knew.

We hugged, and she thanked me more times than I could count. All the while I pretended there'd been nothing weird about me sprinting to catch her three seconds before she'd even fallen. We stared at the puddle by our side, watching as the next drop fell from the ceiling.

"I really didn't see that coming," she said.

"Nope," I agreed. "I guess I didn't either."

For a moment, I almost believed my own words. After guessing she might slip, I'd *decided* to save her. I'd had every intention of staring into her gorgeous eyes. *I* had chosen those things. But the real question was *when* had I chosen? Now? Or back when I was in that dreamworld? The more I thought about the question, the less sense it made. And the less certain I got about how things with D and Bloodshed might end . . . and what say I had in it all.

A final thought caught me on my way back to classroom 4C, bringing an ironic smile to my face: I'd figured out how to gaze across time, and yet there I was, heading into the idiot kids' class for history. Mad ting.

12
RHIA · (15 YEARS LATER)

EVERYTHING IN LINFORD'S house was just so *white*. The spiral stairs, the walls and high ceilings, the tiles in the underground *flippin'* pool. Even Linford, strolling about barefoot in matching ivory jeans. I'd had no clue houses like this even existed in London, let alone half a mile from ours. He'd never invited me over when we dated, and now I wondered if this was why.

The area he lived in was technically East Dulwich but had earned the nickname Peckerly Hills, since it was the street of choice for Western Europe's bougiest Black professionals. His parents weren't home, and his older brother stayed in the basement, which left him, me, and Olivia alone upstairs waiting for the download to finish. Most of the files were Q-encrypted, which meant they were taking ages to unzip. But buried somewhere deep in that trove of data was Mum. I just knew it.

"You know all that time-dilation stuff you were explaining last night?" Olivia said, while the three of us sat in front of the massive data portal in Linford's mum's study. "I think it's happening to me right now. Like, a second ago, I literally thought we'd been staring at this thing for two hours."

"Funnily enough, it's been *exactly* two hours," Linford replied, not even trying to hide his laughter.

And just when I'd thought Olivia was sobering up. Fucking Bakewell tart . . .

On our way in, we'd walked through Linford's kitchen and stumbled across a half-eaten Bakewell tart on the counter. Unfortunately, it wasn't till *after* Olivia had slyly stuffed a whole slice into her face that Linford shared how his older brother had mixed medical-grade neon into the flour, making it so strong that even a dozen of his stoner/banker mates hadn't been able to finish it. According to the internet, neon was pretty harmless—its main trick being that it temporarily switched off the part of the brain that distinguished genius thoughts from shit ones.

The night was already back to front. Olivia was meant to be helping ease the tension between me and Linford, and making sure we escaped with the data quick-time. In the end, it was me and Linford who were babysitting Olivia, and I still didn't have Dr. Esso's records in my hands. I'd been punching myself all week for keeping secrets from her. But now—as I watched her roll across Linford's carpet—I felt a tad less guilt.

I turned to Linford with an exhausted stare. "Should we be worried?"

"Nah," he said. "It'll wear off by the time you lot get home.

"So," Linford continued, spinning a lollipop around in his mouth. "You chatting to anyone at the moment?"

"Nah," I replied. "Not for a while. Things have been quite busy with—"

"I am!" he cut in. Next came an in-depth retelling of how he'd met the new love of his life. I was sighing inside throughout.

This was the Linford I remembered. Petty. Vain. His arrogance his only remedy for his insecurity. It all came flooding back, making me realize how much rosier our relationship looked in the rearview mirror than when I was in the passenger seat.

But I sat and listened politely. I had no plan B for getting Dr. Esso's data. I was still asking Linford a favor, and that favor was still illegal. It helped that I had zero lingering feelings for him. I also suspected the only reason he was showing off and flirting with me was he didn't know any other way to talk to girls. No harm done.

"Fifteen minutes till the download's done," Linford declared. His face lit up as another idea arrived. "Just enough time to finish the house tour!"

We started out front, where Linford gave a blow-by-blow account of the day he negotiated 15% off his matte-black Vespa. 15% of 16 stacks was a lot, to be fair. But it still meant he had a 14-grand scooter parked out front. Mental. No wonder he'd always talked about it like it was his child.

With five minutes left on the download, we headed back

upstairs via some stairs on the other side of the house that opened up into an art-littered hallway. The overhead spotlights chased us as we strolled along the corridor, splashing each of my steps in sparkling marble.

"I love this shade of pink," I said, waving at the accent wall on our left.

"Sick, right?" Linford agreed. "I forget the name. It's gonna bug me all night if I don't remember. We've got some spare tins in the garage, though—I'll find out later."

He ushered us over to the first painting. "You know what?" he said, taking out the lollipop for a second to lick his lips, the way he'd been doing all night. It might have been winter, but nothing justified that level of self-balming. "Even with the Damien Hirst and Modupeola paintings we've bought, this Zita piece right here is still my favorite."

I had a feeling that if I sold my kidneys, I still wouldn't be able to afford what he was pointing at. We truly did live on two completely different worlds and wavelengths.

"See, what I've figured out about art," he added, "is that it's all about metaphors. The artist's job is to find the exact colors and patterns needed to *pluck* the right emotions in the viewer. When it's done right, a piece can transport you—to the most vivid moments of your life and back. And this girl right here? She's all over that shit. And on top of that, she's from ends, like us."

Olivia rolled her eyes long enough for Linford to catch some of the rotation.

"You know my dad came from the baddest block in this

town?" he reminded her. "I was born on ends as well, fam. That's why I'll never forget where I'm from—"

As he was flashing his credentials, a dalmatian, with a spiked collar and veins you could see through its dotted coat, skipped into the hallway. It jumped up at Linford, resting its paws on his belt.

"All right, go on, then, Daisy." He bent down and slid his lollipop into the dog's mouth, letting her lather it with her frothy tongue, before yanking it back into *his* mouth.

I cringed at the thought that I used to kiss this guy. Olivia, on the other hand, was pissing herself with laughter like she'd been doing most of the night.

Linford took a final lick of the (now-slobber-covered) lollipop, then walked to the top of the stairs and chucked it onto the ground-floor carpet, watching Daisy storm after it.

"Everything's a game of fetch with that girl," he said, smirking. His watch beeped. "Coolio," he said, turning off the timer. "Download's done."

Literally saved by the bell.

"You know what," Olivia turned to me, cradling her belly. "You guys go ahead and grab it. I'm gonna use the bathroom."

She must have clocked I was moving to follow her. "It's fine, sis," she said, already halfway down the hall, and walking in an impressively straight line. "That data stick is more important than my potty business. I'll be five minutes. Max."

"Two minutes," I shouted after her. Surely nothing else could go wrong.

• • •

"Olivia?" I yelled, for maybe the twentieth time. I kept a sweaty grip on the data stick as Linford and I carried on our search for my sister around his giant house. We'd reached the garage—the last place left to look.

"That's weird," Linford said. He was staring at a giant cabinet with all sorts of DIY tools and materials in it. It looked like someone had had a field day; half the stuff was lying on the floor. "I could have sworn I locked up this cabinet."

Then came the sound of giggling outside. He and I swapped relieved glances at the same time. Olivia.

But as we followed the giggles out the front door, Linford's happy face became one of pure horror. I *very* nearly laughed, when I first saw what Olivia had done, but I held it in just in time—I owed that much to Linford.

"It's beautiful, isn't it?" Olivia was busy applying a final coat of hot pink paint on the handlebars of Linford's most prized possession. His Vespa. "The big pink swirls on the body are a metaphor for the chaos in life."

Linford gagged. For a second, I was convinced he was gonna vomit right there on the welcome mat. Instead, he just stared, the muscles up his neck taut. Then he let out a squeal so high-pitched Olivia and I had to cover our ears.

After that, it was a chain reaction. First Daisy started barking inside. A few seconds later, a light from the house next door came on. Then the next house. Soon the whole neighborhood lit up like a Christmas tree.

My stomach sank and I swapped a silent look with Olivia. We both knew what happened in a neighborhood like this when a sensor picked up a scream. Especially a scream that sounded as feeble and pampered as Linford's.

Just as I'd feared, the neighborhood sirens started roaring. And my heart sank so deep I thought it might fall out my ass.

"Drone party!" Olivia shouted. She dropped her brush to the gravel and started dancing to a beat that, apparently, only she could hear. "Drone party: get it, get it. Drone party: get it, get it."

My vision narrowed to a tunnel as a full tank of adrenaline and alarm poured into me at once. I was in possession of illegal data. Olivia had just vandalized a resident's property. Neither of us were from around here. I rushed the data stick into my pocket, and just as I was about to check I hadn't slipped it into the one with a hole in the bottom, I heard a buzzing noise.

It started as shapeless sound. But seconds later, a black disk of metal appeared above us. It looked like a tarantula scurrying through the night on six arms, only with spinning blades for toes.

"Stop twerking!" I shook Olivia till she faced me. "That's a Met drone. We have to go. Now!"

I yanked both of us into a full sprint, while Linford stayed behind, hugging his ped.

The drone started a long arcing descent to street level. It was already closer than I expected, moving faster, as well. I was most scared for Olivia. She had ankle boots on and wasn't getting forced into sprint training twice a week like I was. A high-rise was less than a mile up the road. If we got there, we could find cover, maybe even a flat to hide in.

Olivia was wheezing and gasping for air. Her skin had a pale yet sweaty sheen to it. I raced just slightly ahead of her, keeping the gap slim enough to give her hope of catching up, but wide enough that she'd know she really (*really*) needed to run faster.

But the drone was only 20 yards behind us now, and dread was setting fast into my bones. I'd heard stories about those things, read about the "accidents" that happened during arrests. It let out a groan, almost like a door creaking open, which was followed by the *SNAP* of metal parts locking in place. When I turned back, it had rearranged itself into a new shape—the rotors now bunched at the top to make way for twin laser cannons on its ribs.

How had things escalated to *this*?! Ten minutes ago, we'd been perambulating in Linford's hallway, staring at art. Now our freedom was on the line. Maybe even our lives. All because of a slice of Bakewell tart and some pink swirls on a moped?

"You are resisting arrest," the drone announced in a muscular voice. "Your failure to comply leaves me no choice but to engage."

I never thought this was how it would end: seared down by a floating spider in Peckerly Hills.

"You have until the count of three."

I could hear Linford's distant shouts behind us. "Stop chasing them!" he yelled at the drone as if he had authority over it. "The chick in front didn't do anything..." His voice trailed off. "And I think I still fancy her."

I almost tripped when I heard it, but within milliseconds my attention was back on the predator above.

I slowed down to get behind Olivia. We had no hope of getting away with the data, but from here, I could at least shield her from some of the laser fire. It was my fault, after all. My idea to come here and get involved in this madness in the first place.

"Two," the drone declared, cocking one cannon, then the other.

Sorry, Mum, I quietly prayed. *I did what I could.* We braced ourselves, running with our eyes closed, waiting in misery for the robotic *one* to arrive.

But it never did. Instead, all Olivia and I could hear was . . . *barking?*

We finally unscrunched our eyes and turned to see Daisy clawing at the soft plastic underbelly of the drone, the two cannons already chewed off and scattered across the tarmac beside her.

Linford had caught up and was fist-pumping the air. "Good girl," he shouted as the dog ran back toward him with the drone's emergency stop plug in her mouth. *Thank God for her life*, I thought.

Olivia and I kept running. In fact, we didn't slow down until almost a mile later, when we saw a bus going in the direction of Tony and Poppy's house.

By the time we'd climbed to the third level of the bus, we were both drenched in sweat. Olivia collapsed into the seat next to me, and as we caught our breath, I spared a thought for poor Linford. His poor bike. His—

Shit! The data stick!

It wasn't in my pocket. I aired my trouser legs, and it hadn't fallen in there either. It wasn't wedged in my trainers or socks. "No, no, no, no," I said in crushed despair.

Olivia tapped my shoulder. She knew why I was falling apart, but had this annoyingly calm look on her face. She unclenched her palm. The drive was inside. I didn't know whether she'd picked it up outside Linford's house, or at some point along our run. Frankly, I didn't care.

No words were spoken. No hugs exchanged. But she got a nod of profound gratitude that came straight from my soul.

Neither of us had the patience to do anything but open his records immediately. We'd risked too much to hold back. Who knew what could happen between here and home?

I put the stick next to my mobile to establish a wireless link, then watched the screen light up. We scrolled through hundreds of files until we finally reached a video titled: CCT-V_01MD/9124-EVIDENCE.mp4

It took almost two minutes to unzip the single file, but when it opened, we watched a dozen kids standing in the same Peckham alleyway I walked past most mornings. One of them was my mum. Another was Dr. Esso. I didn't recognize the others. They were all just standing there in such static silence it could have been a photo.

Then came the gunshots.

13

ESSO

KATO AND I were part of the first batch let out for lunch. The second and third groups had just joined the queue, which stretched so far down the hallway the end of it got mixed up with the line for the girls' toilets.

Rob slid his tray into the spot opposite Kato and me. "What you lot saying?"

"It's calm, bro," I responded, not bothering to face him. I'd spent all of lunch staring at the entrance, waiting for D to walk in. And so far, there'd been no sign of him or his bredrins. Rumor had it, they'd missed all their classes that morning as well. Meanwhile, four versions of the future were playing themselves out in my head, each time starting with the least likely:

1. Bloodshed and D have let it go. They've changed their minds and deaded the beef . . .
2. As long as I take my beating like a man, I won't go down

looking too moist. I might even get some respect from the mandem . . . which could spell more love from Penny Hill girls as well. Maybe even from Nadia?

3. I can take him. I'll surprise him with that sliding kick that Ken does in *Street Fighter*—I'm pretty sure I saw some guy pull that off in Burgess Park once. I think.

4. I've lost my goddamn mind. With all the trippy stuff that's happened to me today, the one thing I can count on for certain is that I was with a bunch of gang members when they worked Bloodshed. Which means *I'm* gonna get worked. I'm gonna get punched up. Or stabbed. Or worse. In fact, I think that was probably the scene I saw in the Upper World.

I'd started calling it that in my head—"Upper World" flowed better than "Time-Warped Dreamworld Doused in Heat and Lightning." Sounded cooler as well. I still wasn't 1,000% bought into all the stuff Dad had written in his notebook, but I was a lot more believing than when I'd first read it. And I was kicking myself for not bringing it to school, wondering if he'd dropped any other hints. Wondering if a day like today was something we had in common.

The fluorescent light flickered, making us each look up. All the other bulbs on our side of the hall had all packed it in weeks ago, so this one was our last hope.

Kato was combing out his high-top with a black-fisted pick as he rehashed the conversation. "Yo, Esso—tell Rob all that time-travel bollocks you was just tellin' me."

"You're such a prick, you know that?" I replied. "That's why I don't tell you nothing."

Kato slapped his hand on the table and did that laugh where his cheeks and eyes crease up, but no sound comes out. I guess I was naïve for thinking he might be able to help, let alone believe me. He'd already fallen into stitches by the time I'd told him about the Cantor's-branded headphones I'd spotted up there, but at the rate the memory was blurring, I'd had to tell *someone* before it completely faded. Kato had gone on to ask me a bunch of excruciatingly detailed questions, only to then say, "Boss, you took a car to the face today. The sooner you can rub some Vicks on those bruises and back a Red Bull, the sooner you'll stop chatting nonsense." He might as well have patted me on the head.

As the #blackgirlmagic trio—Nadia and her two best mates, Janeen and Kemi—approached our table, I thanked God I hadn't told Kato about the hallway shenanigans with Nadia. We had a special way of consoling each other, which generally involved turning the next guy's suffering into an endless stream of jokes. And Kato was the best at it.

Nadia, who for all money looked set to slide right past without acknowledging I existed, stopped and parked her tray next to mine.

Pop! Pop! The gum bubbles in her mates' mouths burst one after the other. Kemi made sure she sighed long and loud enough that everyone at our table knew what she thought of us. I couldn't stand that girl. No matter the price of popularity, she was always willing to pay, and always ready to judge anyone who didn't just throw it in the bag like her.

"I'll catch you later on, yeah?" The pair looked shocked at Nadia's words, then, once they realized we could see it, rearranged their faces back into nonchalance.

I, meanwhile, focused on taking a quick bite of the sausage I'd been pushing around my plate since the start of lunch. After Nadia sat down, Janeen shook her head one last time, then pulled out her phone to take a photo of the four of us at the table. The pic was bound to end up on the social medias in no time, probably next to her collage of bent-back poses with completely irrelevant inspirational quotes underneath. And no doubt, a quick scroll down from the post would show some laughing emojis and shade from other girls in our year. There was nothing that scandalous about Nadia sitting next to me. But it was the first time it had happened. It represented change. And at Penny Hill, change itself was scandalous.

"You ain't reserved this spot for anyone else, have you?" Nadia asked. Unlike Janeen's and Kemi's plates, hers still had food on it.

As her friends walked off, I caught Mr. Sweeney—the baitest, thirstiest creep in the history of secondary education—checking Kemi out from his patrol chair. She blew a kiss as she catwalked past him, making Sweeney turn red and quickly look away, his gold hair flopping behind.

Nadia shook her head at the whole scene—reading between

lines I saw just as clearly—then pulled her attention back to our table. "Wagwan, guys."

"You sure you meant to sit here?" Rob asked, draping out his pale, vine-like arms to cover her tray.

"I figured since E is on death row, he shouldn't have to eat his last meal alone with you two dickheads," she replied.

Rob pulled his arms away just before she could swat them off, and as Nadia shuffled in next to me, I tucked my arms against my sides, creating as tight a seal around the stench as possible.

"Death row?" Kato asked her, combing out the front edge of his box. "I don't get it."

"Yeah, me neither," Rob said before Nadia could explain. "Is that connected to the time-travel argument you lot were having when I arrived? Also, why am I always last to hear about stuff." As usual, he'd found an excuse to have a moan.

"*Time travel?*" Nadia asked.

In summary: Rob and Nadia both knew about my beef with D; Kato knew about my time-travel madness; but no one (except me) had all the pieces, and they each looked equally annoyed about it. Hashing it out now via a four-way convo was an effort, though. Four times the judgment, four times the number of life-altering questions I still didn't have answers to.

"Abeg, abeg—if I'm really on death row, and this is really my last meal, my final, only request is that we change the subject from all of this. Please."

"Hold up, boss," Kato chucked back. "I'm still stuck on this death row ting. Did you catch some beef, Esso?"

"Just allow him, man," Rob requested. Nadia thankfully nodded in agreement, and by the time I turned to Kato, he was lost in his phone.

"How are you lot feeling about the mock exams coming up?" It wasn't Nadia's smoothest icebreaker, but less bait than bringing up the weather, which had been my plan. "I've been studying the last two weeks, but still feel like I'm barely scratching the surface."

That could mean anything with her. She was capable of pulling a string of all-nighters before a big test, then another week, she'd barely be interested in school. Submit? Or rebel? Those were the two islands Nadia Black swam between each day. Her mum, who liked reminding Nadia she'd had her too young, was determined to make sure her daughter's life was the photo negative of her own. And so, on the one hand, Nadia loathed the overachiever box her mum tried to squeeze her into, and on the other, she couldn't bring herself to be the slacktivist selfie queen that Penny Hill expected either. Only two weeks of studying for the second-biggest exams of the year was definitely on the slack end for her, and I couldn't help wondering if she might be joining us wasters on rebel island for good.

"I'm not too worried about the mocks, you know," I answered. Truthfully, I couldn't even tell her where the surface was, let alone scratch it. "I'm sure I'll do decent, still."

"What you on about, Esso? You know you're failing all of them tests."

Rob wasted no time cosigning Kato's comment with a laugh.

"Piss off, Kato." My right hand was gripping my tray, the other rubbing my sore hip under the table.

Nadia, unfazed by our back-and-forth, shook her head and said to me, "So, how did you do on the practice tests last month? I always took you as one of those quietly neeky ones: pretend like you're not studying, then come out of nowhere and kill it."

"I mean, I was in the top half of the class for art. Didn't do too bad in Creative Writing either—teacher reckons I could do English for A levels if I worked at it."

"Nice one. And the other subjects?" Nadia pressed, grinning.

"Don't watch that, rude gyal," I responded, hoping my over-confident jab would stop her from reaching in for more details.

"You lot are a bunch of tossers, you know that?" she replied.

"Fair enough," Kato responded, genuinely agreeing with her while the rest of us laughed. "Speaking of Creative Writing . . . me, Esso, and Rob are actually going to Youth Club in Camberwell tonight to write our homework stories. You're welcome to chill as well."

"Well, which one is it?" Nadia asked. "Are you working or chilling?"

"Depends on when you arrive," I interrupted. "There's gonna be some 'refreshments' served at the start." I hugged my fingers around the word for effect. "But after that, we'll actually do like two hours of proper writing."

Kato piped up the way only he could. "And just so there's no confusion, Nadia—by 'refreshments,' we mean crystal meth. The theme for tonight's revision session is: Meth and Metaphors."

"That's messed up," Nadia said.

"Maybe Crack and Character Development works better for you?" he responded.

It was clear from how she was folding her lips that Nadia was holding back laughter. She whispered to me, "Please tell me you guys are actually talking about weed, right?"

"Yeah," I said. "Rob stole a spliff from his old man. I don't smoke, but these man swear one puff is enough to turn you into Shakespeare."

"In which case," Nadia said, "shouldn't the theme be: Pot and Plots?"

"Well *played*, Nadia," I acknowledged. "Very well played."

She smiled, then slid a dollop of mashed potatoes past her lips. Her smarts multiplied everything she already had going on. I looked away so she wouldn't catch me staring.

"Ganja and Stanzas?" was Kato's next offering. We each tilted our heads, wondering if we could accept it, but Kato shot again before we could settle the decision. "Fine: Ketamine and Kennings."

"What the blood clot is a *kennings*?" Rob's face looked disgusted—no, disrespected. Ironically, it was the same face I'd put on at lunch the day before when Rob had told us that, based on a photo online, Nines wasn't actually a rapper, but a superagent sent forward in time by East African special forces.

"Nah, Kennings is definitely an English lit word!" Kato insisted.

We all shook our heads.

"For fuck's sake," Kato fired back. "Remember in *Game of Thrones* how everyone called Khaleesi 'Mother of Dragons'? Well, 'Mother of Dragons' is a kenning. It's an old-school English ting, where you basically take a word and replace it with some other joined-up words to make it sound sicker. Take D's little brother, Bloodshed, for example—if my man was born in medieval times, his kenning name would have been 'Slayer of Stepdads' or something. Get me?"

His comment sent a prickle down my backbone, and I had to shake a little to work it out of my system. Every kid south of the Thames knew the story of how Bloodshed had earned his nickname: by stabbing his mum's second husband in the stomach. The headline of the *Evening Standard* the day after had read, *Bloodshed on Brixton Block*. Or something like that. Since he was only 13 when it happened and because his stepdad kinda deserved it, Bloodshed bust his case and was back on road same day. But two years on and the nickname had stuck . . . which D absolutely hated, since, according to rumors, he was out with some chick when it all went down.

"I don't know about all dat," Rob said, still frowning. "'Kennings' is a proper stretch, fam. I think you're just making this shit up."

Nadia stretched her arms high in the sky and let out an

exaggerated yawn, which, we were about to learn, was a warning shot.

"Sizzurp and Similes," she said. "Trees and Themes. Xanax and Syntax." She kept going. And going. And going. With each Uzi bullet, Kato pretended to shudder, shielding his chest and vital organs from the onslaught. Only when she got to "Opioids and Oxymorons" did she stop to admire the pile of mangled bodies around her.

Don't just sit there, Esso. Think of something, say something. The clapping that followed Nadia's round gave me the time I needed to come up with my only contribution so far.

"Acid and Allegory?"

"Dammit," Nadia said. "Been *looking* for one to go with acid."

Riding high and feeling bulletproof, I locked eyes with her. "Well, you know what they say: the couple that alliterates together, obliterates together."

"*Prrrrrrrrrrrrrrrrrrrrrr-aaat,*" Kato shouted, busting gunshots in the air. Rob refused to give him the satisfaction of laughing this time.

Nadia threw her head back. "*Couple?* Bit presumptuous, don't you reckon? Maybe you should study by yourself tonight, E. You can call your session Herbs and Hubris, since that second-hand weed smoke has clearly gone to your head."

"Cheeeeeeees-us is Lord!" Kato screamed, his exaggerated accent borrowed from every African country a British passport couldn't get you into. "We have a winna, ladies and gentlemen, we have a winna! Nadia, Nadia, plis, am beggin' . . . please, come and collect your prize!"

Nadia snatched her imaginary trophy away from Kato. "I'm ever so grateful. And quite humbled as well." She'd put on her poshest voice, cupping her hand into a royal wave between sentences. "First I'd like to thank the British education system, as well as my neighbors back in Manchester—without them, I wouldn't have learned any of these terribly clever quips and wouldn't know anything about these wonderfully harmful drugs."

By the end of her acceptance speech, we were gripping each other's shoulders for support. Nadia almost tipped over on her chair, grabbing the table with one hand and rubbing her stomach with the other.

My laughs were more forced than everyone else's, though. I was still reeling from the pain of her diss earlier on. I mean, "presumptuous"? But what about all those texts between us . . . all those times we'd stopped to chat in the hallway even though we had nothing to talk about . . . me having a vivid vision of her after that crash, then literally saving her life in the hallway? Surely it all meant *something*. The paranoid, spiteful side of me wondered if Kato's superior banter had maybe earned him some ground over me during these last 15 minutes of lunch. Or whether that accidental bum grab in the corridor had been a bit too cheeky (pun mostly intended).

Meanwhile, Rob had had enough. It was time for him to moan about something again. "Not only is this the neekiest conversation I've ever been a part of, but it's also *fucking* problematic."

"What?" Nadia said. We all wore matching faces of confusion.

"We gotta elevate the conversation, innit. For ourselves, for our people. You think Westminster kids are sitting around the table at lunch chatting about Class A substances?"

Nadia wasted no time replying. "First the answer is yes. Those kids love a Class A drug. Second . . ." She opened her comment to the rest of the group this time. "Did I hear him say, '*our* people'? Aren't you Russian or Polish or something?"

We all busted up laughing. Rob, meanwhile, was shaking his head like we were a bunch of toddlers, too juvenile to chew on his medicine.

Kato, still chuckling, added his two pence. "Also, didn't you get dropped into this school by mistake? It's always them man preaching loudest about tough choices who never had to make none."

"Thank you very much," I said to Kato, and then to Rob: "So don't tell me to stay woke, when I ain't slept in three days."

Nadia placed her hands on her chest, like my words had just lifted the lid off her soul.

"Hold on, boss," Kato cut in, placing his Afro pick down on his tray. "Did you just steal a line from Wretch 32 and pretend like it was yours?"

"Nah, definitely not," I responded. "I don't even know what song you're on about?" My Adam's apple started swelling, I loosened my collar, scratched the side of my neck.

"Yeah, that bar was definitely from an old 32 freestyle," Rob confirmed. "You're moving like a sideman right now, Esso."

Nadia looked away. The lid was back on.

After a few more moments of awkward silence, Rob turned to Kato. "But on a serious note: 'Kennings' was definitely a stretch, fam."

Kato carried on making the case for kennings. He prided himself on having the gift of the gab—the ability to "sell thongs to a nun," as he'd put it once. Rob, on the other hand, was born with all his views preloaded and had no plans of ever changing them. That meant all their arguments ended the same way: behind the starting line. Thankfully, that afternoon, their bickering created an opening for me and Nadia to chat to each other.

"Tonight was meant to be my evening off from studying, but I might actually come to your revision thing." Nadia twirled her fork, mixing the beans and mash into a stodgy bronze pile. Her vibe was a bit warmer than before.

"Safe. It'll be fun," I responded, genuinely meaning it. "And educational, obviously."

"Obviously," she said. "By the way, why don't we go to Peckham Library instead?"

"Yeah, why n—" I stopped midsentence. I knew exactly *why not*. And as insane as it was to be planning my evening around what I'd seen in the Upper World, if Nadia pressed again, I'd have to find a way of letting her know we were all staying as far away from that building as possible.

"Also, that chicken shop is next to it, isn't it?" Nadia asked.

"You know the one? What's it even called again?"

"You mean Morley's?"

"Nah, I would have remembered that."

"Oh." I had to pause and laugh. "You're talking about Katie's, innit? Of course. Everyone knows Katie's."

"That's the one! It's mad. When my dad first got his job in London, he was living in a studio just up the road from the library, and I got the bus down from Manny one weekend to visit him, and the first place he took me to eat was Katie's. That chicken is the first thing I ever ate in London."

"Wow, gotta give it to your old man. He really knows how to spoil a girl."

"Piss off, E." She pretended to throw a chunk of mashed potatoes at me with her fork, and her blazer flickered open, giving me a glimpse of the pink bra she had on under her school shirt.

"We'll figure out the venue later, but definitely make sure you don't come too late to the revision ting tonight. I've actually got to head home just before eight. On a film-night riddim with my mum." I rushed the last few words out in a mumble. As embarrassed as I was about people knowing I'd spent every Friday night since I was six at home with my mum eating takeout, I wasn't embarrassed enough to cancel or lie about it.

"Well, mumma's boy . . . I'm glad to see you're so relaxed about everything." She put her utensils down, then turned her eyes away before moving to her next sentence. "I honestly thought you'd be bricking it about this thing with D."

I sighed. "Honestly, Nadia, what worries me even more than D himself is everything that comes with him."

"What d'you mean?"

"You know how these roadman go on—it never ends. Even if I managed to bang up D—and that's a big bloody 'if'—the beef would carry on. Probably until someone got proper hurt. Or worse."

Spark had told me all kinds of stories about what the T.A.S. boys got up to. But the shocked look on Nadia's face told me she had absolutely no clue. I guess they all saw D so often at school, they made the mistake of assuming he was like the rest of us.

My thoughts drifted back to scenario number four: the one where I got worked, punched up, stabbed, or worse. The scenario that matched what I'd seen in the Upper World.

Nadia must have sensed my mood, because she rested her hand on my forearm. The weight of each of her fingers sank in. After weeks of cryptic communication—*she likes me; she likes me not*—I'd been dying for answers. This felt like one, even if it was just the first whisper, and the way my morning had started, I never would've guessed I'd make this much ground by lunch. Kato and Rob saw it, too, then went back to pretending not to eavesdrop on our conversation.

"Sorry to have to leave you. I've got a study session with Mrs. Mwenza, and I'm already late." She got up. "But I'll see you tonight, yeah? Please take care of yourself in the meantime."

"Cool. Thanks. Cool. Cool. Cool." *Stop saying "cool,"* I wanted to scream to myself.

As Nadia walked away, Kato kept his eyes locked on her swinging skirt and jiggling hips and joked, "Bro, I wouldn't mind opening up a bottle of Worcestershire sauce and then lathering it—"

"Piss off, Kato!" I said, already regretting letting him see me so stung.

He laughed, loud enough for the next table to hear. "It's just jokes, man." He straightened his face. "You know my policy anyway: *strictly lighties.*"

I didn't respond. I needed the conversation to die a quick, silent death. I hated when Kato made comments like that, especially in front of Rob. It was like he was sharing family secrets, lifting the bonnet off an engine we all knew was knackered, but drove on anyway. What got me even more vexed was that he was lying. Barely a day passed when Kato didn't conjure up an excuse to drop Nadia's name in conversation, though as usual, he'd only gotten interested in her after I had. If there was one exception to his lighty rule, she was it. But I hadn't openly declared my feelings for her either, so who was I to judge? *I must be closer than him, though*, I hoped. *I must be.* She wasn't on it with anyone else at Penny Hill, and I couldn't overlook how she'd placed her hand on mine when I mentioned the beef with D. Plus, the text she'd sent that morning had *xxxx* at the end. Four of them, for God's sake!

Rob looked nonplussed as he picked up his own tray and

rose to his feet. "Bruv, I'm off as well. I've got to drop the kids off at the pool before class starts." Rob had no shame when it came to his bowels. He must have caught the glint of worry in my eyes, because before he left, he added, "Sorry, mate—I promise I got you after school. But right now, I'm managing a very delicate turtle-head situation."

I shook my head, Kato giggled, and we both watched Rob walk to the exit one careful stride at a time, following behind Nadia. I was glad she hadn't heard Kato's comment about lighties. For Kato's sake more than hers—Liverpool's entire defensive line couldn't have saved him from her attack.

But the biggest reason I was glad she'd left the dining hall? I had just spotted D walking in.

14

RHIA · (15 YEARS LATER)

GOING INTO MY next tutorial with Dr. Esso, I was so angry, and so flustered by it, I could barely speak.

Tuesday training had been canceled, Gibbsy deciding our thighs and the muddy pitches should be saved for the weekend match, which meant there wasn't a single soul in the building, besides me and Dr. Esso. Even the hallway fluorescents, which usually lent a scrap of light to the kit room, had been cut off—leaving just football clutter, a clouded window, and a man keeping a million secrets.

I'd spent all night poring over his records after watching that video. *That fucking video.* The one Olivia and I had watched on the bus with our hands over our mouths. The one we'd risked our lives for. Each time I played the clip, I got enraged all over again. Why hadn't Dr. Esso told me earlier? Why had he strung me along, given everything he clearly knew? But at least now I understood why he was so obsessed with the ridiculous idea of going back in time. Who wouldn't need to believe it with all that blood on their hands?

Almost as concerning was what I *hadn't* found in his files. He had no family albums, no social media profiles, and no teacher registrations, which meant he'd lied his way into this tutoring job like he'd lied about everything else. His records showed he also didn't have much money. He'd bought some Cantor's stock back in 2023, way before they got into 3D-printed chicken and cybernetics, and made millions. Then he did the maddest thing: he gave it all away. And I mean *all* of it. Mostly to schools in the area, including one called Penny Hill that I remembered hearing about since it had topped some academic school ranking recently.

"Okay . . . just relax, Rhia," I muttered under my breath. "He'll do the explaining."

"You know I can hear you, innit?" he said. "As in, I'm right here." He was staring at me like I'd gone stupid, like *he* wasn't the one about to look a fool when I confronted him. "You'd be amazed how often this happens to me, you know. People think just cos I can't see their lips moving, the sound dodges my ears as well."

He reached across the desk to hand me my homework. "Full marks," he said. As if any of that shit mattered now. "I told you you'd enjoy the time-travel aspect of—"

"Just get on with the lesson," I spat out.

His head sprang back, almost snapping clean off the hinge. After a pause, he got back some balance. "Umm . . . cool."

By the time he started speaking again, I already had my

phone in my hand and was tapping on the video icon. It was one of the many Q-encrypted files that had made the download at Linford's house take so long. According to the readout, this single file download would take 84 seconds. A wait that'd be even more unbearable than the first time we endured it on the bus.

"Before we get into everything, I just wanted to say I'm proud of you. I know you're getting more match time, which is sick. And school-wise, I see you smashing these subjects by the time summer exams come round."

His words were pure air to me. I was too busy reminding myself that the broken goalpost on the floor should *not* be used as a weapon on him. After what we'd watched together, Olivia really hadn't wanted me to come tonight—but she'd been fearing for Dr. Esso's safety almost as much as mine.

"I won't lie, Rhia—exam results matter. Without good maths and science GCSEs, half the subjects at uni are off-limits, and a lot of career options disappear after that as well."

While half listening, I watched him hide his hands under the table before continuing in the same careful tone. "But it's even deeper than all that. If you don't get numbers, you can't see through the lies they're spewing on the socials. And them man there will just keep feeding you with bookie stats, convincing you your community's broken beyond repair, and that without their help, we'd rip ourselves apart. I grew up more scared of the boydem on my block than the paigons who crammed us all in there then moved us all out. I didn't know any better."

Whatever he was saying was coming from the chest now.

"Look, there are things I'm trying to teach you . . ." He pointed his finger at the window that was clapping to the beat of the rain. "Things that no one out there understands. Stuff I've been wanting to explain since we met."

My ears perked up.

"Rhia, have you ever stopped to think about what maths *really* is?"

Just as I thought he was about to fess up about Mum, he'd veered back into his standard nonsense. 60 seconds left on the download. 60 whole seconds listening to this bullshit.

He leaned forward, gut pressed into the table. I leaned back. "In one sense, maths is just a weird-looking language we made up in our heads to help us do useful shit. Some diggers not too long ago found a 43,000-year-old bone with 29 cuts on it buried in a mountain in Swaziland. Turns out, the first humans to ever use maths were some African ladies trying to track the moon for God knows what reason."

He was so smart. And yet sometimes . . . so, so dumb.

I felt a line of sweat down my side. Somehow the wacky ideas and hopes he'd planted in my mind still had some grip on me.

45 seconds left.

"Then you have the equations the Ancient Egyptians used to build the pyramids," he droned on. "The same line of maths that Pythagoras made famous centuries after. Look at the Ifa prophets who communicated with 256-bit binary code centuries before computers were invented." The words were rushing out almost uncontrollably. "Or take the Muslim mathematician who invented the numbers 1 through 9 so traders would have a way of talking money, then turned everything he learned into a subject he named Al-Jabr. People invented maths as a tool to make our lives easier, but then something happened: our creation started walking and talking all on its own. It started doing unreasonable, unnatural things."

I looked up from my phone to see him almost levitating off his seat, his voice getting shakier with each word.

"Just think for a second how insane it is! A guy like Albert Einstein jots down some random equations about light and time—the same ones we've been working through—while working at his desk job. Then some men who needed bigger guns took his doodles and created an atomic weapon that killed over 100,000 people.

"100,000 people," he repeated, snapping his fingers. "Gone in a flash. Physics has this *godly* power. It can explain the past, predict the future. It can give life. And it can snatch it away."

Five seconds left. My heart was banging against my ribs.

"You have that kind of power in you, Rhia. And once you realize it, there's—"

"You knew my mum, didn't you?" I placed the phone faceup on the table. And after waiting too long for his lower jaw to rise, I pressed on. "You two were at that murder scene together that night 15 years ago."

"How on earth did you—"

"Answer the question," I butted in. "And don't you dare try lying."

I hit *play* on the 13-second CCTV clip and let him listen to the gunshots. To the screams. Only God knew how anyone could have survived that scene. And yet here he was.

"Turn it off." He couldn't see the flash of red light that flooded the screen midway, but he was clutching his temples like he could feel it. "Please."

But I didn't lift a finger. I'd had to suffer through it to the end. He would too.

A final glance at his feet was all the confession needed. I waited for silence to charge the room before speaking again. "I want an explanation. And I want it now."

He sat up. "Fifteen years . . . that's how long I've spent waiting for this. And I *still* wish I could have had another week to get you ready for it."

Ready for what?! I'd have screamed if I wasn't already paralyzed with anger.

But despite his wish for more time, sitting in front of me was a man who now looked scarily prepared. No. More terrifying than prepared—he looked . . . eager.

"I guess it's time for me to tell you why I'm here," he announced. "And about what happened to Nadia."

He slid a notebook from his rucksack as he spoke—the same tattered notebook I'd seen in his bag the night I met him.

"I wasn't even sure you were alive. I was about to give up. On you. On everything." He exhaled as he lifted the book. "I thought about burning this thing every other day. Even put my lighter to it a couple times. But then one night I heard the TV next door switch on, and a Scouser newslady reporting from the other side of my bedroom wall. She mentioned a young sports prodigy from Peckham. Apparently, this 'future football legend'—her words, not mine—had never played club football before but scored two screamers on her debut. The presenter described how the girl had been in Care for pretty much all 15 years of her life. And that her surname was Black. And I knew straightaway it was you."

He stared down at the table. "So I tracked you down, and figured a couple hours of tutorials each week would be the best way to get to know you, to be sure you were her. But from the first moment we met outside, when I heard your voice, my heart almost exploded."

That was when his feet had gone dodgy that first night. I'd been right all along. But that only cranked up the fear already paralyzing me.

I wasn't here for an easy time, I reminded myself. I was here for answers.

"What about my mum?"

He gulped. "Your mum and I went to school together. We were in the same year at Penny Hill Secondary, before it turned into a science academy. Nadia was the first person I properly talked to about this time-travel stuff."

He paused, and a somber smile came to his face. "She loved you, Rhia. She loved you more than sci-fi films or TikTok dance challenges or *Moesha* reruns. And trust me, that last one was a big deal to her, still. She was tough. Smart. Sometimes even kind."

He couldn't see the tears rolling down my cheeks, but one sniffle was enough to turn his head toward me. Somewhere between his words, I'd gone from knowing I once had a mum to actually knowing *her*. Apparently, she was obsessed with cheesy retro TV. She loved me. My mum was bursting with dimensions, and for the first time, she felt real.

"So, what happened to her that night?" I said, my stomach now touching the desk. There'd be time to sort through my emotions when I got home. Right now, I had to focus on the facts. The details. "My mum got checked into St. Jude's Mental Health Care Home on the twenty-fifth of October"—I double-checked the date stamp on the video—"the Monday after this was taken."

His feet hadn't flinched one bit.

"There was a flash of light in that video, wasn't there?" he asked. "Right after the first gunshot?"

"Yeah, lit up the whole screen."

"Well, something happened to both me and Nadia in that moment. I don't know what. I blacked out, and I only have foggy glimpses of the place my mind went to. But I remember waking up and knowing everything had *changed*."

"Changed how?" Rain was tapping against the window, hammering the silence between his answers.

"There's still so much about that night I can't remember. In the end, they were rolling me into an ambulance, and I could hear her screaming behind me. I lost my vision that night, and she lost her mind." He shook his head. "I wish I could explain it better."

I had the same wish. I was hanging on his every word, clawing at them for meaning and finding nothing.

He took another deep breath in. "From then on, it was like Nadia was only *partly* there. I mean, you could tell she knew exactly what was going on around her, but her mind was clearly lost in something way too big for the rest of us to understand."

I knew how it felt not to be understood. I wished I could go back to be there for her; I wished she could be here right now for me.

"Only 2% of the UK died from the mutant virus strain that year. But almost a third of the patients at Dulwich passed away. She had you by some miracle. But not long after, she . . ."

"She died," I finished, drawing a hesitant nod from him.

"I saw her a week before that. She was writing peacefully at her desk, but I could tell she was unwell . . . like *really* unwell. She said she wanted to take a photo somewhere nice."

My mind went straight to the one tucked away in my drawer.

"I couldn't see, so she lined up the camera for me, then sat on the bench and spent a whole minute settling herself down for it." He was sniffling. "She said she was taking the photo for you. I don't know where it is, but I know it was her last gift to this world, Rhia. And she gave it to you."

I sat in shock as the dots connected. Everything he was

saying was true. From his feet to his face, it was obvious.

"I'm sorry for not telling you this straightaway. I know the way I've gone about all this is proper dodgy. I was shook that if I just came out with it—with no time to walk through things step-by-step beforehand—you'd run a mile."

Even at the rate he was filling them, there were still so many gaps. So much to process.

"I should have been there when they took her away. To tell them the pain she was feeling was real . . . as was the strange world her mind kept drifting to." He shook his head, looking more distressed than he had at any point so far. "But by the time I got out of hospital, they were more interested in locking me away for agreeing with her than they were in listening to my reasons." He choked up again. "After a while—like her—I stopped talking about it to anyone. But I knew I had to find you so I could tell you what I know. I know that the world my dad wrote about in his book is the same one I saw that night, Rhia. The same one your mum, Nadia, saw. And I knew the only chance I had of getting you to see it, too, was by getting you to believe the physics first."

It's one of those things you have to believe to see—the exact words he'd used in our first tutorial.

Then he decided it was time to tell me about a place he called the Upper World. That was when I stopped crying and sat up.

He described it like it was a place that still existed. The Upper World—according to Dr. Esso—was a place where the thread of human consciousness stitched into the fabric of space and time. A world where understanding the mathematics of reality could let you see it. All of it: your whole life laid out in front of you from start to finish. It was where space, time, energy, and all the physics he'd taught me in our lessons came from.

"My memories from up there are still choppy. So I'm partly going off this notebook, which I scanned so I could listen to it," he confessed. "But I'll never forget the heat I felt, like a cloud of Hidden Energy was following me."

"Why are you telling me this?" I asked, pushing my chair back an inch. It was too much to take in even before he'd started on this new path. "None of it makes sense."

"And yet it does. Doesn't it?" he replied, steady as stone. "Rhia, have you ever had déjà vu that was so strong you could have sworn you'd actually experienced the moment before? The kind of déjà vu that makes you wonder if there's more to reality, to time, than you think?"

"I'm not sure," I said, repressing the memories of the many occasions I'd felt exactly what he was describing.

"Then I'm guessing you never questioned *why* déjà vu can feel so real to us."

In fact, I had. And the only half answer I'd gotten was from Olivia. She once said that the reason we get déjà vu is because when we're born, we see our whole lives flash across our eyes. And that it happens one last time when we die.

"I've felt it, Rhia." He was hugging himself, like he had to stop his truth exploding out of him. "It comes from a place just beyond our fingertips. A place that sits on the other side of this one. Sits *above* it."

This isn't how this was meant to go, I was thinking. My compass was drifting farther and farther away from the familiar. I was meant to still be angry. And he was meant to be giving me straightforward answers. But now I was too sucked in to go back.

"Electromagnetism, the fixed speed of light, time dilation, everything I've taught you is real physics. You can confirm it in any textbook or any pop science video online. But what I'm telling you right now—about seeing the world the way physics describes it, about tapping *into* that—you won't learn anywhere else."

His phone went off, jolting him like he'd been jabbed with a needle. He tapped his feet while reaching into his pocket, and by the time the noise stopped, he was preaching again.

"In your last assignment, you used a special Tesla to describe how we travel through time."

I knew the metaphor he was referring to; I'd come up with it using what I'd scribbled on the napkin during my chat with Olivia at the stadium. But why was he mentioning it now?

"You said that at normal speeds, the Tesla has more than enough battery to power the engine and the clock on the dashboard." He was reciting the words I'd used in my homework from memory. "But once the car gets close to light speed—its max speed—the battery strains and there's not enough juice for the clock. And so the clock slows down, which, for this make-believe Tesla, means time *itself* slows down as well. Time dilation, basically."

"I did," I mumbled. But I was also wondering: How on earth was I still going along with this? Why was I listening to the same man who'd spent the past month lying nose-flat to my face?

"And finally, you said that if you ever managed to reach light speed in this special Tesla, time would completely stop. That the start, middle, and end of your car journey would get squeezed into zero seconds: a single moment."

I jumped as a ball fell from the table beside us. Even the kit was bugging out.

Dr. Esso didn't flinch, though. And each notebook page he turned was like a guillotine falling, my sanity breaking off chunk by chunk. The man was dismantling my mind, because he wanted to reshape it.

"We normally see life in three dimensions," he continued, finally settling on a dog-eared page. "But at light speed, your whole life gets squished into a single picture, letting you see both ends of the fourth dimension as well—*time*."

He flexed the backbone of the notebook to make sure the open pages stayed flat on the desk. And the longer I stared at the horrifying landscape sketched in pencil across the page, the fatter the goose bumps got on my arms.

"Well, 15 years ago," he said, "I managed to look out the window of your special Tesla, and this is what I saw." He placed his fingers at the base of the drawing. "The Upper World. The only place where I can stop your mum from getting shipped off to an asylum where she'll die a preventable death. The only place I can prevent those bullets from ever reaching their targets and stop anyone from dying that night. And I need your help getting there."

15

ESSO

THE TEACHERS KNEW the scraps and all-round ghetto behavior usually happened at lunch. That's why Mr. Sweeney and Ms. Russel sat on high chairs at opposite sides of the hall, sniffing for the slightest scent of beef.

From the corner of my eye, I watched D walking into the dining hall. He was with his boy Marcus, the one who looked just like the season-three fugitive version of Dushane (to me, but no one else). Marcus was one of those very rigorous guys: a straight-A student who only bopped with people who gave no Fs.

He split away from D and walked to the end of the dining hall where Mr. Sweeney was now patrolling. After glancing side to side with a devilish smile, Marcus dipped his hand in his pocket and yelled at the top of his lungs: "Scrammmmmmm-bllllllle!"

For the uninitiated, Scramble was a stupid, stupid game played at school. It started with the Scrambler—and anyone could be the Scrambler—throwing a one-pound coin on the floor, then shouting, "Scramble!" as loud as they could. A horde of kids then dove, skull-first, after it—using their fists, elbows, legs, everything they had to win the coin. On a bad day, you might smash your nose up or catch your finger under someone's foot. On a good day, the game ended with a few minor scratches, plenty of jokes, and a modest transfer of wealth.

But where Marcus had taken the piss was by throwing in a *two*-pound coin. It was like driving a truck full of live goats past fasting lions. A heap of kids piled up in front of Marcus, while the rest of the hall jumped out of their seats to see who'd float to the top, money in hand. Even Ms. Russel and Mr. Sweeney were part of the stampede.

The room's center of gravity shifted to the far end, and in the commotion, I lost sight of D. I looked down at the rough sides of my arms and saw the hairs standing up, something I'd always assumed only happened to people in films. Something was clearly setting me off. And even though I was sitting 30 yards away from the danger, I still felt like I was drifting into a trap.

Before I could think to call him back, Kato was already at the far end of the dining hall, hustling, like everyone else, to see the action before the scramble mountain crumbled.

"Prick," I muttered under my breath. Sure, Kato couldn't see how fast my heart was racing, or my knees knocking under the table, but he knew my situation with Bloodshed, and how scared I was. And yet he still left me to watch some kids fight over a two-quid coin. The exact same way he'd bumped me every other time I made the mistake of trusting him.

I reached for my tray, and a dark shadow fell over it.

It was D, his gold tooth glistening like the necklace draped over his school jumper. His eyes traced me top to bottom— starting with the sweat on my forehead and ending at my untied laces. *Better here and now*, I thought, remembering my bone-chilling premonition . . . *versus in a dark alleyway tonight.*

"What you sayin'? You were with them Peckham yutes that rushed my brother." His voice had always been low and gruff, like he mixed broken glass in with his breakfast cereal. He stared at me, his eyebrows arched above big, vein-stained eyes. "Man would wet you up right here if we weren't in school."

He said it all calmly, like it was as obvious as the square root of nine. It still didn't make sense to me how we'd gone from family friends to fatal enemies in less than a week.

I exchanged the shock on my face for puppy eyes. "It's not even like that, you know. Ask Bloodshed—I was the one telling everyone to allow it—"

"Don't call him that," he said, raising his voice, then bringing it back down again so it could ride with his original train of thought. "You lot proper disrespected my lil bro. *And* in West End. *And* in front of a couple gyal. Do you even know how much of a violation that is, bro? Did you really think man would let that slide?"

He grabbed the carton of purple juice off my tray, then punched a hole into it with the straw. *Is this guy really gonna drink my juice and make me watch him finish it before he rushes me?*

But instead of putting the straw to his mouth, he just stared at it, then back at me, then back at the carton again. And after one final pause, he turned the container over my head and squeezed its contents onto my scalp.

I shuddered as the cold, violet liquid ran down my shirt and into my lap. And as it dripped into my eyes, D's laugh got louder and louder.

Without thinking, I shot up from my chair, twisting so I was face-to-face with him.

"Fight! Fight! Fight!" The chants began a few meters away, then started echoing around the room.

"D and Esso are about to rock!" someone on the table behind shouted. I could literally hear the phones swooshing out of people's pockets, everyone ready to post highlights online. More people joined the crowd, and the growing intensity gave me an almost divine revelation: *This is my time.* By settling things now, I could avoid the future I'd seen in that vision. The vision I'd gone from mocking to mostly believing. And I'd have the element of surprise on my side as well. D would never expect me to make the first move.

I dug my heel in, felt the rubber squishing under my feet. Before I could talk myself out of it, I swung around, hitting D's cheekbone so hard I almost split my fist in two. He moved too late to duck, and his whole body followed his head to the side.

Not even five seconds passed before he was back upright, dazed for sure, but perfectly alive and sadly on his feet.

He slid two fingers in his mouth, and when he pulled them out, they were coated in a glossy red film. "Little dickhead," he said, directing the insult as much to himself as to me.

Well, that punch didn't go to plan, I thought. I started plotting my next move, started guessing at his. I knew he wasn't stupid enough to bring a shank to school. Or was he? Even without a knife, I wondered how far he was willing to take the fight. He was fast, powerful, ruthless.

I took a step back, looking for safer ground. *Keep your hands up, stay crouched, stay woke*, I reminded myself, bracing as a wave of rage drowned his face.

He flew forward, his fist balled up by his hip. I'd watched enough UFC fights to be able to read a telegraph, and just as I expected, the fist he'd kept in his pocket came out, tracing a line aimed at my jaw. I had just enough time to bring my arms up to shield my face. But just as he got in range, he dropped his body into a lunge, lodging his fist so deep in my stomach I heard my intestines squish.

I was wheezing, bent over with my back flat enough to lay a pint on, staring at the juice puddle at my feet. I would have sold my soul for a breath of air. But my lungs refused to lift. It was the kind of pain where just talking about it could make the spot tingle again.

"Pussio." He laughed. "My guy really tried it with that cheap punch."

He must have known I was paralyzed from the waist up, because he didn't waste any time going to work again. As his knee made contact with my temple, I could hear my brain rattling inside my skull like a metal tab in an empty Coke can. Turns out, when you take a hit to the head, and I mean a *proper* hit, you see stars. I'd always thought that was just some gimmick they did in cartoons to be funny. No, you actually see stars. Bright yellow sparkles everywhere. Another fun fact: when you're hurting in two places, your brain picks which one is worse and makes sure you only feel that one. So my only consolation from getting a knee to the head was that I couldn't feel the ache in my stomach anymore.

I dropped to the floor.

"*Perfect*," someone shouted, congratulating D for his punch like it was a Fire in the Booth punch line.

"Finish him," another girl yelled. Each syllable drooled out in slo-mo to my ears.

I lay there on my back, trapped. I made out four phones with camera lights on, and at least a dozen more faces watching. Along with the screaming, and the bitter taste of bile in my mouth, the pain was back as well, wrapping itself around my stomach and squeezing. The throbbing in my head felt like the same throbbing I'd had when my cranium hit the bonnet of the Range Rover that morning. Two head injuries before 2 p.m. What a start to the day.

As I drifted further and further out of it, waiting for D to finish me off, I heard one voice scream: "His eyes!" And another frightened one reply, "Oh my God . . . they're turning dark."

Then the dining hall dimmed to night.

I'm still on my back after copping that knee to the head, but now it's dark and warmer than a sauna.

Then a gleaming bullet whizzes toward me. Well, "whizzes" is an exaggeration: it's only moving as quick as a bowling ball, but it's close enough to make me almost shit myself.

More bullets appear, each one rippling through the air like a shark's fin cutting water. And one by one—like spotlights shining around a stage—faces come into view. Targets.

The first bullet is aimed at Spark.

The second is on path for Bloodshed, standing opposite him.

Rob and Kato are there as well, mouths stretched wide as four shells race at them.

And crouched next to me is Nadia, clutching her stomach with her eyes closed and her cheeks stained with tears. She looks like she's praying it's just a dream, hoping the bullet parked in front of her forehead might evaporate.

A blink later, and the dining hall surged back in full color. My shirt was soaked through with sweat. It felt like a thick, static energy had filled the hall, like the humidity in the Upper World had followed me back. D stood over me in the same spot I'd left him, probably wondering just how knocked out I really was.

If I had known how things would play out, I would have stayed down. If my priority was de-escalating the situation and swerving my future away from that grim moment with D and Bloodshed by the library, staying down was the only call.

But I could still taste the purple juice on my lips. I could remember the look on D's face as he poured it on my scalp. I accepted that he would never let this go and that no one at Penny Hill would ever let me forget what he had done to me. I remembered all the bullshit I'd gone through the whole day, the whole week. And so I decided: *I'm not having it anymore.*

I got up and leapt at D so fast he was still grinning when I tackled him to the ground. And even though I was still getting my balance after a sludgy transition back to real life, I crashed down on him like an ax, letting my hooks melt into one nauseating blur over his lifeless body. It was like everything was going at turbo speed, like I was hitting him so fast, one moment of time was crashing into the next.

If not for the ache in my arms, I'm not sure when I would have stopped. But when I finally did, I saw and heard something that terrified me.

No, I told myself. *Go away.*

The dining hall was there in full brightness; I could even see Sweeney running toward me. We weren't in the Upper World anymore, so why was I still hearing hailstones crashing around me? Why was I staring at D's forehead and seeing a bullet hole in the middle of it?

The fork that fell to the dining room floor jingled so long and loud we could have sung the first lines of a funeral hymn to it.

My shirtsleeves were covered in red specks. They seemed

to get bigger the farther down my arms I looked. My knuckles, usually smooth and creamed, were so sliced up I could see the white tissue under the skin. I was lost for words about what I'd just done, just seen.

But when I looked back down at D, his eyes were no longer rolled back, and the gory tunnel through his head had disappeared.

Now all I could see was clear, brown skin.

But before I could process what had happened and why I was seeing flashes of dead people while wide awake, Sweeney grabbed my collar, yanking me off D and clear of the crime scene.

"Man like Esso!" Kato shouted from behind the table, bringing me back to the present. He was pumping his fists in the air like a tennis player after an ace, proud of himself for doing absolutely nothing.

But I couldn't really take credit for what had gone down either. I still had no idea what had happened and definitely hadn't done it on purpose. Was I really seeing glimpses of the future? Where had that superhuman strength come from? It had made it feel like I was punching at light speed, while D was moving through porridge. Even more worrying was that this time, not only had I visited the Upper World; it had also visited me. I'd thrown those punches and seen those visions in the bright, clear light of the dining hall.

Sweeney tightened his grip on my collar. I was still close enough to D that I could see him starting to come to. There was no sign of a bullet wound, but the rest of his face was swollen and battered with blood leaking out of the gash on his cheekbone. As he rose to his elbows, I wondered what I was feeling most—relief or disappointment?

Meanwhile, Marcus had barged his way into the inner rim of the crowd and had to grope for something sturdy to hold when he saw his mate broken on the floor.

Sweeney grunted as he tugged me along, only loosening his grip once D and I were no longer in striking distance of one another. On our way to the exit, we walked past a long wall of stony faces. I knew what they were all thinking because I was thinking it, too: *Shit just got real.* And none of us was prepared for what would happen next.

I'd thrown that first punch thinking it would swerve me away from the future I'd seen in the Upper World. But what if I'd just steered right into it?

D climbed to his feet, shrugging off Marcus and the teacher as they tried to help him up. After a lumpy cough, he spat a red gob to the floor and straightened to his full height. Mr. Sweeney rushed me faster toward the door, but I turned around one last time only to see D smiling at me.

Then, without breaking his stare, he raised his hands and threw up the T.A.S. gang sign.

Part III:

MATTER

FROM BLAISE ADENON'S NOTEBOOK

To Esso,

At many points during my childhood, I was told the story of Eve—a girl who lived in a village where everyone saw time.

As the legend goes, in this village every child was born being able to see the past, present, and future at the same time. They would feel the warmth of their mother's womb right next to the cold seeping into their elderly bones.

Then one day, a girl named Eve was born. Unlike other children her age, Eve only cared about one thing: an icy evening, decades in the future, when she would fall off the edge of a mountain and die. Reliving those moments of freefall tormented Eve in a way that no one in her village could understand. To them, every moment and every emotion were sewn together. Dying on Tuesday was no sadder or more painful than finding a pebble in your shoe on Monday.

Desperate to escape her fixation, Eve taught herself a trick—a way to forget death. She pushed all her visions of the future outside the main chamber of her mind. And the one WINDOW that could let her see them again, she buried inside a memory she knew she'd forget. With further practice, she learned how to narrow her mind's eye to one sliver of time that she called the "present," and she vowed to only ever walk toward her last day in single steps. Henceforth, she lived in hazy recollection of the past and blissful ignorance of the future. She even forgot about death altogether—its inevitability, its stench, its calm—which freed her from the only fear she had ever known.

She rejoiced. She wept. She loved a man. She cherished her children. She truly lived like there was no yesterday or tomorrow.

But soon after her third child was born, the village fell under the shadow of a long drought. Eve, desperate to find water for her dying boys, set out to the only place she knew she could find it—the icy sheets at the top of a mountain north of the village. Her family and neighbors told her to stay, insisting the drought was always how they were meant to die. But Eve ignored them.

As she neared the peak, she had a moment of déjà vu, a chilling sense that she had seen this moment before. That split second of distraction caused her to slip on a loose rock, and Eve fell silently to her death many miles below. Her village mourned her, of course, but not with any more pain than they had the day she was born.

16
RHIA · (15 YEARS LATER)

THE WINTER FROST had burrowed into the fleshiest parts of my fingers. But it wasn't the wind or the cold that was making me fumble my stupid house keys. My nerves had been on fire since the end of the tutorial, when Dr. Esso had dropped all of his bombshells about my mum, about me. I was still regaining my feet, and in the rare moments I managed to cool down, I'd feel myself swinging so fast between hope and horror I didn't know where to land.

Chill, I told myself, slowing down so the brass key in my hand wouldn't miss the keyhole a third time. I desperately needed a late-night dissection with Olivia before I could calm down enough to come up with a plan. But as I shouldered the door open and stepped in, I decided it probably made sense not to tell her the physics part straightaway.

What Dr. Esso had told me—about reality existing in four dimensions—had somehow made *sense*. I thought back to just before our first tutorial. I'd sent him my location, a pin that showed where I was in terms of longitude and latitude on the

map: the first two dimensions. Then I'd told him we'd be working in the kit room on the top floor, so he'd know where along
the third dimension—height—we were headed. Finally, we'd
agreed to meet at a specific point in *time*: the fourth dimension, which, ironically, he'd ignored and arrived when he'd
liked. Since I could use those same four dimensions to locate
every event in my life, it wasn't too far-fetched to believe we
might live in this 4-dimensional space-time thing he wanted
to cross. What had *actually* blown my mind was the trail of
bread crumbs he'd used to guide me to that conclusion.

It had started with our first class on electromagnetism,
which he'd managed to turn into a lesson on light. Then he'd
spent the next session getting me to betray my common sense
by accepting that light travels at the same speed for everyone
("no matter what"), while time doesn't. I'd then worked out the
next takeaway by myself: that if you move fast enough, time
slows to a trickle and an entire journey squeezes into a single
image.

But Dr. Esso had then gone a leap further by showing *that*
image in his notebook. The Upper World, he'd called it. A
place where you could step outside the present, and into any
other moment in time. A place where I might actually—I had
to pause before even daring to think it—where I might actually find my mum.

And maybe even save her.

I still had so many things to ask Dr. Esso. But I'd also gotten
so many earth-shifting answers from him tonight that I'd been

almost grateful when Tony's message popped up telling me to rush home.

The promo screen on the wall by our front door replaced the weather forecast with a personalized ad for Tony: *Dream House: Devon Edition.* I rolled my eyes . . . this week's pipe dream.

An angry crosswind tugged the front door shut behind me, and the kitchen door creaked open, stuffing the hallway with the smell of shepherd's pie. Poppy stepped out and into my path. "Hey," she said, removing her mitts. She'd gotten a new dye in, a shade deeper than her natural ginger.

Behind her, Olivia, still in school uniform, was tiptoeing from our bedroom into the corridor. She flashed a hand signal at me, where Poppy couldn't see it.

Juggling? I wondered. *Maybe she's trying to tell me to juggle the situation?*

After years of tippy-toeing around the Hayes household together, we'd created a chunky dictionary of secret sign language. On a normal day, I would have deciphered her coded message in seconds. Not tonight, though, not with the backlog of puzzles already grinding my brain.

After performing the same motion three times and earning nothing but a confused stare from me, she started mouthing it. But the moment Poppy turned around, Olivia's eyes were innocently focused on her Vantablack fingernails.

"Tony's waiting for you in there," Poppy said, pointing to the living room door. I could hear a laugh track blaring from the TV on the other side.

I had no idea what I was in for, but also didn't have it in me to waste energy guessing.

We walked into the front room together and found Tony in a diagonal slumber on the couch. The open can of Boddingtons in his fist seemed to be defying gravity and geometry—standing righteously upright as he snored. His forehead reflected the blinking light from the Christmas tree in the corner, reminding me I had a week to fill the four stockings hanging from the bottom branches.

Poppy shook Tony out of his nap, and he rose to his feet. His beer hand cast a hammer-shaped shadow on the floor.

Bollocks! I realized. That was what Olivia had been trying to warn me about: I was in for a bollocking from Tony. I faced forward, a bit better prepared even if I didn't know what I was in trouble for yet.

"Were you with your tutor this evening?" he asked.

"Yeah, I was," I replied, all of a sudden feeling nervous. "Why?"

"Would someone *please* turn off that blimmin' telly," Poppy moaned. As Olivia answered her call, I centered my weight on both feet.

"I got a call from Care this evening." Tony referred to all my social workers as "Care." "She's been trying to reach your tutor for a month to get a physical copy of his teacher certificate or something or the other. She got tired of him dodging her calls, and so she done a search through his CantorCorp records herself, and guess what? Came back blank. The man's a con."

Poppy was shaking her head; Olivia was biting her polished nails.

"Jesus," I said, bending my mouth into a surprised O shape that I hoped looked authentic. But inside I was panicking. And all I could think was: *What else did they find out?*

"Look, I know you're a fan of the guy. I haven't seen you working this hard for school since . . ." Tony paused to dig deep into his memory. "Well, since—ever, I guess. But Care was absolutely adamant that you're not to see him again."

"If he's a con, why would I want to?" I asked. Tony didn't need to know that Dr. Esso had, just tonight, given me a number of unignorable reasons.

"Because you're hardheaded," he replied. "And sometimes too quick to forgive." He let through a lazy smile. "Please stay away from him, though. If Care finds out you've seen him again, then I—"

His left eye shut first, and the second one put up a quick fight before falling as well. Just like that, he was asleep again. And this time, not only was his can still upright, so was the rest of his body.

"Tony!" I said, short of a shout but vicious enough to snap his eyes back open. "You were in the middle of telling me off."

He stood up straight, checking the corner of his mouth for drool. "Ummm . . ."

"You were about to tell me the consequences of getting in touch with my tutor?" I reminded him, trying not to laugh.

"I know," he replied with professional calm as he glided back into our discussion. "If Care finds out I let you interact with that tutor again, they'll dock more points off my account. And we really can't afford that right now."

I softened my jaw so he wouldn't sense the rage heaving inside me. Of course that was the only thing he cared about. Of course, just as I'd found the truth, just as my lifelong search for my *real* mum was paying off, here he was, trying to snatch it all away. I'd risked everything to find out who Dr. Esso was— only for this lot to climb out the woodwork long after I needed them, assuming they knew him better.

I imagined the bleak future Tony was demanding of me— the one where I never spoke to Dr. Esso again. In that future, I'd learn nothing else about my mum, and would forever wonder if this Upper World was real. I knew what Olivia and I were fetching him these days barely covered groceries and utilities, and that Poppy was already working way more hours than the legal limit. I understood all that, I really did. But this was just *bigger*.

As if reading my mind, Olivia intervened, this time pretending to throw a pill in her gob before fake swallowing it.

Plan B, I realized, thankfully much quicker this time. *We'll figure out a plan B*, was what she was telling me.

Satisfied he'd said enough, Tony sagged back down next to Poppy.

"I love it when you use your tiger voice," Poppy told him, rubbing the patch of his bicep not covered by his polo shirt.

I turned to Olivia, slyly pretending to vomit.

● ● ●

Two days later, a letter arrived in the post. I'd read through it at least thirty times already, but this was Olivia's first. She sat straight-faced and cross-legged on the bottom bunk, wrapping as much of her pointy self into the quilt as possible. She'd been playing devil's advocate so well all day, I'd started to wonder if it was even an act. I, on the other hand, was pacing back and forth across our bedroom, leaning against the radiator every few laps to top up on heat.

Tony was still panicky about getting his Care pay slashed and had warned me in clear terms not to contact Dr. Esso under any circumstances. The higher-ups in the Care system hadn't taken his deception lightly either . . . and their feelings mattered the most. Until I aged out, my real mum—in the eyes of the law, at least—wasn't Nadia Black, or even Poppy, but Southwark Council. And as a ward of Southwark, all it had taken was one click from my social worker to block incoming and outgoing communication between mine and Dr. Esso's phones. She'd even gone as far as messaging Gibbsy and the academy staff to warn them not to let him on the grounds.

I'd all but given up until Dr. Esso found a way around it: sending a letter addressed to me inside a reused bank envelope.

It was a massive relief to have more of the truth in my fingers, but terrifying at the same time. Not only was there the question of how and what to write back to Dr. Esso, but if I should at all.

"I still don't reckon it's worth it," Olivia declared. "The guy's a nutter."

"I'm not saying he's not a nutter," I replied in a hushed, bitter voice. We could hear the TV next door, so it wasn't far-fetched to think Tony and Poppy might pick up our argument as well. "But if there's even the tiniest chance he's right, I *have* to know."

She shook her head. "Read the last page of his letter again . . . actually, it might have been the second-to-last . . . the page where he gets all serious and tries convincing you to write back, basically." She got up and put her ear to the door, to make sure no one was coming, then signaled for me to start.

"'Nadia never spoke much after that night. But on the few occasions that she opened up to me about the Upper World, I could tell how much she believed in it. The last time I visited her, she kept saying the same thing over and over: "Rhia will tell you—she'll tell anyone ready to hear."

"'You were just a baby at the time, so it made no sense. But it does now. There's nothing I've thrown at you that you haven't overcome. And you're the only person who needs to find her even more than I do.

"'I know that the WINDOW I climbed through 15 years ago to get to the Upper World is still open. On quiet nights, I swear I can even hear its humid wind seeping through a sill in my mind. I need to get back there, Rhia. I've learned every-thing I can from the physics and from my dad's notebook, but they haven't told me what I need to know. And that must be because your mum was right: you will tell me.'"

I let the letter drop to my side. "So, what's your point?"

"Look," Olivia said, shaking her head. "I was there when we watched the CCTV video from that night. It was effed up. And I mean really effed up."

"Again, what's your point?" I said, not caring how irritated I sounded.

"My point is: the man's obviously got a massive case of that post-traumatic stress thingamajiggy, as in, proper bad. I mean, how can you not see that? You don't think it's a coincidence that the same day the stuff in that video happened was the same day he claims to have gone to this magical Upper World?"

I shook my head at her.

"And ain't it weird," she continued, "that besides some Greek dude two thousand years ago, Dr. Esso's the only other person to ever even mention this place?"

I'd known explaining it to her was gonna be an uphill battle, but I hadn't expected her to be rolling boulders down at me.

When she saw she wasn't getting through to me, she pressed even harder. "I mean, did he even give you any proof?"

"Yeah, I already showed you." I struggled for a simple response. "Most physicists believe time isn't actually structured the way we experience it—"

"Rhianna, I'm not talking about a maths proof. Real-life proof."

I wanted to respond saying the two were the same. I almost did. But the sentence sounded daft even in my own head. This must have been how Mum felt when she tried explaining herself.

"Well, how about him buying that Cantor's stock and it going up 50,000%?" I challenged.

She straightened out her pajama bottoms and leaned against the flowery wallpaper Poppy had laid down the day the council had told her she was getting girls. "So he likes gambling and got lucky once. Even a broken clock is right twice a day."

Instead of these half-baked arguments, what I really wanted was to scream: *This is about my mum!* But even the idea of shutting down the conversation that way felt selfish. Unfair.

"Listen," Olivia went on, "from the looks of it, and even from his own reaction, he was *kinda* . . . to *blame* for what happened that night. And the poor bloke has spent the last 15 years unpicking every bit of physics that lets him believe he can go back in time and fix it."

"And who better to trick into joining him for his insane joyride than me?" I replied sarcastically.

"That's not what I meant."

"I think it might be exactly what you meant, Olivia." I looked into her eyes, refusing to turn away.

"You're angry, I get it." She bent down to the bed like she hadn't even noticed my stare. "Come sit down."

After holding out for a while, I plopped down next to her, barely flinching when a loose mattress spring poked into my thigh.

She edged closer to my end of the bed. "Look, sis—I get it, you want to understand who your real mum was. God knows I'd kill to know as much as you've found out."

I'd been so careful about not mentioning my mum too much

to Olivia, trying not to remind her of everything she was still missing. But of course, she'd known all along. She probably knew me better than I knew myself.

She put a hand on my shoulder. "But you can't keep doing this. It's not healthy, it's not safe, and it's not *quite* as logical as you might think. Plus, honestly, we kinda have everything we need here already."

"What, those two doughnuts in the front room?" I replied, laughing for no other reason than to style out the pain.

"Yeah, actually! I mean, don't get me wrong—they're about as far from perfect as you can get. But Tony's never laid a finger on us, and Poppy keeps us clothed and fed. They care, and they're *right* here."

Before meeting Dr. Esso, getting adopted was what I'd always wanted most. And as my time here added up, I'd come to see Tony and Poppy almost as parents. And Olivia as my sister. But even if or when it became official, would I really stop looking for a way back to my real mum? Did I actually have a chance of finding anything more than a memory of her somewhere in space-time? Of rewriting the whole of history for one woman? I lay down, covering my face with my palms. I would have happily jumped into a black hole just to get some sleep. For the next minute, we both stayed quiet, but I knew Olivia was listening. We could go a whole hour in silence and come out knowing we'd heard each other.

While tracing my fingers along the printed grain of the wooden plank that held my bunk above hers, I finally responded. "Yeah. It could be a lot worse, I guess." I at least agreed with her that there was a lot I'd taken for granted, a lot I had to lose.

"Plus," she said, beaming, "you've still got me!" She locked me inside one of her mercilessly tight hugs.

"You know I hate hugs, Liv. Please."

"Well, you hate baby goats and double rainbows as well." She squeezed even tighter. "And you deserve them *aaaall*."

"You're such a piss taker." I still couldn't bring myself to hug her back, but I was tired of taking out my anger on her. Tired of being tired. I didn't agree with everything she'd said, but I couldn't ignore the fact that, unlike Dr. Esso even, she'd been 100% truthful throughout.

"I guess it's still sisters before misters," I said, reciting the words she'd told me during the Dons match. Even if she couldn't understand how bad all this was twisting me up inside, the words still applied.

"Always," she replied, finally releasing me. "Also, can we *please* go back to me being the crazy bitch and you being the sensible one?"

That one got me. We both laughed until our cheeks were sore. At one point, Poppy even came in to check Olivia hadn't choked on gum again.

Before the night was up, I promised Olivia I wouldn't write back to Dr. Esso. And she promised to chuck out any other post that came from him. Days later, the Q-encrypted file with all his info on it would self-destruct—just as Linford had told us. And I would let it.

But secretly, I would hide away the envelope with his return address, ready for the day I'd need to write back.

Knowing I couldn't risk landing Tony in trouble or getting myself kicked out of his house, I would pretend I was keeping in line. I would act like everything was perfect, and if Olivia doubted it, I would lie. The part of me needing answers would burn hotter than it ever had, and I would find a way to smother it. So everything could go back to normal. For a while.

17

ESSO

HEADMASTER CRUTCHLEY

The words were engraved in thick square letters on a bronze plaque. Mr. Sweeney, who was now clutching my arm, looked even more shook of the man on the other side of the door than I was. He put his ear to the door and listened for a few seconds before knocking.

A muffled voice finally came through from the other side, and as Sweeney twisted the knob, two kids from the year below burst out like confetti, just missing him as they flew past.

"Watch where you're going, you two!" Sweeney shouted.

The one in front stopped laughing and did a double take as he brushed past me, switching between the message on his phone and the newly anointed badman that the message was about. He lifted his chin at me. Playing the role, I nodded back, and in a small, almost spiritual way, I felt like I'd just entered manhood. As if at some point in that dining hall I'd stumbled into VIP and was now chugging champagne with the rest of the household names.

On my walk to the head teacher's office, I'd been stuck trying to make sense of the miracle of violence that had taken place in the dining hall. That strange stretch where I went from being humiliated to being on top. It had all happened because of the Upper World, which clearly had more to offer than just peeking into time. It was some Superman-type madness, what I'd pulled off. *I might actually be*, I thought, *the first real-life superhero*. And from Narm, of all places.

Thinking back to what my dad had written in his notebook got me buzzing. At some point, he'd probably gone through the same journey from doubt to baffled belief that I was going through. I *was* ending up like him, just like Mum had warned. But did that make me crazy or just finally sane? I tried picturing Mum's face if I told her everything that had happened since she'd handed me his diary, but I couldn't pinpoint her reaction. What exactly did she know? Even if she didn't believe in the Upper World herself, she must have read about it in Dad's notebook. She'd have surely heard him babbling about it at some point when he was alive.

Sweeney scowled at me after spotting the smirk on my face as we walked into the waiting area. He wasn't wrong to be judging me either. The paranormal visions I'd had in the dining hall had been anything but cheerful: a sky full of bullets headed at Nadia and my best mates; D with a hole in his head? And yet, with those visions of carnage playing around me, all I'd cared about was knocking D the fuck out. *What's happening to me?* I wondered. *What am I turning into?*

"Come in!" yelled the headmaster from the far end of the

room. My questions about the Upper World would have to wait. For now, it was all about pretending his demerits were the scariest thing in the world. Between the premonitions, my promising chat with Nadia, and whatever was about to happen in the headmaster's office, there were quite a few balls in the air. And I couldn't drop any of them.

There was more polished wood in Crutchley's office than the rest of the school combined. I sat down; Sweeney didn't. I was weirdly calm. It wouldn't take long for Crutchley to come to the only rational conclusion: D engineered the fight; I was just defending myself. A hundred eyewitnesses could back that up. I just had to shut up, and in 10 minutes I'd be back with my mates, basking in the admiration of the stunner I'd pulled off at lunch, while figuring out how to save my night.

Crutchley sat his bearlike frame down in his swivel chair, then unbuttoned his tweed jacket to let his belly dive freely over the belt. To understand how men like him and Mr. Sweeney worked, you had to know how they were made. Back in the year 2000, a ten-year-old boy named Damilola Taylor was walking home to his family's flat in North Peckham Estate—just down the road from our flat. He'd been studying at Peckham Library and had walked part of the way home with John Boyega—yep, the same *Star Wars* Boyega that Spark's friends had been talking about in West End on Wednesday night. If I had to guess, young Damilola was probably looking forward to doing what all ten-year-olds like doing at home. Taking a nap. Tucking into some rice and stew. Playing a few rounds of *FIFA* and finishing his homework before his parents got home.

But he never made it home. Two boys a couple years older than him shoved a shard of broken glass into his leg and left him to bleed out on a stranger's stairwell. A true story. So it goes.

Back then, more and more stories like that kept coming out, and the government decided they couldn't ignore the outcry or waste the opportunity. They responded with a war on black-on-black crime in London, with Penny Hill Secondary plopped right in the middle of the two main battlefronts: Brixton and Peckham. The expensive new crime prevention program that rose from the ashes was called Trident (which just so happened to be the same name the government gave to the fleet of military submarines ready to drop nuclear bombs on Britain's enemies). It was Trident, and its extra funding, rules, and supporting programs, that had brought men like Crutchley and Sweeney to Penny Hill.

"So, Mr. . . ." The headmaster paused to glance at the report cards on his desk before continuing, "Mr. Esso Adenon. Where's that name from, out of curiosity? *Esso?*"

"It's from Bénin," I replied. "A little country between Togo and Nigeria."

"Does it mean anything? The name?"

"Yeah, in Gen—a language people speak there—it means 'yesterday' and 'tomorrow.'"

"Well, which one?" There was a moment of silence as he

and Sweeney leaned in for my response.

"Both," I replied. "That's what my mum told me, anyway."

"Well, that's awfully confusing, isn't it?" He chuckled, and Sweeney, once he knew it was safe, laughed too.

In my mind, I was kissing my teeth. It wasn't the first time I'd been through this, not the first time someone had asked me to rip up my name into smaller, plainer pieces they could swallow. I knew exactly what nonreaction I had to give to keep this tiring bit of small talk as small as possible.

Realizing I wasn't up for his posh-boy pleasantries, Crutchley sat up in his seat. He tossed a file across the cherrywood table, and for a second it looked like it was going to fall off at my end, but it stopped just short. *He's done that before*, I thought.

"So, tell me how you've gotten yourself into this mess, Esso." After waiting four or five seconds, he raised his voice. "I asked you a question—how did you get yourself into a brawl in my dining hall?"

"I didn't get myself into anything," I shot back. "You can ask anyone in the dining hall—everyone knows it wasn't my fault."

"Ah, 'it wasn't my fault,'" he mocked. "If I had a pound for every time I've heard that sentence, I wouldn't be here working for 30 quid an hour with you bundles of joy."

Sweeney grinned thirstily, exposing the coffee-stained tips of his two front teeth.

"What do you make of all of this, Sweeney?"

"I um...I..." Sweeney stuttered. He clearly hadn't expected to be asked to do anything but smile.

"We haven't got all day," Crutchley warned him.

"I'm . . . I'm not really sure who started it, sir. By the time I got Esso under control, Devontey Teno was already on the floor, unconscious."

"Ah, Devontey Teno. Another wonderful surprise. We'll come back to him in a second. And Ms. Russel, where was she when all of this was going on?"

"She got to the fight even later than I did, sir. There was a commotion at the other side of the dining hall—a silly game they play called Scramble, where they essentially fight each other on the floor for a pound coin."

"Ah," Crutchley said. "I see you're getting down with the lingo, Sweeney."

"Just enough to do my job, sir." He was blushing. "Ms. Russel and I were busy breaking up the Scramble, and I saw Devontey and Esso fighting on the other side of the dining hall, so I had to go and address that."

"Righto." Crutchley swiveled his chair back to me. "Esso, if you take a look inside your file there, you'll notice a curious trend: an increase in detentions and demerits, coinciding with declining test scores. You've done a cracking job of shifting your focus from success to self-sabotage."

It clearly wasn't his first time using that line either.

"I hate to say it, Esso, but I've seen this all before. From half the kids here. Not only is it bloody depressing, but it's also just *boring*. Like watching car crashes that take years to end."

He rested his forearms on his table. "You might think I'm

just some crusty, heartless old git, but I do care about what happens to the pupils at this school. I genuinely care if you succeed or not. If you live."

The way he said his last sentence and the way he and Sweeney exchanged looks made me wonder just how much he knew about my cold war with D and his brother.

"Esso, we're in all sorts of mess in this school." He put his finger to his chin. "And not just demerits and suspensions kind of mess. I'm talking Her Majesty's Prison mess. And we need you to . . . help us . . . help you."

Sweeney couldn't hide the confusion on his face, but by now I was already five steps ahead of Crutchley. He wanted information on D and the T.A.S. boys. The boys who'd been running riot at Penny Hill all year with impunity. And he wanted it from me.

"Let me be plain, Esso. I don't believe any of this is your fault. Devontey has sat in that same chair you're sitting in more times than I can count. I'm well aware of what that beastly boy is capable of." He smiled. "In fact, as you were on your way here, I had Purdy go through his locker. Can you guess what she found?"

I kept my head down, waiting for him to answer his own question.

"A list of things *I* can't even legally own. Surprise number three," Crutchley said. "It's safe to say you won't be seeing him at Penny Hill anymore."

Madness, was my immediate reaction as I thought about what that meant for D. For some reason, the second place my mind went to was his mum, and how cut up she'd be when she found out her oldest son was school-less. She'd find a way to blame herself like she always did.

But as bad as I felt for the two of them, it didn't hold a candle to how afraid I was for myself.

"Your locker was clean, of course," Crutchley added.

I nodded back casually.

"But your disciplinary record is anything but."

Crap.

"If you add that to the demerit that I'm thinking about giving you for today's fight," Crutchley went on, "I have more than enough to make a case for your permanent expulsion."

Crutchley pulled out a sheet of paper and placed it on the desk. It was blank except for the school crest printed at the top. As he put pen to paper, I could just about make out what he was inking in black.

Early Christmas list

From: Esso

To: Mr. Crutchley

Just below those words, he scribbled the number *1, DEVON-TEY TENO* next to it. Then he continued numbering down the page.

The wait was killing me.

Finally, he rotated the page and slid it my way.

"I've only put one name on this page, and I'd like you to help me *guess* the rest. Everyone you know in the Think After Shooting gang."

T.A.S. was the best-known set in Brixton, but I was still

impressed he knew the name and how to spell it out. I'd heard it used to stand for Think After Shanking. I guessed once the cash price for an unmarked stick had dropped to a few pinkies, even acronyms were moving differently.

"You can choose to tell us because it's the right thing to do, or because you want to avoid getting expelled. Or both. Your motivation is entirely up to you. And for my part, I can guarantee complete confidentiality."

Confidentiality. I played with the word in my mind, then sent it far, far away. Everyone knew what happened to singers. The code of ethics was graffitied on every brick wall between here and home, the stories scribbled on our little hearts.

Like the one story about that Indian girl who saw her friend get shanked on Camberwell New Road and told Crutchley. I'd heard he'd promised her confidentiality as well. But that didn't stop the detectives from dropping her name in front of their prime suspect during his interrogation to buy leverage. The following week, she got taken out in broad day outside her house. No other witnesses came forward.

My knuckles were throbbing—still bleeding in places— and a dense fatigue was yawning through my body. Uninvited, the daymare of D and Bloodshed walking toward me in the night crept forward from my memory. I could almost hear the cracking of hail on the pavement, almost see Peckham Library in the background. If that premonition came true like the first two already had, I was set to run into them after the sun went down—a future that felt even more likely after what I'd done at lunch.

I was now stuck debating two hideous choices: I could grass on D and get splashed, or I could keep it real and get kicked out of school, and probably out of Mum's house as well. *That's life*, I thought. You're given a problem, you find a solution for that problem. But then your problem and your solution have sex when you're out the house, and you come home to a litter of new problem children to take care of.

Who could I even turn to for help with my new demonic problem children? Mum? Her pastor? Definitely not Rob or Kato . . .

None of them, I decided. I sat back in my chair and let out an exaggerated sigh that caught Crutchley and Sweeney off guard.

"Sorry, but I don't really do Christmas gifts," I said, facing Crutchley. A 10-second stare-off kicked off between us, focused and quiet enough that I could hear the clock ticking and Sweeney itching.

Crutchley broke first. "I'm disappointed in you," he said, shaking his head. "But not all that surprised. I just wonder when you people will learn that if you want to play at Wimbledon, you have to wear white." He looked at Sweeney. "Please take him to the detention room and supervise him until the end of the day. And make sure he gets a bandage for his hand. He's already dripped all over my carpet."

Crutchley shared his final words of advice as he tailed me to the door: "I'll give you until tomorrow morning to think it over. You can come to me or Mr. Sweeney when you change your mind. It really is a worthwhile opportunity, Esso—Penny

Hill would be sorry to see you go."

He folded the paper twice, slid it in my side pocket, then sent me back into the wild.

The detention room was on the top floor, and every few steps Sweeney turned back to me with that thin-lipped, close-mouthed smile of his.

Our meeting with the headmaster had done something for him. He had a new bounce in his step. Not only had Crutchley trusted him enough to let him in on his plan, he'd also asked for his help in executing it. Sweeney was probably already calculating how much his take-home pay might jump once promotions were announced.

"I hope you'll do the right thing here," Sweeney said as we got to the final flight of stairs. "Mr. Crutchley and I weren't bluffin', you know. You should be more scared of what *we're* capable of than anything those T.A.S. hoodlums are threatening."

The slimy look on his face gave me an idea. A plan.

I slid my palm along the railing, wondering how soon I could put it to work. Too early and Sweeney would think I wasn't slick enough to pull it off. Too late and he'd think I didn't have the bottle. In the end, though, the perfect time announced itself when Sweeney put on his smug grin again, and I decided it was the last time I could stomach it.

"Kemi Harper," I said. It was barely loud enough for him to hear, but I knew he had.

"Excuse me?"

"Kemi Harper," I repeated. "You know her, don't you?"

His eyes darted around as he scratched the crown of his thin mop. His wide strides turned into nervous shuffles, his soles scraping the floor every other step.

"I'm not really sure what you're playing at, Esso. I mean—"

"How about Jodie Pyne? Hope Ngozi? Leanne Davies?" I offered. "To be honest, the Leanne thing was more of a rumor. Might have been complete bollocks, actually, but I could throw in some other guesses if you like?"

"Shhhhhhhhhh!" He grabbed my arm, yanking me through the doorway of the nearest empty classroom. "Esso, you don't know what you're on about." He turned to double-check no one was in earshot. "And you don't have any proof for these bloody allegations either. So just keep your mouth shut before someone hears you!"

"Are you having a laugh?" I replied, not bothering to lower my voice. "Half of Penny Hill knows about you. You think that just because they're legal by a few months, you're safe?"

He was still clamping my arm, and tight enough that it would start tingling soon. But I let him hold on.

"I just hope you do the right thing, Mr. Sweeney. Crutchley ain't the kind to bluff. Trying to remember who I heard that from recently."

That one turned his face *all* the way upside down.

"Look," I brought my mouth close to his ear. "I'll keep quiet about your creepy and *pathetic* extracurriculars." I had no intention of keeping that promise; Nadia already had plans to tell on him, and I'd be there to cosign whatever she said. But I still needed to sell it hard. "All you gotta do is make sure I don't get expelled. Whatever sneaky plans Crutchley has for me, handle that, bruv."

Sweeney's skin was graying. He didn't deserve to keep his freedom, let alone his job. He nodded frantically, shaking me out of my thoughts and waiting for my final words.

"Now," I added coolly, "get the fuck off my arm."

18

RHIA · (15 YEARS LATER)

I'D BEEN TRACKING my delivery on my way home, so I knew it had already arrived. I ripped apart the packaging like a cave girl, moving closer to the corridor light so I could see my new football boots shine. Maria was the only other girl on the team with these. Actually, hers were the 240-quid Predators and I had the half-price Adidas Preditos with the side ridges painted on instead of molded. Going for the classic black, red, and white had been a no-brainer. Once you strayed from that, you might as well get them in Burberry print and stick neon lights on the toe caps.

It was the day before Christmas Eve, and this was my present to myself. Poppy had given me the cash to order them that same morning—*minutes* after Gibbsy had sent a video note telling me I was starting in the Academy Cup final in two weeks. By the time I got to school, Olivia had told everyone. She might have been even more gassed than I was. She knew my cardio schedule and stretching regimen. And when she came home from a movie with her friends, she was used to finding me asleep in bed with a pulser strapped to my thighs and a creatine shake on the desk, ready for my morning workout.

I leaned my soggy umbrella against the wall. There was tinsel running along the hallway and around the door frames. Even though the sparkly decorations warmed my heart, a part of me was looking forward to the holiday passing. The new year provided a chance to reset . . . to restrategize.

Only a few days had passed since I'd opened Dr. Esso's letter, and I was already brainstorming ways to communicate with him secretly. But I'd also promised myself I'd let things cool down first, enjoy the holidays properly, and resist doing or even *thinking* about doing anything till after.

I headed toward my room, impatient to try on my new secret weapons and to make sure they'd made the right boot half a size bigger like I'd asked. On my way, I spotted Poppy's flats outside the front room, and lined up next to them, Tony's boots, and Olivia's Docs.

Strange, I thought. They were all home, but it was so quiet. No TV blaring; no Olivia chattering on the phone and Poppy telling her to quiet down; no groggy hum of Tony snoring on the couch. As I crept into the front room, I had the alarming thought that a burglar might have tied them up on the floor and gagged them. But there they were—the three of them on the couch, in their usual spots.

Olivia was staring out the window. Poppy's face was buried in her hands. Tony was the only one looking dead at me.

"What is this? An intervention?" I joked, my heart fluttering.

My biggest worry was that they'd somehow realized I still had plans to contact Dr. Esso and were now teaming up to stop me.

"Sit down, Rhia." Tony pointed at a chair in the middle of the room that he'd unfolded for whatever this meeting was.

I turned to Olivia, hoping she'd give me some kind of warning signal: another pair of bollocks, or maybe she'd "lie" on her side, our code to fib if it came to it. But instead, she carried on pretending she couldn't feel my eyes poking her.

Then a sniffle leaked out from inside Poppy's palms. She was crying. This wasn't an intervention, I realized suddenly.

It was an ambush.

"Rhia, I think you might want to sit down," Tony repeated.

I could already feel my fight-or-flight instincts gripping me. "I'm all right."

"Trust me. It will make this easier."

"This might be your first time doing this," I replied. "But it's not mine. I'll stand on my two feet."

Poppy's weeping got louder.

"That's fair." Tony stood up, the floorboards bending beneath him. "As you've probably noticed . . . I've been in a bad state for a while. And Poppy's been picking up my slack for longer than she deserves." He massaged the back of his neck. "Next month, we're moving into a small place in Devon. We've always wanted to do it, and Poppy reckons the change of scenery'll help. But the bit that breaks our hearts is that we can't take care of you anymore. We've barely scraped together enough for the move." He paused. "And if we sacrifice any more, it'll break us."

I wanted to explode. The last four years I'd tripled as this man's chef, cleaner, and therapist. I'd literally wiped chunks of his vomit off the kitchen sink.

He would do the same for me, I'd always reminded myself. *He cares.*

"I'm sorry," he said, a tear dropping from his chin to the ground with a *thud*.

Poppy looked up from her hands, mascara smeared around her crystal-blue eyes. "I'm so sorry, Rhia." She was shaking. "I know this isn't fair. I just wish there was more we could do."

I remembered my first one-on-one with her. I'd told her the number of foster homes I'd been through, and she'd promised me (through messy tears just like these) that I would never have to find a new home again.

In the corner, Olivia had dense bags below her eyes. We were two mismatched socks that Tony and Poppy had tried on for a while. But we'd never looked quite right. We'd always been one inconvenience shy of getting chucked out. We'd just forgotten.

I knew the time for looking back and analyzing the "if onlys" and "what ifs" and "next times" would come soon. For now, I was expected to be a good sport. That was what they always hoped for going into these chats. And so I dug deep and found a way to serve my most lenient smile.

"So I guess Olivia and I owe you a farewell party, then?"

Tony and Poppy exchanged glances. Olivia sank into her seat, her eyes squeezing shut.

"Um . . . Plymouth Council said they could pay for one foster child. But only one." Tony cleared his throat before finishing. "So Olivia's staying."

Each syllable pushed the knife deeper into my back. The room suddenly felt like it was expanding around me till I became a tiny speck. Invisible. Lost.

I should have known, I told myself. Olivia was a fighter, after all, and she'd have done whatever it took to nail down that spot. I wondered how long she'd kept it from me. All the times I'd been out playing football, she'd been here on this couch, pulling away at Tony and Poppy's heartstrings. She'd convinced them that their friendlier, prettier, simpler daughter was obviously the better pick.

Maybe she'd told them about the letter I'd gotten from Dr. Esso, about my real mum, or any one of the million other secrets I'd locked away with her. I thought back to the countless times she'd bandied around words like "sister" and "forever." All the times she'd come home in pieces after one of her waste-cadet friends or flings put her down.

I was always the one to put her back together.

It was *my* shoulder she cried on every night. Every. Fucking. Night. *Mine!* And now she wouldn't even look me in the eye. I was too angry to feel anything but hate toward her. And I couldn't wait to get to our room, so I could tell her how I felt using words she'd never forget.

"C-C-Care called," Tony continued, choking through his words. "They, um . . . they said there's a bed for you in one of the group homes nearby. They can hold it for you till Monday. And we're gonna make sure we give you a good last Christmas weekend."

Those two words—"group home"—resuscitated something buried deep inside me. Somewhere in my DNA was the imprint of a Rhia who'd tasted that carnage and had narrowly escaped it, vowing never to go back. My right eye started twitching, spasming up and down like a broken camera shutter. It was like my body wasn't sure whether to let me see this catastrophe unfolding or to hide it from me.

It stung that a few days ago, Olivia had asked me to turn my back on Dr. Esso—the one person who could connect me to my real mum . . . only to now abandon me herself. It hurt that I didn't have the strength to stay the weekend like Tony wanted, that I'd be leaving for the group home tonight, missing Christmas.

The silence hung as I crossed the room, past Tony, past Poppy, past Olivia, before stopping by the tree. The fairy lights were dancing. Virgin Mary watched me from atop in ceramic blue. The gifts I'd wrapped for them—a sharper razor for Tony, a foot massager for Poppy, a retro photo album for Olivia packed with our best hits—all rested there, untouched. As I untied my own stocking from the lowest branch, I had a thought so sad it made me smile: I'd arrived a year before Olivia. And they still chose her.

I walked out without letting a single tear drop.

My next home would have no room for that.

19

ESSO

MR. SWEENEY AND I had spent the last two hours alone in the detention room, avoiding talking or looking at each other. I still couldn't tell for sure whether I'd made the right call threatening him. Before my uncle got deported, he used to quote West African proverbs that always involved animals for some reason. One, in particular, came to mind: "If you have a snake in your house, open your front door and guide it out—because if you trap it in a corner, it will leap at your throat." By blackmailing Sweeney, I'd left him with three choices: come for my jugular now, later, or never. I'd banked on him being too moist to take the first or second options, but I couldn't help thinking, *What if I'm wrong?*

Then again, what other options did *I* have? Penny Hill was already the roadest school in the area, so where would I go next if I got expelled? But if I ratted like Crutchley wanted me to, I'd have to bet on all the T.A.S. boys I wrote down on his snitch list either dying or becoming born-again pacifists over the weekend. Those weren't choices. They were different-colored tombstones. I'd won the fight with D this afternoon but couldn't shake the feeling I'd set myself up to lose a much bigger battle tonight.

Once the school bell rang, I left Sweeney and joined over a thousand students trying to cram their way out the school's front doors. Out the corner of my eye, I spotted Rob and Kato snaking their way through the crowd to catch up with me.

"Baaaaaaaaaaaaaws man!" Kato shouted, his fists muffling the chant from his mouth. "I ain't never, ever seen a comeback like that in my life, bro."

"Is it?" I asked. The fight felt like it happened a million years ago. I wondered if the bangs I'd taken to the head were setting in because each minute that passed made the memories harder to retrieve.

"You were like a blur, fam. Man was left-hooking like Joshua, uppercutting like Fury. At one point, you were standing over D with blood up your sleeves, and these dark-gray-looking eyes, fam. I had to pinch myself to make sure my head top weren't loose." He stared at the ceiling in thanks. "I swear down, that whole lunch was too peak."

"You look proper mash up, though," Rob added.

Their comments rolled over me. I was still so lost in my thoughts I could barely register what they were saying and almost missed the fact that everyone walking past us was pointing and staring at me, too. It's funny how when you get something you've always wanted, it never feels the way you expected. Nobody tells you that. How much victory collects.

Nadia walked past, gripping her backpack straps. She didn't see us, but Kato's eyes tracked her down the corridor, while he directed his next words at me.

"You reckon she'll look at you now, bro? Now you're a bad-man and all."

"What did you say?" I was fuming. I'd heard every one of his words but wanted to give him one last chance to de-escalate before I did the opposite.

He looked me dead in the eye and, without uttering a word, grinned.

"Fuck you," I said, shaking my head and walking away. It was all I could do to stop myself exploding. I was used to Kato chatting shit and throwing the odd low blow. But something about the way he'd said it this time, the look on his face. It was too far. Especially after all I'd been through, after all we'd been through.

"It's calm, boss." He lunged after me and grabbed my arm. "Why you being all sensitive? It was just banter."

It *wasn't* just banter. He was putting me in my place, under-estimating me like everyone else had all day. And he knew it.

I spun back around to face him. "Was it a joke when you linked Kaylie behind my back as well?"

He dropped his gaze to the side, quietly hissing with that goddamn smirk still on his face. "Come, man, that was like three years ago——"

"And you *still* ain't apologized! I'm not letting you spoil what I got with Nadia."

He refused to look me in the eye, but I was at his nose now, staring him up and down. Sure, he didn't know quite how big the fire was that I'd spent the last 24 hours trying to put out before he'd helped splash petrol on it. But for the first time in our five-year friendship, I finally felt like I knew everything I needed to know about him. And I was ready to share it.

"I've been connecting a lot of dots today." I summoned the same calm gullyness I'd used on Sweeney a couple hours earlier. "And I realized something: every time I actually try hard at something, try to be good at *anything*, you're always the first one to cuss me. Calling me a neek when I ask questions in class, always finding ways to chop me down when it comes to girls. But now I know why you do it—you need me to feel like shit so you can feel better about yourself. Because deep down inside"—I used my finger to stab his chest—"you know your life ain't worth the gum on my shoe. You're dirt, bruv. You're less than dirt, and you know it."

"It's calm, bro," Rob intervened. "Just chill out."

"No!" I shouted. "I'm not listening to you neither." I pivoted across to him. "At lunch, I told you to stay with me. You knew what was up, you knew I needed your help, and you fucking left me."

"Bruv, I didn't know D was gonna rush you like that," he said, sounding genuinely bent up by my accusation. "It's not as deep as you're making it out."

"That's the fucking problem! Nothing's ever deep unless you decide it is. You spend the whole time on your high horse talking down at everyone when you're literally shit at *everything*. You've never even pretended to give a shit about anything I care about. You're a selfish, useless waste man." We each stood there, like three rocks planted in a river while the crowd flowed past.

"Know what? I'm not having you two dragging me down anymore." I walked away, glad that they'd have to watch me striding through the front door with the rest of school gassed for me.

The sky looked nothing like it had that morning. The rain clouds were gone, replaced with puffy dots painted on a blood-orange canvas. When I finally re-spotted Nadia, she was halfway down the main road. We'd left things off in a decent place at lunch, and I was keen to see if I could cover more ground. After the day I'd had so far, I also just needed someone sensible to talk to. Someone smart. Even if it was going to add 20 minutes to my journey home.

My phone vibrated. I yanked it out of my pocket so fast I almost fumbled it, but caught it just in time to see the notification pop up.

Mum: We still on for FFCF at 8 p.m.?

Knowing how stubborn she was, it was a proper big deal that she'd extended the first olive branch.

The response I drafted in my head read something like: *I'll order the fish and chips. You pick the film?* But none of my Upper World visions had come with time stamps, meaning I didn't know where I might be at 8 p.m. To make matters worse, Nadia was pulling away up ahead.

Given everything I'd seen and foreseen, this could be my last chance to really speak to her. To really be with her. Mum's text would have to wait.

To keep up with Nadia's gangly legs, I had to go from a gentle jog to a very uncool sprint, sliding around another group of kids from school, when she turned onto the side road.

"Who are you, and why are you following me?" she said, not facing me or breaking stride.

"It's me. Esso."

"Jesus, E." She swung around and her cackle-laugh melted away any awkwardness from my creepy entrance. "I thought you were some kind of stalker."

"Just wanted to say wagwan, innit. We didn't get to finish our chat earlier. Anyway, what you saying?"

"Are you really asking me that?" She glanced down at my knuckles, covering her mouth when she saw the red blots on the bandage. "I heard about the fight. You okay?"

It hurt worse than it looked, but I replied, "You should see the other guy," adding a smirk.

"You think you're sick now, innit," she said, shaking her head. She pulled her bag straps close into her body, and a few steps later, stopped in the middle of the road, adding extra weight to her next line before dropping it. "You gotta be careful, though, E. You said it yourself—D and them T.A.S. boys don't squash the passa till it's done." She placed the slightest bit of extra emphasis on the final word, and I felt a lump rising in my stomach.

I knew she was right. Of course I did. I knew the smartest move would have been for me to offer my humiliation as a peace offering to D. I should have stayed down after his first punch, then taken the never-ending giggles and pointed fingers that followed on the chin as well. But that was the past now.

"If I get back after half term and either of your seats is empty, I'm gonna be *pissed*," she said.

"Since when d'you care so much about me?" I asked, thirsting for her to take the bait.

Instead, she shoved me away. "Both of you need to just not die, innit."

She was being serious. I kicked a stone along, thinking a bit more deeply about it myself. I definitely didn't want anyone to die, and maybe D didn't either. Going to war wasn't as glam as they made it look in the films or songs. The truth hurts, and the *whole* truth is excruciating. I thought about Spark and the time he boasted to me about the first kid he'd "put it on"— and I mean properly, permanently put it on. But behind closed doors, Spark couldn't sleep, couldn't eat, didn't leave his house for weeks.

Nadia craned her neck forward. "Are you even listening to me?"

"I am, you know. Just got a lot on my mind I'm trying to figure out right now. You honestly have no clue."

"E, you annoy me sometimes, you know that? I've told you so many things about me. Some proper embarrassing stuff as well."

I stayed quiet and kept my eyes on the traffic as we walked. I couldn't tell her about the visions, especially the one in the lunchroom with her facing off a bullet. In addition to making her wonder just how often I dreamed about her, she'd probably call me ments and freak out. I could figure this out myself.

"Do you think anyone else at school knows I'm diabetic?" she asked. "You think I even considered inviting Janeen and Kemi to our sci-fi movie marathon last month?"

"No. I guess not."

"Exactly. But *you* know. So now it's your turn: spit it out."

"It doesn't matter, Nadia."

"Well, I'm guessing it does. Otherwise, you wouldn't be thinking about it this much." She looked at my lips expectantly.

She had a good point, and it wasn't her first time making it. Deep down, I wanted to fess up. I wanted her to know and understand everything about me. But deeper down still, I wanted her to drag it out of me, inch by inch. I'd given up the info way too easy to Kato, and look how that had turned out. She wasn't a prick like him, but if she happened to do me the same way, at least I'd know I'd been careful.

"You promise you won't laugh at me or take the piss?"

"E, you know I can't promise that." A wicked grin spread across her face. "But I can promise I'll keep it between me and you."

"Fine," I said, satisfied I'd put up enough of a fight. "So, I actually got hit by a car this morning." I had planned to stop the story roughly there, but that sentence alone had lifted so much weight off my shoulders, I suddenly wanted it all off. "And since then I've been seeing random glimpses of the future."

After a pause, Nadia shook her head. "You are such a dickhead sometimes, E."

I stopped walking, untucked my shirt and pointed at the discolored lump on my hip. "Look: this is where the car smashed into me." I couldn't read her reaction, so I carried on with more force. "And after I got hit, I woke up in this dreamworld and saw a bunch of projections of myself, including one that was wearing headphones from Cantor's for some reason, and when I stepped into one of the projections, I saw three visions of the future. It was sort of like time traveling but where only your mind goes on the trip. And now two of the visions have actually happened in real life. As in *happened* happened, both today. And it can't be a coincidence that this is all happening the same day I found my dad's diary, and read a page where he talked about this mental place called the Upper World."

I'd made the pit stop to catch up on air, but found her staring back at me in polite disbelief. "Honestly. And later on at lunch, when D punched me, I was knocked out cold, but when I got up, I started having more visions. Then while I was fighting back, I was super hot, like volcano hot, and I also felt like I was moving through time at a snail's pace. Anyway, that's mostly it."

"So, is *this* why you lot were talking about time travel at lunch?"

I nodded nervously.

"Hmmm." She rested two fingers on her chin. "Well, the precognition-slash-time-travel stuff you mentioned might actually make logical sense. Plus, you showed me solid proof that the car crash happened. There's only one thing I still don't get: Why is the skin on your hip so damn ashy?"

"Piss off, Nadia."

She bent over laughing and took her sweet time collecting herself. I felt like an idiot. I didn't enjoy the looks of pity she kept giving me either.

"I'm sorry, E. I shouldn't have made that joke, man. Look, I obviously don't believe you. But I can tell from that stupidly serious look on your face that *you* believe you. And that's probably what matters most right now. And I'm sorry about the accident this morning. That's shit but I'm glad you're okay." Her serious face was back on. "I just need you to slow down so I can understand it a bit better. Like, more explanation, more details."

"Honestly, I ain't got no explanations yet. I'm not even sure I can say it any better than I just did."

"And you're sure you ain't got concussion symptoms? No problem remembering who the current prime minister is?"

"*Nadia,*" I groaned. "You gonna chat to me about this or what?"

"You're lucky, you know." She was gazing up at the sky.

"Time travel is, by far, my favorite sci-fi theme, so I'm actually overly up for a chat on it."

Of course she was. This was the same girl who'd told me she was thinking about applying to a redbrick uni to study physics. Nadia, who when she wasn't babysitting her little brothers, had her head stuck in a 400-page novel. I was kicking myself for not thinking to ask her sooner, then got hit with an idea that might just about make up for it.

"How about this. If you can explain how time travel works in all the movies and books you've read, then, after our revision session tonight, I'll tell you *everything* about the mad shit I saw when I time-traveled. Deal?"

"Deal," she responded, shaking my outstretched hand.

Her face went tense. She pressed a finger against her lips. One second passed. Two. Three . . . Five . . . I begged myself to keep quiet so she could think in peace. Finally, she came back.

"So, on a basic level, there are two types of time travel."

"Okay," I said, dubious about how far she'd get with the little I'd told her.

"The first kind of time travel is the kind you get in films like *Hot Tub Time Machine* or the *Avengers: Endgame* movie. Although . . ." she said, trailing off. "I'm not really sure if anyone understood what the hell was going on with the science in *Endgame* . . . Anyway, with this first kind of time travel, you can go forward or back in time and change things. So, like in *Hot Tub Time Machine*, they travel back to the eighties, and one of them uses his knowledge of the future to invent Lougle, which is just his shameless copy of Google, and he goes on to become like a multigazillionaire."

"Yeah, I watched that film after you recommended it. Was funny, still." My phone vibrated a few more times in my pocket, but I ignored it. Nadia was still going.

"The second type of time travel is the kind you have in *Harry Potter and the Prisoner of Azkaban*."

She could probably tell from my hanging jaw that I was waiting for the details like my life depended on it.

"So, Hermione and Harry use this magical device to travel back in time, but they eventually realize that even though they can travel to the past, they can't change things they've already seen happen. In that version, it's like once you see any part of your past or future, it's kinda set in stone."

"What about the bits of the future that you *haven't* seen?" I said. "Are those set in stone as well?"

"If you asked the ten smartest physicists in the world that, they'd disagree on the answer."

What hope do I have, then? I wondered. We weren't far from Camberwell Green—I could tell by the finger-shaped branch that leaned over the park fence as well as the strengthening smell of barbecue ribs. I still had to grab the bus to get home, but Nadia lived only a few minutes' walk away. I was working on borrowed time.

"The weird thing is," she continued, "a lot of the famous scientists who've gone proper deep into time travel end up going . . . kinda mad. No one knows for sure how fixed the future is, or which of the two types of time travel is right." She peered up at the clouds. "I can't believe we're having a practical conversation about time travel right now—"

"I'm worried it might be the second one," I replied, my voice shaky. I wasn't exactly keen to share the details of the near-violent vision I'd had with her. Those details could wait.

"Worried?" she asked, now looking a bit worried herself.

"Well, you said the past and future are 'set in stone' . . . When I got hit by that car and woke up in that dreamworld, I'm pretty sure I saw it—that stone. I swear down, there was this giant structure that reached up into the sky, and when I went into it, I saw flashes of my life . . . of the future. Get me?"

Her eyes darted back and forth as I spoke, her brain ticking even faster than when we'd started. After a few moments, her face lit up again.

"What you just said about this big 'structure' thing . . . it kinda reminds me of the Block Universe."

"The what-a what-a?" I asked.

"Stay with me on this one. So, Einstein pictured the universe as a massive block that's made up of everything. And not just the space that the planets and stars and you and I sit in, but all of *time* as well. And it's all just mashed up together into a single block." The look of confusion on my face must have told her it wasn't quite clicking, so she went back to the start. "Basically, in this Block Universe, if you went to one corner of the block you might find yourself in Persia in like 5000 BC. Go to another edge, and you're in Thailand in the year 2090.

But every part of the block, every bit of history and our future destinies, already exists; it's all just sitting there, waiting to be explored and understood."

It was impossible to miss the resemblance between what she was describing and what I'd seen up there. "I think that's it," I announced.

The air twitched with honks from black cabs and red buses, each fighting for room in rush hour. The interlacing roads of Camberwell Green were less than a hundred yards ahead.

"I've gotta go get dinner ready for my little brothers," she said. "Thanks for the neeky chat, though."

Bun your little brothers! I wanted to say. The worst thing that could happen to them was they'd go hungry for an extra hour. There was so much more at stake for me, maybe even for her, if I couldn't maneuver us into a better track for the future.

"Promise me you'll get your head checked if you start feeling sick, yeah? See you at the library tonight, otherwise."

"Cool," I replied, biting my lip. "Man's there." I was so busy sifting through my new worries I almost missed the word "library."

I'd planned to tell her, Kato, and Rob at lunch to stay as far away from that place as possible, but hadn't found a decent explanation. And maybe I didn't need one. There was no way Rob and Kato still wanted to chill out after our dustup. So the only thing left for me to do was use the 20-minute bus ride home to pick a different venue for me and Nadia to "revise," then convince her to come anyway.

Meanwhile, Nadia was ready to say bye and searching for signs of life from me. I reached my knuckles out to spud her, not realizing she'd started coming in for a hug . . . which meant I punched her in the middle of her chest by mistake. From the look on her face, she must have been wondering exactly how many times I'd hit my head. Desperate to fix the situation (and not lose my chance of having my chest against her boobs), I quickly wrapped my arms around her. But by that time, she'd already dropped her hands, which meant we spent the next few seconds with her strapped down like she was in a straitjacket, my BO swirling around her like a pack of homeless dogs.

I watched as she walked off. It was the fastest I'd ever seen her move. *You clown, Esso.*

Desperate to distract myself with anything but the thought of our final moment, I pulled out my phone to check who'd texted me earlier.

Gideon: Fam get sumwere safe quik. D and mandem r lookin for you! AVOID CAMBERWELL

The final words in the text made it clear I was fucked.

The fact the text had come from Gideon, rather than Rob or Kato, made it clear I was fucked and alone and had no one to blame but myself.

20

RHIA · (15 YEARS LATER)

IT HAD BEEN almost a year since I'd last had the dream.

It always started out blurry. I see a grayscale outline of someone in front of me. I squint harder and realize it's a woman on her knees with both arms raised up to me and crying out my name. It's Mum. I have no proof of it, but I know it's true in the way you just do in dreams. But as things come into focus, I notice that the smile I've seen so many times in that photo in my drawer is gone from her face. And where her eyes are meant to be, there are circles filled with inky blackness. She's not weeping anymore. She doesn't even seem to recognize me. The world starts spinning around me, and I wait to wake up in my real-life bed, drenched in sweat and crying.

Two weeks had passed since Tony and Poppy evicted me, and it still felt fresh. But I had a new house, new roommates, and a new life to get on with. Today felt especially new—my first match on the SE Dons premiership pitch. The groundsmen had mowed the grass up into an emerald chessboard, the angles switching every five-odd meters. And the smell of it? The only proof I had left that there might still be a God out there and that she did, sometimes, give a crap.

We'd gone into the second period tied one—all, and Gibbsy had made a halftime speech so gangster it made me wonder what she'd done for a living before coaching. She roasted Maria for not taking more pops at goal and the entire midfield for not sticking to our patterns. The only words she saved for me were: "Cracking finish," but then, "don't stop working."

I'd gotten lucky with my goal, and she knew it. After running back lazily from a clearance, I'd somehow found myself on the end of a through ball, which I'd then finessed into the corner.

If I hadn't been so knackered, I'd have done a backflip or at least a quick slide to the corner post—it was a cup final, after all. But I'd slept barely an hour the night before and had to wake up extra early to get to the stadium since the commute from the girls' home took so long. Chuck in the leg cramp threatening to pull me out the game, and I was funding the second half on debt.

The key was focus. My job was to push through the pain and, more important, not let anything that happened last month distract me. Not Olivia's Judas kiss, not Tony and Poppy ditching me. Not even Dr. Esso's promises, which now felt hollower and more distant than ever. Getting attached was too risky, I'd learned. *There's a famine in Scotland right now*, I kept reminding myself. *Real shit. Now get over yourself.* In Gibbsy's words, this game would define our lives. This was what the season had been building up to: a hundred suicide runs, a thousand passing drills, close to a million crunchies, and it all added up to this match against Arsenal Girls' Academy.

This team, this game, this chance at a contract was all I had left. But as tempted as I was to think forward to the full-time whistle, when everything would be sealed, I couldn't yet.

There were 20 minutes left, the game was still drawn, and there was enough heat pouring from the home crowd to fry an egg on the crossbar. The Bayer Neverlusen manager was watching on from the north stand. So were the Tottenham scouts, although no player with working feet should have to sink that low. I rushed toward the touchline to get on the end of a goal kick and had to squint to see the ball as it cut through the sun. I plucked it out of the air, letting it fall to a weightless stop on my laces.

It didn't take much to skip past the first player. I cut a line toward goal, ready to sky up the final two defenders. But before I could decide which foot to put it on, their blond captain in center-mid nabbed the ball from me. Again.

It was maybe the tenth time she'd done it that game, and I still hadn't figured out how. Her legs were half the length of mine, yet always managed to find their way to the spot I was cradling the ball. It was like she knew what I wanted to do even before I did. Each time she stole the ball, she'd pass it back to her sweeper, pretend not to hear the crowd applauding, then swing back round and smack my bum, teasing, "Unlucky, love," or something just as patronizing.

"Pass it!" Maria shouted the next time I was on the ball, throwing her hands up when I got tackled instead. Mio, our left wing, made the same complaint a minute later.

"Easy now, Rhia," the captain taunted. "Everyone's watching you. Remember?"

I unballed my fists, refusing to face her. *Don't do it*, I told myself, feeling my shoulders lumping up. By the time I got back to halfway, the adrenaline in my veins was mostly watered down. A minute into injury time, I couldn't let anything or anyone confuse me into second-guessing myself. None of this other stuff mattered—all I needed was one more shot at goal.

Then out of nowhere, an unusual pattern emerged on the pitch—a constellation of moving bodies about as rare as all eight planets lining up. I almost pinched myself to make sure my grogginess wasn't making me see what I wanted to see. But sure enough, the tide of our midfield was drifting forward, the opposition's offside line was drifting back, and Maria's hips were square in my direction. The hairs on my arms stood on end as my core stiffened. Even the air felt thicker, like a hurricane was approaching, ready to sweep me up if I was ready. This was *it*.

I opened a long, arcing run down the left flank, pointing to a spot a few meters ahead, so Maria had no doubt where I needed the ball to land. And despite all our petty passa that season and her having a lane to go alone, she passed it—a perfect cross to put me one-on-one with the keeper.

My heart was thumping. I had to beg my nerves to simmer down. The goalie was screaming for backup, but there was no way it would arrive in time. She turned her feet to the spot I was eyeing, and after seeing me fake in that direction, threw her body at the far post . . . leaving an open goal for me to caress the ball into. The crowd were already on their feet, screaming. I grinned as I cocked my foot back.

But when I looked down, the ball was gone. It took me a second to figure out what had happened, but by the time I had, the same girl who'd been robbing me all afternoon was one-two-ing with her teammate toward the opposite goal.

I didn't have the space or time to calm down, to think through a rational plan. All I had was the resolve to make myself an unbreakable promise: *I. Am. Not. Having. This.*

Not after faffing an open game-winning shot at goal. Not with the month I'd just been through. Nothing was going to stop me from stopping her. Not this time. I was ready to push my legs till they broke, to demand that time itself snap in two; whatever it was going to take to get her.

I carved a straight line down the field and watched the world get blurrier each time I found another gear. Relative to me, everyone else on the pitch might as well have been going backward. When I reached the box, the blonde was back in possession and shaping to shoot. All I had to do was nudge the ball away, and most important, nudge it before I hit her.

Even if I shattered both her ankles while sliding in, the ref would call it a clean tackle as long as I'd clipped the ball away first. I thought about slowing down, knowing if I mistimed it this close to goal, it would be a sure penalty for the opposition and certain death for me. But I rolled the dice instead, sped up, and let my weight fall until I was as low as the shears that had mowed the pitch before kickoff.

It was way closer than I would have liked, so close that the entire time I was sliding in, I was convinced I'd messed it up.

But I did it.

I actually *did it*.

I clipped the ball away from her feet a split second before cutting her down to size with my new boots. I couldn't believe it. I'd actually saved the day.

I let a smile cross my face as I rose to my feet, but then watched the referee sprint past me and toward the penalty spot, pointing manically at it before sounding her whistle.

This doesn't make sense, I thought, not able to move or even blink. *What's happening?*

To my disbelief, the ref was marching back toward me, stopping once she was close enough to shove a yellow card in my face.

I was frozen on the spot, unable to say a word in response. I thought back to when their captain had tackled me. I'd promised not to have it, not to let what was happening *right now*, happen. And as a giant cloud stormed forward above, covering the pitch in darkness, I realized that that promise was all I had left.

Then it was like a switch flipped in me, and before I knew it, I was sprinting after the ref. "Miss, that was a legal tackle," I shouted at her back. "Everyone saw it!"

She pretended she couldn't hear and stepped away. A few of my teammates ran in to form a barrier between us, genuine pity in their faces. Even Maria looked like she felt bad for me. But none of them spoke up in my defense.

The ref was wrong and I was right. It was as simple as that. What was happening was unreasonable. Unimaginable. Unjust. And this was coming from someone whose life up to that point had been nothing but one broken domino crashing into the next.

I'd lost enough already; I couldn't lose this.

"Nah," I shouted, breaking free from the half a dozen grips on my arms. I was livid with the blonde, but no word could describe how I felt about the referee, who, in that moment, embodied everyone who'd left me with this piss take of a life.

"That's not a bloody penalty. Change the call, bruv—I'm not having this." My words were sharpened with hate and hardened by the certainty I was right.

Finally, I pressed my nose against hers. "CHANGE THE FUCKING CALL!"

She took a long, pained look at me, the same pitying face as everyone else. Then she reached into her pocket and pulled out a second yellow card. Then a red.

Game over.

I'm not proud of what I did next.

Without pausing to think, I loaded a ball of phlegm onto my tongue and spat it on her face.

The assistant coaches had to run on, each one tugging me away from the referee with all their strength. Meanwhile, the ref drew the string of phlegm from her right eye, her face turning from shock to disgust to fury. I was shouting like a jackal, fighting to break free so I could run after her again and spit in her other eye.

In the end, it took six grown women and men to pull me off the field, and I spent the entire drag to the sideline shouting threats at the opposition.

Their captain stepped up to take the penalty. Hoping gravity could hear me, I reached out and prayed for space itself to bend, praying that by, some miracle, I could guide her shot safely over the crossbar.

She gazed down at the ball . . . took three measured strides forward . . . then slotted it clean past our keeper. And just like that, everything our team had worked for was lost.

A chorus of boos, mostly from our home crowd, chased me off the pitch and down the tunnel. None of my teammates could bear to look at me. Only Gibbsy followed me upstairs into the room where I sat muddy and weeping, alone. It was the same room where I'd had my lessons with Dr. Esso.

"Give me that jersey," she demanded, looking about ready to peel it off herself. "You never deserved it."

I left the grounds that evening knowing Gibbsy was right. Knowing I'd lost everything.

21

ESSO

FOUR ANCIENT ROADS crisscrossed at Camberwell Green. As the evening light dimmed, more and more cars and buses were crowding through the dark.

Usually, bodies and traffic move in rhythm: a bus arrives, forcing people to either jump on, get off, or impatiently check their phones. But the ten or so yutes at the bus stop were far from on beat; they were lurking instead. Their confidence was practically flooding the square, and from that extra dip in their steps, that added weight in their laughs, it wasn't hard to guess what was in their pouches. Skengs weren't exactly hard to get either; they were giving them out with Happy Meals up north, and even feds didn't dare touch the roadsides strapless.

One of the boys started walking in my direction. Another kid followed on an electric scooter. They were moving too slowly to be chasing me, but they were getting closer, almost close enough to pick my face from the crowd.

I pulled my trousers up. *Think*, I told myself, then pivoted on my back foot and spotted a pub sign a few yards back in the direction of school. The Piglet's Arms. I squeezed between two men vaping at the doorway and snuck into the redbrick tower. Without thinking about how ridiculous I must have looked, I jogged to the window, peeking through a gap in the curtains to watch the kid on the scooter roll past next to his friend.

"Phew," I sighed and, while turning, found myself eye to eye with a guy who didn't look too pleased with the energy I was bringing to the place. *He must be the pub owner*, I decided, based mostly on how much he seemed to care.

He stepped forward like he was gliding on ice. "And how can I be of help to you, sir?" His front dreads had silver streaks like a witch, and the bass in his voice pounded like a speaker pressed to your chest.

"I'm meeting some mates here in a second," I said, shuffling away from the window. "Was just—err—looking out for them," I added unconvincingly.

Arms already folded, he shifted his weight from one stringy leg to the other. "Need some ID before I can serve you."

"No need, mate," I said, using a cockney accent I thought made me sound older. "Not drinking, just having dinner. Heard the fish and chips are pukka here. Can I actually grab a table upstairs?"

Before he could make his mind up, I was on the fifth step.

They'd clearly invested in a fresh coat of paint for the top floor, although it still smelled like decade-old cigar smoke. It was empty, besides a young, gothy couple sitting at the bar sharing a mound of shepherd's pie. I hated that dish. It was afflicted by a lack of seasoning, and something about the ratio of meat to potatoes had never sat right with my spirit. But after missing out on half my lunch, the shepherd's pie looked more than peng enough, each clank of cutlery on the ceramic plate making my mouth water that little bit more. I picked the table with the clearest view of the bus stop and, when the waiter came around, ordered fish and chips, as promised.

I was staring at my phone so hard that when I chewed down on my lip, I drew blood. As the coppery taste filled my mouth, I sat wondering whether to text Gideon back, debating how much more I wanted to know. *There's no other choice*, I decided as I tapped the screen.

You: Love for dat. What else you heard?

Gideon: Some T.A.S. boy found ur paper. It had D and headmasters name on it. Word is you snitched fam

I chucked my mobile across the table like it was possessed. And after burrowing my hands into my pockets, I realized Crutchley's snitch list was gone. I dug deeper, double-checked each corner, but when I pulled my fingers out, they came back with nothing but lint. *Crap!* It must have fallen out when I'd pulled out my phone while trying to catch up with Nadia.

Gideon: True say D is on a MERK TING bro

It was the only possible sequel to his first text. Half measures weren't taken with snitches; justice was total and swift. It had to be, to make sure everyone had an opportunity to learn.

Rule Number 1: You never rat.

Rule Number 2: They disrespect you, get 'em back.

I couldn't even remember the next bit of the lyrics, but I remembered singing them with a smile like everyone else, never realizing how it felt to actually be about that life, to be a slave to those rules. Instead of responding to Gideon, I shrank into my self-pity, wondering how the strangest and shittiest day of my life could have gotten even stranger and shittier. As my steaming strip of cod arrived, I couldn't help staring at it and thinking, *Just a couple days ago, you had no idea you'd be dead.*

The young couple left, and the night evicted whatever life was left on the pub's top floor. The beige wallpaper looked duller; everything did, and my appetite was so limp I could barely find the will to lift my fork. My phone lit up with a new notification.

Gideon: Should be safe in Peckham. Texted Rob and he said theyre goin library tonight for revision. You cutting tru?

I almost swallowed the chip in my mouth whole. I'd forgotten to text them about the library. I'd just assumed they wouldn't go ahead without me.

I reached for my phone on the table, desperate to warn them, but met it already vibrating for my attention. I prayed it might be Gideon calling with better news. Or even Nadia or Kato ringing to share some kind of genius escape plan. I had first noticed my hands trembling when I'd cut my cod in half, and each second since, the shaking had gotten weightier, to the point where I could now barely hold the phone steady enough to read the caller name.

INCOMING CALL: UNKNOWN

I thought about ignoring it, I wanted to, but my reflexes got the best of me, and a second later I was poking at the *answer* button.

"Evening, Esso." The voice was shaky. And white—I assumed. *Who the* . . . Before I could finish the thought, they continued: "It's Mr. Sweeney. I'm calling with bad news."

Bad news? I pressed the phone closer to my ear, gripping the table edge with my free hand.

"I told Crutchley about your, ummm . . . *unwillingness* to cooperate. Based on that, your fight with Devontey today, and your prior demerits, you're expelled."

Expelled?

The word didn't feel real to me.

"You'll get a letter at home on Monday, so don't bother coming into school after half term—you'll be turned away. Oh, and I already warned Crutchley that you threatened to make up lies about both of us. You had a chance to get to him first, but you didn't." I could literally hear the smugness. "But don't beat yourself up about it. He'd never have taken your word over mine anyway. Good luck with your life, Esso Adenon."

The voice vanished, and the screen turned black. I hadn't said a word.

I felt the phone slide from my fingers and drop to the floor. A web of cracks ripped across the screen. There was too much shit coming at me all at once. Too much for me to bear.

The table next to me started blurring and spinning. Bile crawled up my throat, the sour taste making me nauseous.

A second later, it was like someone had wrapped their hands around my neck, squeezing tighter and tighter, until I couldn't down another molecule of oxygen. And the more I tried ripping the hands from my throat, the more I just scratched at my own skin. On the cycle went—my fear feasting off my pain and my pain cranking up my fear, and with each new loop, the pair grew fatter and hungrier, hungrier and fatter.

Is this what a heart attack feels like? I wondered. *Am I dying?*

I wanted to spring out of my chair but I was stuck. It was like I was trapped inside my own body, my darting eyes the only part of me allowed to move. While struggling to break free, the full impact of the visions finally hit me with lethal force: not only were they all real, they were also inevitable, unavoidable, unstoppable. The gory vision I'd had of Preston getting run over had already come true. So had the one with Nadia and me in the hallway. That meant I was maybe an hour away from D and Bloodshed pulling up on me in Peckham, and my mates showing up for the massacre as well. Everyone had been right about me. My mum. Mr. Sweeney. My primary school teacher who once joked that if I didn't somehow find a way out through football, I'd eventually end up dead or in jail.

Clearer than anything else right now was death. D was going to die. Nadia was going to die, along with all my friends.

We were all going to die.

22
RHIA · (15 YEARS LATER)

IN THE THREE weeks that had crept by since Tony and Poppy had let me go, I hadn't witnessed a dull day at Walworth Home for Young Ladies. On my first weekend, a fight broke out in the shower room over a stolen earring that looked like a WWE women's championship match—choke slams, torn-out hair, the lot. Most of the beef was between Bloodshed girls and competing sets. So those of us not inked knew keeping our mouths shut and chins tucked was our only bet for dodging the cross fire.

There were all sorts in here. Like this one skin-and-bones girl down the hall. She'd do these magic tricks (them ones where you picked a random card and she guessed it), but she always guessed wrong. The worst part was having to pretend you were impressed when she finally got it right on the fourth go.

Then we had this girl who sat opposite me at lunch every day and refused to stop staring at me while I ate.

And finally, there was my roommate, who (unfortunately) reminded me a lot of Olivia. She never stopped sharing the detailed layout of the five-story mansion she was going to own when she was rich. During the day, she was bouncy, bossy even. But after lights-out, just as I'd be slipping into the deepest, lushest part of sleep, she'd wake up screaming. Top of her lungs, screaming. I had learned there was no point trying to calm her down either—you just had to wait till she was done, then watch her wander the room in confusion like she was searching for the part of her childhood she'd lost.

Dr. Anahera's office was on the top floor (pretty much the only room in the house not decorated like a cell) and had a nest-level view of the lone tree in the care home's backyard. With the day near done, only the sun's top edge floated above the horizon, the rest of its tired corpse buried in dirt. We all had to do therapy once a week, and I usually signed up for the late sessions—there was less time to think after, that way.

"We talked about the concept of 'choice' last week. Have you had any interesting reflections since?"

"Yeah, actually," I replied to Anahera. "I don't think free will exists. We don't choose shit." Looking back at everything that had led me here, like Dr. Esso showing up with all that hope just before it all evaporated, there was clearly an inevitability to my doom. An unavoidability.

"Well, that's an interesting development." I could imagine her practicing that fake smile in therapy training, probably in the same course where they'd taught her to prevent her patients learning how she really felt about them. She always looked chirpy but concerned—a flight attendant serving you drinks while the plane was in free fall.

"Lemme explain, Miss Anahera—"

"It's 'Doctor,'" she interrupted, in her thick New Zealand accent. "I don't like making a fuss about it, but it's either 'Doctor' or 'Professor' that goes in front."

"My bad. So, Dr. Miss Anahera," I continued. "I think I've actually got proof."

From beneath us came the crash of exploding dishes. Another fight in the kitchen was my guess. Anahera and I both shook our heads before she told me to carry on.

"I found a physics book in the library that talks about this thing called the 'clockwork universe' theory. I actually came up with a cool thought experiment to show you how it works."

She probably didn't give a toss, but she was the only person I could find for miles who was getting paid to pretend she did.

"So, imagine you took a super-detailed MRI scan of my brain right now," I instructed, "and you got a printout showing you exactly where every atom in my head is, how heavy each atom is, and how fast they're all moving."

She gazed up from her notes and blinked—therapy speak for "I'm listening."

"Now, here's the cool bit," I continued. "For our physics homework last week, we had to use this one equation to calculate where two snooker balls would end up after colliding with each other. And I had this realization that—theoretically—anyone could take that MRI scan of my brain and, using the same equation from my homework, predict how all the atoms would collide with each other, and where they'd all be a second later. And you could just run that calculation over and over again on all the atoms in and around our brains to figure out where they'd be at any point in the future. And since our brains are made up of nothing but atoms and our brains make all our decisions, you could basically predict every decision I'll make between now and when I die."

She paused to take in a deep breath and waited a few seconds before pointing her biro tip at me. "If I'm getting this right—you're implying that it's equations and forces out of our control that determine our future. Not us."

"Yeah, I think so." I was plucking at a saggy wrinkle in the leather armrest, which, at the right angle, kinda looked like the folds in a pug's forehead. "What do you think?" I asked, a bit nervous as usual about the notes she took while I spoke. "And I'm not asking for your algorithm's answer either. I actually want to know what you reckon, what you feel about what I'm saying."

She crossed her legs and put her pen to the side. "What you're describing is the classic free-will-versus-fate debate." I could see her auditing each word before letting it out. "And I tend to agree a bit with both sides. There's a nice quote that goes, 'Life is like a game of cards: the hand you're dealt is fate; the way you choose to play them is free will.' I guess I believe that no matter how stingy life is, it always gives you at least a few choices. Even if you have to go deep inside yourself to find them."

"Hmmm," I mumbled. After looking deep inside, I still felt that what she was saying was a heap of nonsense. And the statistics were on my side. "Look, I don't think it's a crazy exaggeration to say that 98% of the kids who are born into shit situations grow up and die in the same shit. And 98% of people who are born lucky—surprise, surprise—stay lucky."

She looked over her glasses at me. "And what about the other 2%?"

"You're being serious?"

"You can assume I am if you like," she replied. "Or you can assume I'm joking. In which case—please, humor me."

"Honestly, who gives a flying fuck about that 2%? All anyone ever wants to talk about is the other 2%. I literally just told you that 98% of people in this world don't get a choice. 98%! Why the fuck are we talking about that lucky 2%?"

I could feel my temperature rising, and I wasn't sure I wanted it any other way. Nothing of what she'd said rhymed with reality. None of it fit into the declining grooves that shaped *my* life. I'd had that football contract in my hands, Tony and Poppy ready to adopt me. I'd been killing it at school, topping my class in subjects I used to be bottom set in. I'd had a complete stranger walk into my life, revealing everything I'd never known about my birth mother. And then, like atoms smashed together, it had all split apart again so quickly. Like clockwork, I'd circled back to where I'd always belonged.

"Rhia, I've spent most of our short time together focusing

on one thing: slowly dismantling the shame you carry around, which is clearly linked to difficult things you've had to endure throughout your life. But today, you've swung to another extreme, where you now believe we live in a predetermined world with no choice and no hope. And I'm afraid I can't support that either."

"Where's this going, Dr. Anahera?"

She grinned at the cheek of my response, but wasn't letting it distract her this time. "My point is, I've seen you figure out concepts that I hadn't even heard of until I started my PhD. I've watched you do a thousand kick-ups on that lawn out there, while barely looking at the ball. It's frightening how capable you are. How powerful you could be."

A memory pinched me—Dr. Esso claiming something similar in our last lesson. Both of them were infected with that same optimism.

"But?" I asked. There was always a "but." Sure, I wasn't attacking people in the showers like the other girls, but I wasn't the easiest fosty to sell either.

She looked at me with pained eyes, then started tampering with the device on her ear. "You already made tenure," she mumbled to herself. "And it's not like they ever pay you on time anyway."

The gadget flashed red, repeating, "Do not manually deactivate," loud enough to hear from where I was sitting. Two beeps later, she dropped her arms back to her lap, the light on the earpiece now off.

"I'm sure you already know what this thing does," she said

pointing at it. "It's got an AI brain that pulls from a database of over a million therapy sessions just like this. Each time you speak, the Thera-Bot tells me what response to give, the exact words most likely to have you leave here not feeling too sad or too happy." She undid her top button. "So me freestyling like this without my device on could earn me a reasonably firm slap on the wrist. You follow?"

I was so surprised by the casualness of her words that I forgot to respond.

After waiting a moment, she added, "Please nod if you understand what I'm saying to you."

"Yeah, I understand," I replied, a little anxious.

"Rhia, there's this old theory in psychology . . ." She unclipped the earpiece and lobbed it on her desk. "It suggests that when you experience a traumatic event in your childhood, a part of you gets stuck at that age. It's like on one hand, you're too afraid to face that extraordinary moment in your past, but on the other hand, you're too afraid to move forward from it. And so you just stay there, trapped in time."

I hated when people used words like "extraordinary" to describe horrid things. But that didn't explain why my heart was hammering and why I could hear my teeth screeching. I looked down at my feet, making sure they didn't twitch or find another way to expose how I was feeling.

"Take your old tutor, Dr. Esso, for instance. From everything you told me in our last session, he clearly hasn't accepted what happened that night. He's still trying to change events that took place when he was 16, as if *years* haven't passed since then." She paused to take off her glasses. "And sometimes when I look into your eyes, Rhia, I see an infant."

I turned to the window, wrapping my arms around my ribs in a tight hug. All of a sudden, there was a long list of places I needed to be.

"I see an infant who dreams about her mother's embrace and refuses to let go. That small child in you is afraid of the future. And rightly so. But she's wrong to tell you that you have no say in it."

"You're chatting shit," I said, eyes shifting to the side. The thought of her words being true terrified me. Because if I was responsible for my future, it meant I'd been responsible for my past, too. All those foster families that had passed on me, everything that had happened to Dr. Esso, to my mum. "You don't know what you're on about."

"I don't know much about physics, if that's what you're accusing me of. And I'm not sure anyone's figured out who wins the match between free will and determinism. But what I do know and believe—with every atom in my soul—is that just because you feel stuck right now doesn't mean it has to be that way forever."

I'd had enough. Enough of adults telling me about my life, before disappearing from it.

She was in the middle of jotting something down when I walked over to her chair and smacked the notepad off her lap.

"I swear if you write one more word about me in your

fucking notepad, I'm gonna tear this room apart." I pointed my finger between her eyes. It shook along with the rest of my arm.

Without breaking my gaze, Anahera stood up and slid off her heels, before rolling her sleeves up one careful fold at a time. I stretched to my full height over her, clicking my knuckles one after the next.

She looked at me dead on. "What do you want to tell her, Rhia? What have you wanted the younger you to understand all these years? What does *she* want to say?" She opened her bronze arms in a show of surrender. "The words might be in there. Or they might not, and that's okay. Just give her a chance."

It was such an illogical request. And yet it was ripping me in two. I wanted to storm out, but something was wrapped around me and fixing me in position.

I broke free and turned to cover the three meters back to my seat when the room started spinning. Even the ceiling looked the wrong way up. My legs went weak and before I knew it, I was on the floor. And then it was like 15 years of hurt were raining down on me all at once.

One day, I thought. It was all I'd ever wanted. One day when I got to go to sleep, knowing that when I woke up, I'd be enough. I couldn't do this anymore. It was too much. I tipped over on my side, chest aching, sobbing on the carpet.

"I'm sorry," I said, finally piecing together the courage to speak out loud. "I'm sorry I messed this all up, Mum."

"There's nothing to be sorry for," Dr. Anahera replied a few seconds later. "Just confusion to work through."

For the next hour, she watched me cry all manner of lies into her carpet. Some of them were buried too deep inside me to dislodge. But the few that came out dissolved into the nylon fibers with no way back. I was lying on my side, my fingers curled up like a T. rex, my bottom lip quivering, and my flared nostrils trying to sniffle up two snot trails slimed over my cheek. Anahera couldn't hug me—she'd broken enough rules already. So instead, she knelt next to me and stayed silent when the next girl banged on the door. And the next.

We just rested there. Weightless.

At one point, I even spared a thought for Dr. Esso. I'd abandoned him the same way I'd been abandoned. I pictured him lying on the floor somewhere, weeping for the same reasons. Where was he now? I wondered. Did he still care about me, about my mum? Did he still believe that he could save her? As if reading my thoughts, Dr. Anahera spoke up.

"If there are past wrongs in your life that you think you can right, be my guest. But just know there's a wild and precious future out there waiting for you as well."

I rose to my feet and said thank you. And as I walked out the door, I knew the first person I needed to see.

23

ESSO

"BREATHE, BREDDA, JUST breathe. Thaaaat's better." It was the same man who'd eye-harassed me on my way in, but his mood—and his accent—were totally different now. Gone was the cold stare he'd given me, replaced with a look of concern as he took in my violent shaking, the fear on my face.

"That's much better," he repeated in his calming Patois baritone, one hand on my shoulder.

I wiped the sweat from my chin and forehead, inhaling as he'd instructed until the pub came back into high resolution. "How long was I out for?"

"Not sure. I came upstairs just now and, man, I thought ya having a fit. But I seen plenty fits, I seen plenty panic attacks. *You?* Definitely having da latter."

"Panic attack?" I whispered. It was the kind of thing I'd thought only white people got. "Is it permanent?"

He grinned. "Nah, bredda. It's a stress ting. *Extreme* stress, in fac." He paused a moment, letting the smile slide off his face before continuing. "Tell me, what's a handsome yute like you doing stressin' at ya age? You should be out playin' wit your mates, chattin' up girls, eatin' dinner at home with your madda."

I fake chuckled. "Stress" was a wicked underestimation of what I was going through. Where could I even begin to explain everything to him? I could start with the premonitions I'd had after the car crash, then move on to the bullet-filled vision from lunch, then tell him about how I'd just gotten expelled and had a price on my head, and that all my friends were scheduled to get shot tonight as well.

"I can see ya got a lot on your head," he said, sparing me the misery of putting my worries into words. "Listen, young yute. I ain't no doctor, but I have some understanding for you: Tings are what they are, and only a fool worry about tings him cyan't control."

He raised a cheeky eyebrow. "But then again." He paused another second. "If ya do have control, you gotta rise to dee occasion."

After checking me up and down one more time to make sure I wasn't about to have a panic attack again, he reached for the flimsy paper on the table with £9.49 written on it and scrunched it up. "It's on me. Ya good to go."

He went back downstairs to attend to his bill-paying customers, and I sat alone with the words he'd left me. There was some hidden hope in them; I could *feel* it. And they were timely to the point of being almost . . . prophetic.

I thought back on all the visions I'd seen over the day. Some of the details seemed to have been replaced with static. But I remembered enough—I remembered D and Bloodshed walking toward me in a hailstorm with Peckham Library looming in the background. And I remembered the bullets aimed at everyone in the last vision I'd seen, at lunch.

One sight stood brighter than the rest: D lying dead on the ground. I tried to shrug off the gory image of the hole in his head, but it came out as a cold shiver.

I thought back to the D I used to know. The D in the baby photo above the TV in his mum's front room. The D before he became head of T.A.S., before his brother Xavier became Bloodshed. Life had stolen away the little they'd started with.

As I was getting ready to spare a similar thought for everyone else I'd seen in my visions, a revelation flashed in front of me: *I'm the link*. When it swung around the second time, it stung like acid to the face. *I'm the one connecting it all. I* had been there when the Peckham boys slapped up Bloodshed in West End, kicking off this whole road beef. *I* went to school with D and had humiliated him at lunch before basically getting him expelled. And it was my snitch sheet the T.A.S. boys found that escalated things further. It was my warning text to Spark that morning in the loos that meant his boys would be strallied up in Narm waiting for T.A.S.. And my best friends, Nadia, Kato, and Rob, were heading to the same place to meet *me*.

More misery washed through my veins as I sat back in my seat. I was the reason my two best friends, a dozen kids from

Brixton and Peckham, and a girl I was almost sure I loved were all about to go. There was no coincidence or luck about it—*I, Esso Adenon*, was the why behind it all. And by making fearful decisions based on what I'd seen in that stupid, fucking Upper World, I'd only made things worse.

Looking at my two options, I realized that if I teamed up with Spark and his boys and we clapped back at T.A.S., people would die. But if I ran and hid, people would die.

It was lose-lose. And not just losing a game—losing my friends.

Nah, I thought. *That can't run.*

That. Can. Not. Run.

The thought of any harm coming to my people snatched me from the doom and gloom I'd soaked myself in, and up to my feet. There *had* to be a third way. Some path where everyone, including me, went home tonight with our bodies untorn and our souls intact. It was wishful thinking; I knew it was. But I *had* no choice but to think wishfully, to hope. If I'd single-handedly created this situation, I was the only one who could fix it.

I was the only one who personally knew both D and Spark, and they were the only ones who could call back their boys. As poor as my chances were of getting through to them, I had better odds than anyone else in the known universe. And if the Upper World had confirmed anything, it was that *some* version of tonight existed where I could find D and Spark in the same place—Peckham Library.

I knew by going to Narm now, I was risking it all. Even thinking about it felt dangerous. But the risk of not going felt even deadlier.

These weren't Superman fantasies I was having. I didn't care about being a hero; I just couldn't tolerate a situation where *anyone* got killed. Every one of their lives was worth "rising to dee occasion" for.

I'd been taught that people like D and Spark, who lived by the sword, almost always deserved to die by it. But I knew both of them. I knew neither of them had ever asked for swords in the first place. We'd all grown up with the same choices: survive or die. There had to be more.

Surely there was a part of D that wished he'd never touched the roads in the first place, a part of Bloodshed that wished he could go back in time and stop his mum from ever meeting the stepdad he'd been forced to harm. My heart started racing— maybe *that* was the revelation that could change everything.

Maybe—just maybe—I could offer them something in exchange for laying down arms: a different future; a better one. It required me to believe that we lived in a universe forgiving enough to, once in a while, let us change our mistakes. A world operating on the first type of time travel Nadia had explained. But more than just believing in it, I would have to make it happen. And that meant figuring out how to get back to the Upper World—or, better yet, finding a way to bring the Upper World to *me*, so I could use the same power it had given me in the dining hall.

It might work, I told myself as new branches of possibility sprouted in my mind. *It has to work.* I found myself standing taller, burning with fresh purpose. Everything I'd worried about the whole year at Penny Hill felt like vanity now. Even getting expelled didn't matter anymore. Not next to our lives.

I swiped my phone off the table. In my new, almost reckless mood, I decided there was one more thing I had to do, words I'd held in too often that needed to be shared.

You: Sorry mum. I love you.

I still felt bad about the things I'd said to her during our argument. But after the day I'd had, I could see things much clearer: she'd been trying her best all along, just like I had. She worked her ass off every night for me. She cooked for me, prayed for me, cleaned up for me—on second thought, I actually did most of the cleaning up, but the fact remained she was the best mum in the world. The sacrifices she'd made so I could have it better might never earn the interest they deserved. But the one thing I could do in return, just in case I bowed out, was let her know I saw her. And though her words still stung like hell, I saw those differently as well. I probably *was* on the same downward spiral as my dad, and if I didn't find a way out ASAP, I was going to end up dead, just like him. Maybe she'd given me his notebook so I could better understand his choices. So I could better make my own. For the hundredth time that day, I wished I had his diary with me, that he could be here to help.

Within seconds, Mum was ringing me, her imagination

probably running rampant wondering what kind of disaster could have caused her son—her desperate, defiant only son— to send that kind of message. I didn't pick up, knowing she'd probably be more worried than helpful. And I had the beginnings of a plan to get on with.

I walked out and into the night, refusing to look back.

24

RHIA · (15 YEARS LATER)

THE PLOT WAS surrounded by green on all sides, and the mansion itself stood dully in the middle, most of its windows boarded up or broken. A fox was watching from the long grass—probably wondering what the hell I was doing here; what anyone would be doing here. But I couldn't stop staring at the bench in front of me. The same green bench from my only photo of Mum. It was right there in the garden of St. Jude's Mental Health Care Home. Just like Dr. Esso had said.

I had dared to believe it. Now I was seeing it.

And seeing it in the flesh changed everything. In none of my dreams had Mum ever felt this close. Even standing there with my eyes wide open, I could hear her calling out to me with the same tender voice she spoke within my sleep each night.

She was still out there somewhere, begging for me to believe in her, to find her. She had to be. I felt inside my coat pocket to make sure the oil-stained envelope with Dr. Esso's return address hadn't crawled out in the five minutes since I'd last checked. And, for the umpteenth time that evening, I said a quiet thanks for my decision not to throw it away.

Gravel bounced in the distance behind me. Those were Olivia's footsteps. I stepped back from the bench, reminding myself to keep my zoo of emotions at bay. If there was any chance of fixing our friendship, it would require my calmest words and undivided attention.

Less than a week had passed since I'd peeled myself off Anahera's carpet, and my head was still spinning. In fact, it was only a few hours earlier that I'd womaned up and gotten in touch with Olivia. I was lucky I hadn't waited any longer. She'd messaged straight back saying their U-Haul was arriving in the morning, making this her last night in London, our last chance to see each other without spending 84 quid on a train fare. I didn't know whether seeing her face would lighten the sting of everything that had happened with Tony and Poppy, or just rip that wound open again. Either this would be the night things went back to normal or when we both realized there was no normal to go back to.

The most likely case, I figured, was that we'd make nice and promise to keep in touch. And over time, we'd let weekly catch-up calls turn into monthly ones, then annual ones, until all we had left was a faint twinge of guilt each time one forgot the other's birthday. *That might have to do*, I thought to myself while picking a fir cone from the damp grass.

The footsteps were only meters away now.

Big smile, I reminded myself. *Be nice.* And just as I completed my half turn, Olivia collided into me.

"Oooof." I was lucky to still be on my feet after the whip from her running hug. "You're . . . choking . . . me."

She stepped back, stopping to check nothing on my face had changed in our weeks apart. Then she got serious.

"Listen—I didn't know Tony and Poppy were leaving till that same night they told you. And I never told them any of your secrets. I swear down. But still . . . I should have fought harder for you. I messed up. I was selfish and I was scared and I . . ." She paused to clear her eyes. "I'm sorry, Rhia. I'm so, so, *so* sorry for leaving you. If you ever need me again, I'm here. I'm on that next train no matter the time of day. I mean it, sis. I love you."

After hesitating as long as I could before it got rude, I replied. "Yeah . . . same here." The grudge had gotten too heavy to hold. And imagining myself in her shoes, I wasn't sure how much I would have done differently.

She was screwing her heel into the pebbles, and I noticed the beginnings of a smile on her face. "Not gonna lie, it would be pretty amazing to hear you say the actual words. I mean, you definitely don't have to," she clarified. "It's just . . . you know . . . I did call you 217 times over the last month with no answer. And honestly, I'm not sure you've ever said *I love you* back to me before. I guess a verbal confirmation would just *really* help lock down the—"

"Come on, Olivia." She knew I hated this soppy shit, which

was partly why she was forcing it. But she also didn't look like she was going to back down any time soon.

"Fine—I love you too."

She stood waiting for spare details.

"And I mean it from the bottom of my cold, cold heart."

Olivia laughed first, the giggles less and less nervous each second. It wasn't long till I was bent over with her. I'd forgotten how squinty her eyes went when she cackled, how miserable I'd been not hearing the snort that came after it. It was like we'd been transported back in time, to a better time. An idea I'd been thinking a lot about lately.

After we managed to straighten up, Olivia looked around and asked: "Where the hell are we, by the way? I couldn't even find this place on the map."

"St. Jude's." I pointed my eyes at the green crosshatched bench to our side. "Where my mum stayed before she died."

Olivia covered her mouth. "That . . . that's the bench from the photo."

I nodded, thinking about how dazed I'd been when I first saw it. I was *still* dazed.

She rushed over to the bench to get a closer look, while I stood back, trying, for the sake of chill, to fix my eyes on something less intense—anything else.

What my eyes landed on, about 15 meters to our right, filled me with the sort of panic you'd only know if your mind had also been torn apart so violently you weren't sure it'd ever piece together the same way again.

Olivia followed me over to a statue of a woman on her knees, reaching up with both hands. Both eyes were hollowed out and black.

"No," I said. Weak with awe, I dropped to my knees. "That can't be right. No way."

I had no way of explaining how this figure I'd seen so many times in my dreams, and nowhere else, was right here with us in real life.

I thought back to another of Dr. Esso's warnings: about there being more to life than met the eye.

Now everything that seemed impossible was coming to life—my dreams, my mum, even the Upper World felt one outstretched arm away.

Olivia was still speechless. Maybe now she was ready to believe the crazy things I wanted to tell her. Maybe now we could get to the answer.

The evening sun was bouncing off the top floors of the Shard like it was a prism. Farther off, I could make out the meaty chest of a cloud with edges so dark it risked leaving a permanent stain in the sky.

"English breakfast?" Olivia pulled out a flask and two mugs from her rucksack and wiped the wet off the bench before pouring the rounds.

After a minute of worrying that touching the bench might make it vanish into thin air, I finally sat down. The whole garden still felt fragile, scary even, especially after finding that statue. But being there had also added to my determination. All around me was proof I'd been right not to give up on my mum after all.

"Thanks," I said, sipping the hot tea so fast it fried my front taste buds.

I knew I wanted to see Dr. Esso. But what I needed to figure out now, hopefully with Olivia's help, was what I wanted to tell him. Or, to put it in Mum's final words: what I was *meant* to tell him. I had one or two half-baked ideas, but like a splinter in my heel, the harder I plucked at them, the further in they went. Mum was somewhere out there in the fabric of space and time—that much was a fact of maths. But the hope that we could get there somehow rested on much shakier ground. As Olivia was discovering.

"So, according to Dr. Esso," she started. I wondered if she was doing her typical thing of politely clarifying the facts before she shat on them. "Your mum said: 'Rhia will tell you.'"

"Yep."

"Which means *you're* meant to teach *him* something?"

"Yeah."

"Okay, that part's clear enough." There might have been just a *lick* of sarcasm in her comment. "And you reckon the message you're meant to tell him has something to do with time or energy?"

"No," I replied, impatiently shaking my head. "Time *and* energy."

She almost choked on her own spit as she burst out laughing at how serious I sounded.

"Olivia!" I shouted, poking that spot on her ribs I knew she hated. "The difference is important."

"I'm sorry," she said, apparently accepting I'd sunk to Dr. Esso depths of physics obsession since she'd last seen me, since we'd both seen what was in this garden. "Please just explain how you arrived at this time *and* energy thing."

I couldn't decide where to start. In the end, I went with my most recent discovery. "So, a couple nights ago, I was watching videos on gravity for homework and somehow got lost in a deep internet spiral. You know them ones?"

She nodded solemnly. She'd poured out twice as much liquor as me for time lost down there.

"And I stumbled across one article that Albert Einstein wrote about a century ago."

"The $E = mc^2$ guy, right?"

"Exactly. So the title of this paper was, 'Does the Inertia of a Body Depend on Its Energy-Content?'" I spread my feet, bracing myself for her reaction. "Isn't that manic?"

"I quit physics after GCSEs, remember? First boat out. You're gonna have to make this very simple for me, Rhia."

"That's fair," I conceded. I'd had the privilege of a few days to think about all of this. "Well, basically, 'inertia' is just a fancy word for something being sluggish and heavy. So Einstein's title—in plain English—is basically: 'Do Heavier Things Have More Energy?'"

She continued staring with eyes that screamed: *Simple, please!* I had to try harder.

"Well, I guess I never saw 'being heavy' and 'having energy' as necessarily going hand in hand. It's not like if I gained 10 kilos next month, I'd suddenly be more energetic because of it. In fact, I'd have guessed the opposite."

I was rambling. "Anyway, what really threw me off about the title was the question mark."

"The question mark?" she checked.

"Yeah. It's a weird choice. I mean, this ain't no average bloke. This is *Albert Einstein*—the kind of person who gets to end their sentences in full stops. And yet for some reason, he was so shook by what he'd discovered about energy that he wrote it as a question. Almost like he was hoping he was wrong."

She squinted at me, probably wondering what had happened to me and what I was gonna come up with next. The craziest part was I was only sharing a fraction of the madness I'd dug up online. Scrolling through it all, a terrifying trend had emerged: all the people who went too deep into the maths of time or energy had messed-up shit happen to them.

Take Leibnitz, for example. He invented a branch of maths called calculus, then right after, decided to change his surname from Leibnitz to Leibniz, claiming he was deleting the "t" since he no longer believed in time. But if you asked me, that wasn't the action of a nonbeliever. That was the action of a man so scared of the truth he had to check himself into witness protection with a different ID.

And Einstein himself, a month before he died, wrote these chilling words about a friend of his who'd just passed away: "He has departed from this strange world a little ahead of me.

That means nothing. For us believing physicists, the distinction between past, present, and future is only a stubbornly persistent illusion."

Then there was the really dark stuff. Like what happened to Boltzmann. Boltzmann studied energy and was also the guy who figured out why we feel time the way we do—i.e., always flowing forward rather than back. He lectured at a uni in Austria and, according to his colleague, lived in constant fear that one day while up at the board teaching his students, he'd suddenly lose his mind and all his memories. Just before the start of one school year, Boltzmann went on holiday with family. And while his wife and daughter were out swimming, he hanged himself in the hotel room without leaving a note.

"There's something about that title," I continued, pacing across the grass. "Something about a guy secretly crapping himself while talking about physics . . . The only other time I ever saw something like that was the night Dr. Esso told me about the Upper World."

"I see." She looked away. "So you think that your mum predicted that one day, you'd be so good at physics—with Dr. Esso's help, obviously—that you'd single-handedly figure out a way to harness time and energy and then go back to save her?"

"Hmmm," I said with a stare. "That sounded like a harsh judgment, wrapped inside a rhetorical question, dressed up as a friendly clarification."

"I've missed that humor of yours," she said, reminding me

there was still the thinnest sheet of frost between us. "Look, Rhia—I hate being the doubting Debbie here, I just don't get how anything you tell him could give him the ability to go back in time." Her hands were pressed to her hips. "I know how important this is to you, and I swear, I want it all to make sense. I just don't know how."

As tempted as I was to jump back with a tidy response, I couldn't. I didn't have one. A blubbery flapping noise came from my lips instead. The last time she'd seen me this excited yet deflated must have been the night we queued for two rainy hours outside Peckham Belly, only for the doorman to confiscate our fake IDs.

"You know what," I said, proper spent. "Let's call it for tonight." I was barely making sense to myself, let alone Olivia, and the crazy ideas I'd been chucking about wouldn't have impressed Dr. Esso either if he'd been on the other end of this bench. I'd have to figure it out on my own and on another day.

I filled her mug with fresh tea, but by the time I lifted it to her, she was wandering toward the fence.

"This place is manic," I heard her say while gazing into the eyes of another statue at the edge of the lawn. "They just need to fix it up."

"Be careful," I warned. I'd seen two driverless bully vans on the way here and wasn't feeling a repeat of our evening run from Linford's. "If a drone tags us here, Linford's dog won't arrive in time to save us."

That one lightened her up. "I wouldn't even bother running,

you know." She pointed to the mansion in the distance. "I'd climb through that window at the bottom and hide, fam. Pass the time filing my nails or suttin'."

All of a sudden, my fingers went slippery, and the mug in my hand fell to the bench, smashing and crackling like fireworks.

"Jesus!" Olivia shouted. Seconds later, she was at my side. "You okay?"

"You're a genius!" I replied, my hand still shaped like the cup was in it.

"What?"

"Even when we're stationary . . ." I grinned. "We're still passing through time. We're *moving* through time."

The maths was pouring through my head faster than I could shape it, but I had to.

"Boom, so there's this one bit of Einstein's theory of relativity that says everything in the universe basically has two speeds: the speed it moves through 3D space, and its speed through time. And whenever you add up those two speeds, it always adds up to the speed of light. Never more. Never less."

I grabbed four stones from the ground, then scooped a dollop of mud. "Hold your hands out, please."

Even if she was just humoring me, she obliged. I watched her face crease in disgust as I massaged the mud into her nearest palm, then plopped all four pebbles on top.

"I want you to pretend this muddy hand represents your speed through time. And your other hand, the clean one," I continued, holding her empty palm, "that represents your speed through 3D space."

"Please know I'm only doing this cos you told me you love me."

"I *still* love you," I replied. I'd have said it a million times if I weren't so anxious to get out what I was processing.

"Now look: physics says that the faster you move in space, the slower you move in time." I took the pebbles from her dirty "time-hand" and placed them one by one in her clean "space-hand" to represent her speed shifting from one domain to another.

"Hold on, this is that thingamajig you explained with the Tesla when we watched that match." She paused to search for it. "Time dilation, wasn't it?"

"Exactly." It warmed me that she'd been listening. "And d'you remember me saying that once you hit the maximum speed possible in space—which is always the speed of light—time stops completely? Cos you've maxed out your quota."

"Yeah, I remember," she said, staring at her time-hand, which was now empty.

"Now look what happens when we start slowing down again." I moved the pebbles back into her dirty time-hand one at a time. "It all goes in the other direction: since you're moving slower in space, you start moving faster through time. Until eventually, you're passing through time at . . ."

I stopped when I saw it in her eyes: she knew the answer. She was just too scared to say it in case she sounded daft. "The speed of light?"

"Yes!" I screamed. "You know what this means? Even though we're both standing still right now, we're actually moving through time at the speed of *bloody* light."

"Umm, that doesn't feel right." She was shaking her head while I was trying to calm my heart palpitations. "I mean, wouldn't we *feel* it? If we were traveling through time that fast."

It was a fair question, packed with common sense. But I remembered what Dr. Esso had taught me about common sense—how it can sometimes play tricks on you.

"Not necessarily. I mean, right now, the earth's spinning on its axis at about 1,000 miles per hour. And we don't feel *that* at all, do we?" It was all coming together. "We've basically spent our whole lives moving through time at light speed, so we don't know any better. We don't know how it would feel if it were any different."

She flipped her lips into a *fair enough* shape. Until I hit the punch line, that was all I could expect.

"And here's the key," I continued. "If we're both traveling through time at light speed right now, there has to be some source of energy pushing us forward at that pace, right? Even if that energy is hidden from us. And it couldn't be just a little bit. You'd need a crap-ton of that Hidden Energy to keep everything in the universe ticking along through time."

I thought back to when Dr. Esso had described the Upper World. He'd actually used the words "Hidden Energy" to describe the heat he'd felt up there.

Judging by Olivia's darting eyes, I couldn't tell if she was catching up or thinking ahead. "And you reckon there's a way to tap into it? That Hidden Energy?"

"Yeah," I replied. "And I think that's what my mum wanted me to tell Dr. Esso." I stopped to catch my breath. "That if he allows himself to believe everything I'm telling you right now, he might be able to somehow get back to the Upper World and help her. Because once he's there, he'll have power beyond his wildest dreams."

I took the biggest stone from her hand and dropped it on my left foot, striking it and watching it soar into a glass window, setting off a loud, echoey *clank* inside.

"Jesus," Olivia whispered, her head tucked in. "Weren't you the one warning me about drones spotting us?"

"I'm sorry," I replied. She was 1,000% right, but I was already thinking about the next thing.

I needed to see Dr. Esso. He'd been right all along. There wasn't an ounce of doubt in me now.

According to everything I'd read online, the restraining order that Care had filed against him would have tagged his address. That meant that if I got too close, I'd trigger a proximity alert at the nearest police station. Even if I turned off my phone or took the fuel cells out of my shoes, they could find some other way to pick me up. I'd have 15 minutes (max) to get in and out before police arrived, and I'd have to make every minute count.

And every day I waited brought more risk. Every day that passed would bring me closer to a day when it was all too late.

A high-rise nearby had gone up in flames the week before. What if his was next? What if he left London? Or the UK altogether? What if something bad happened to him, or worse, he *let* something bad happen?

I'm going tonight, I decided. Nothing would stop me—not even having to go alone. Although, if I was being honest, I really wanted Olivia there. It just seemed so reckless to involve her in something she didn't believe in and didn't fully understand yet. And with our relationship still needing more time to mend, I felt shady asking her for a favor this soon and this big.

Thunder roared down, filling the sky with rain. The storm I'd seen earlier was almost on top of us. I thought back to what Dr. Anahera had said—how no matter how stingy life got, it always gave you a few choices. *Now* was my choice.

"I'm gonna go see him," I told Olivia.

"And I'm coming with you," she replied, smiling while she zipped her jacket to the chin. "There's no way I'm missing this."

Part IV:

ENERGY

FROM BLAISE ADENON'S NOTEBOOK

To Esso,

I believe, like our ancestors did, that the earth never hides the things we need, but instead provides them in abundance. Light energy rains on us from the sun; chemical energy is digested from the harvest; electrical energy strikes in lightning. But Hidden Energy? Mother Earth concealed that from our eyes for millennia.

Then a new generation came along. Products of the Steel Age, you could call them. And one among them, Einstein, had the most original of ideas, followed by the most dangerous of afterthoughts.

Einstein took a well-known fact—that light travels at a constant speed for all observers—and went on to reveal that space and time were fluid. Exactly three months later, he published a speculative article that ended with $E = mc^2$.

I must emphasize just how abnormal this journey of discovery was. Imagine finding a loose string in your rug and pulling on it. As you pull, the thread arrives in a rainbow of brilliant colors, none of which you've ever seen on the surface. You keep pulling and pulling until your entire carpet has unwound and you finally realize the thread is tied to something underneath your floorboards. And when you lift the plank to see what you've been tugging on, you discover that buried under your living room is a bomb.

That's what Einstein's equation said: hidden inside even the tiniest bits of matter is an ungodly amount of destructive power ready to be unleashed.

I'll admit I didn't think much about Hidden Energy when the elders explained this all to me. Not until a few years ago, when my fellowship paid for a trip to Hiroshima—the city where it was first revealed to the world.

We had been taught about the first atomic bomb the world dropped on the Japanese in World War II. Our teacher told us it killed around 146,000 people. But she left out one small detail: most of them were kids. They leave out those child-sized details in the textbooks as well. Like the burns. I had heard of first-, second-, and third-degree burns before. But visiting Hiroshima was the first time I learned there is such a thing as **fifth**-degree burns. That's when your flesh turns straight into charcoal. They don't show you the photos of the rain that fell that evening—each drop sticky and soot-black. The kids were so charred and thirsty that they opened their mouths to the heavens, drinking in as much of the radiation-soaked water as they could. Many died from it. The ones who survived that suffered from diarrhea for months. Then they died, too.

My child, I have read about Japan's cruelty toward its enemies during war. Believe me. I have heard people say that by dropping the bomb, we ended the war early, that countless lives were saved. But none of it seems to wash that bitter taste of Black Rain from my mouth.

146,000 people.

146,000 people.

146,000 **people.**

If you sat the bodies of those kids down in double-decker buses and, starting from Peckham, lined up the buses end to end, you'd cover the 4.5 miles to Piccadilly Circus and back. And it took less than a kilo of nuclear material to erase all those souls. Less than a kilogram. The approximate weight of a human heart.

$E = mc^2$

Look at it, how bland and tiny it looks. Three letters followed by a tiny number that even a toddler can count to. You have to look closer to understand how it creates its terror. Written in words, the equation simply says:

Energy = mass × the speed of light (squared)

So, for 1 kilogram of explosives that's:

Energy = 1 kg × (300,000,000 m/s)²

Which, when you multiply it out, gives:

Energy = 90,000,000,000,000,000

That final number is ninety quadrillion. Or put another way: 90 million, billion units of energy. Staring at the maths, you realize—it's the speed of light, that c in the equation, that fucks you. That's what killed those kids. 300,000,000 is already a devilishly large number; then the equation takes liberties and forces you to square it. They never stood a chance.

My colleagues tell me I have a habit of mixing my science with my voodoo. But I believe all of us can feel the Hidden Energy around us, flowing past us, through us. When someone you love walks into a room, you feel that surge, that tug on the fabric of space-time between you. I tell you all of this because if I could have spoken to my younger self, I would have warned him. I would have asked him to find a less destructive way. Old Eve might have been the wise one all along. She knew some things were better left forgotten.

25

ESSO

BY THE TIME I stepped outside the pub, the streets were hollow, and a ghostly wind was scavenging through the skeletons of buildings. I unknotted my tie and tossed it in my bag, knowing that whatever I might have to do en route to Narm, I'd be better at it feeling loose.

The number 12 bus approached the corner. *Just in time*, I thought. *My first bit of luck all evening.* Against the backdrop of dim streetlights, the bus looked like one of those glow-in-the-dark caterpillars on *Planet Earth*. It even moved the same way, snaking around the bends and corners of Camberwell Green. I hopped on through the back shutters and saw a little girl using her fingers to carve triangles into the steamy window. The seat opposite her was open. As I moved in, the woman I'd be sitting next to squeezed her handbag. So I decided to stay on my feet and think in space.

What had worked in the school dining hall with one boy caught off guard wouldn't work on the roads with two packs armed to the teeth. I'd been lucky with D; odds were, I'd get no run-up next time, no back doors, no chances for an injury-time comeback.

The bus driver was rounding corners like he *wanted* to tip over the bus. It took a while for me to build up enough courage to let go of the handrail and type. A few jumpy scrolls later, and I found *MANDEM FIFA 18*—the message group me, Rob, and Kato had made when we first became friends. We'd never gotten around to updating the name.

@MANDEM FIFA 18: Currently patching shit up with D.
Stay away from Peckham library area

I'd missed a few opportunities to warn them earlier, between chasing after Nadia and my breakdown in the pub. Still, it felt satisfying to tap *send*.

@MANDEM FIFA 18: Also I'm sorry for what I said earlier
I was being a prick

I thought about finishing with a line about how I hadn't meant any of it. But staring at my phone's keyboard, I couldn't do it. Some of what I'd said *had* been real; lots of it still was. And something felt off about putting a straight-up lie right after a sincere apology—the same kind of dickhead behavior that had gotten me into this mess in the first place. And I couldn't afford to gift Kato and Rob an overly moist text as ammo for however many days of teasing I had left. So, in the end, I went with something simple.

@MANDEM FIFA 18: If anyone asks . . . I went out like a
G. Love for everything

The driver took a sharp turn onto Peckham Road, then slammed hard on the brakes as he pulled up on the stop. The swing/jerk combo launched my thigh into the hard edge of the seat in front of me, and a stinging sensation shot down my leg, reminding me how sore and bruised my hip still was from the car crash. It felt like my body had aged a decade since morning, and it felt like that much time really had passed.

The engine hummed to life again, and the driver went back to carving up the streets. Only when I stopped massaging my hip did I look up and see that two boys had gotten on. The kid in front was massive. He was wearing an all-black tracksuit with thick yellow scribbles across the chest that made him look like an Addison Lee van. He was gripping his pouch, which was bent up and stretched by whatever was inside. *Hold up—is that Vex?* I'd never met Vex, but I knew his name. Everyone did. Between the stories of him knocking out three counterprotesters with one punch each, him pulling up on one of Spark's guys, the case he bust last summer, and the rumors about his strict diet of Ting and vegan food, his name got around.

If it *was* Vex, that was very bad news. He was one of Bloodshed's guys. I still couldn't see the kid behind him, but I was lucky neither of them had spotted *me* yet. I cut my losses, distracting my eyes with my home screen.

No new texts. But two notifications: an *imjustbait* video and a follow request from my uncle in Bénin. I rejected the request and watched half the clip. Kemi had also posted the Sierra-filtered photo of me, Rob, Kato, and Nadia sitting together at lunch. I took a screenshot and saved it.

Meanwhile, I was wrestling the temptation to look up and see what the two boys were up to. I thought back to a story from Sunday school, the one where God's about to destroy a city and sends an angel to tell Lot's family to run and not look back under any circumstances. One of them does look back (obviously) and immediately gets turned into salt. Was God testing me the same way? Or was my paranoia getting the best of me? I waited a few more seconds, then looked up—and sure enough, Vex was staring straight back at me.

"Shit," I muffled under my breath, holding myself back from full-blown panic. In my periphery, I could see Vex turning to his friend, nodding. I still hadn't seen the other guy's goddamn face, but I also couldn't afford another look.

I've gotta do something, I realized. *And ASAP.* There were four more stops until Peckham Library, and no way I'd last those ten minutes. I was certain it was Vex now, which removed hand-to-hand combat as an option. The guy looked like he sparred with bears for practice.

I could run, though.

"Next stop, Peckham Park Road," the digital conductor announced overhead.

Dear Holy Avengers, remember my prayer this morning asking for forgiveness? I hope that request got cleared, cos I really need you to cover man's back right now.

When the bus stopped, and the doors slid open, I stood perfectly still with my head low.

One . . . I counted, as the main batch got off.

Two . . .

On *three*, I sprinted at the exit, sliding between two ladies flanking the opening just before the doors slid shut.

Before I knew it, the bus was back in gear, the wheels rolling on with me safely on the pavement. "Thank you, Iron Man!" I shouted at the sky. I might actually get to figure out this time-travel shit and live to see another day. A day when I'd play FIFA with Rob and Kato again, tell Mum I loved her again, and if I got really lucky, maybe even ask out Nadia.

I'd barely made it 20 yards into my jog before I heard banging and muffled shouts from inside the bus behind me. "Let us out, you batty-man! Open the fucking door!"

You could hear the strain in the bus's joints as the blows to its frame got louder and harder. After putting up a brief fight, the driver pulled the hydraulic brakes, and the bus let out that African-auntie-kissing-her-teeth noise—followed by the two boys.

The decision was all but made up for me. My best option now was to force them to chase me all the way to Peckham and play on home ground. At least, according to the Upper World, my destiny was to be in front of Peckham Library tonight, alive. I'd have to figure out how to bend the rules of time back in my favor once I got there, but for now, running would just make that fate arrive sooner.

Before they could roll down their balaclavas, I saw that the other kid had been Bloodshed all along. My heart rate climbed into a frenzy.

The chase was on. And the end, hopefully, was near.

26
ESSO

A STINGING PAIN shot through my injured hip as I launched into an ugly sprint. "Mind over matter," I counseled myself. It was the kind of pain that would have slowed me down on any other day. But Bloodshed and Vex were too close behind. Too motivated.

Even with a wobbly leg, I fancied my chances in a race against Vex—I'd banked on that before jumping off the bus. But Bloodshed was gaining, his long legs swallowing up the gap so fast that within a few seconds, I could hear him breathing.

Above us sat an empty black sky that looked like it was creating spheres of rain out of nothing. One pudgy drop fell from a leaf into my eye, blinding me for a moment. Even the trees were against me. In primary school one time, my teacher said that William Blake had come to Peckham as a kid and claimed he saw angels in the trees. Running down that stormy, desolate road, clinging to my life, I wondered where Blake's angels had gone.

A lightning bolt spread its branches across the sky, staining everything white. Thunder followed a second later, and what had started out as trickling rain turned into a downpour. I kept running, powering through a stitch in my side that felt like it might burn a hole through me.

"Where'd you think you're running to, fam?!" Bloodshed shouted. He was within snatching distance; I could feel it. I wasn't about to make the mistake I'd made on the bus and risk turning to salt again. So I faced forward and somehow—from somewhere—found a last bit of fight.

In the distance, I made out the profile of a heavyset man carrying supermarket bags in each hand. He had on a stone-washed jacket and matching jeans.

Is that . . . ?

By the time I got close-up, his familiar, beaming smile confirmed my guess. It was the same smile I'd seen him wearing as he argued with the chaperone after the car crash, the same one he'd worn after taking the piss out of that Vietnamese kid, Tom.

"Preston!" he shouted gleefully in his full denim suit. "Haafa, bross? Is everything . . ." He looked behind me and, on seeing Bloodshed, let his shopping bags drop to the ground.

About to speed past him, I yelled, "Sorry, bro. Can't stop."

"Don't worry, bross." His accent still came with a generous serving of plantain. "I got your back."

I turned and watched him shove himself clumsily into Bloodshed's path, forcing him to sidestep into a passing pedal bike.

Bloodshed and the cyclist crashed into a heap on the main road, and a line of cars screeched and skidded around them. I wanted to laugh, but held back, knowing how pissed my lungs would be if I wasted the oxygen. The West African man, seeing his job was done, ran away in the opposite direction, waving.

Keep faith, I told myself. After that massive piece of luck, my plan might actually work.

I threw my guardian angel a thumbs-up, then focused on winning the race to Narm.

The next time I looked back, the two yutes were no longer in sight. I decided it was safe to slow down a bit and started thinking about where to veer off the main road. The oversized, overlit Burger King backing the £1 shop came into view, meaning I was a 10-minute walk from home. But 10 might as well have been an imaginary number—D and Bloodshed both knew where I lived.

Slowing down was the worst decision I could have made for my body. I had a headache in my hip, and a migraine in my thighs. Pretty quickly, the best I could manage was a quick hobble, one leg dragging behind.

I'd walked these streets a thousand times, and never seen them so empty. Everything felt different. It was like the universe had sucked all life from the storm we were walking into, the vortex I had created.

I finally reached the walkway leading to Peckham Library. And even though I hoped none of my mates were in there, it brought some small comfort imagining Kato and Rob in that odd-shaped lump of pastel-colored copper. Not that they could do anything to help me. But just like no one likes watching a horror film alone, I kinda wanted someone with me in case the boogie monster showed up. A friend to smile over me as I breathed my last breath.

The same number 12 bus I'd jumped off 10 minutes earlier sped past. The driver gave me a nod, mouthing: *Good luck.*

Farther ahead, in front of Katie's chicken shop, was the hazy silhouette of a familiar girl, also nodding at me. *Is my brain playing tricks on me?* I had to check it wasn't constructing a reality I wished was real, by filling it with the one person I wanted to see most. But as I got nearer, the mirage didn't disappear, it solidified. It became Nadia.

"Why you limping like that?" she said once I got close. Her smile cut a sharp contrast to the chaos I'd just been running from. "And why you so out of breath?"

I was knackered, but seeing her pumped fresh fuel into my cells. I knew this would be the only chance I got—the only comma in a breathless chapter of a day. I wanted to reach for the one thing that might bring light into the void I was in, even if it was just a flicker.

Tomorrow wasn't promised, after all.

I glanced behind me: still no sight of Bloodshed or Vex. And so I grabbed Nadia's hand and pulled her into the narrow alleyway behind the chicken shop. She complained about there being no cover and about her hair getting wet, but she said it all while laughing.

I stopped and stared at her, peering into her giant brown eyes. It felt like the walls were closing in on us, space conspiring with time to strangle my last opportunity. This really was the last thing I should have been thinking about. Bloodshed and Vex couldn't be far behind—what if they spotted us? What would they do to me? To her?

What if she didn't feel the same way I felt about her? What if she'd never felt the same way?

But what if this was my last shot, and I might die never knowing? Never trying? Every instinct in my body was telling me that now was the *only* time.

"You're scaring me, E. Can you just tell me what—"

Before she could finish, I pulled her into my arms and pressed my mouth to hers.

She froze.

Maybe from the shock, I hoped. My lips were freezing wet, after all, and I'd come in with no warning.

But with seconds flying past, there was still no sign of her reaction. *Crap!* I screamed silently and pulled back to see her face stunned and confused. I'd come on too strong, probably too soon as well. I'd messed this up the same way I'd messed up everything else.

But just as I was accepting defeat, she pressed her chest to mine and fell softly into me. She kissed with purpose, almost like she was stealing me. My unbandaged hand wandered down to the small of her back, and she snatched it—not to pull it away, but to guide it farther down, sliding my palm across the denim holding her bum. I squeezed, and she lifted onto her tippy-toes, giggling. It was barely first base, but it felt sweeter than all my life's wet dreams combined, a magical moment we were both sheltering under the blanket of rain. It was perfect.

But it also felt—*almost*—too perfect. The sort of flame that can't sustain itself for more than a few moments. With time against us, how long could it last?

Something cold smacked my forehead. *Was that a stone?* I thought. Then one landed smack on *her* nose, and she tilted her head back. The icy wind that had been searching through Camberwell earlier had found its way into the alleyway, stripping the heat off our skins and away from our embrace. I looked up to a sky peppered with hailstones the size of marbles.

This was the hailstorm I'd seen in the Upper World.

This was it.

Nadia brought a hand to her mouth. She was staring wide-eyed over my shoulder at something, or *someone*, that I couldn't see, and judging from how her face sank, it could have been the devil himself. Whatever it was grabbed my arm. A beat later, I was spun around and pulled away from her.

It was D, with Bloodshed jogging close behind. Filling the other corner of my view was the orange surfboard on top of the library.

Déjà vu, I said to myself. Then I faced what was in front of me.

27

RHIA · (15 YEARS LATER)

PECKHAM, LIKE MOST towns in London, was split into four quadrants. In the first quadrant, the obviously wealthy families owned condos and semidetached houses built for obviously wealthy families. The second quadrant was where the artsy kids pretended to rent flats their parents had already mortgaged for them. People like Tony and Poppy settled down in the third quadrant, the grimy-yet-up-and-coming neighborhoods, which always seemed to be upping and coming, but never quite arrived. Then you had the final quadrant, the end farthest from the river—*the* Ends. And the bit where Dr. Esso lived was Ends HQ, especially after dark.

In space, the 78 bus stop by his house was agonizingly close. In time, we were on an endless journey, stopping every 10 seconds. Assuming Dr. Esso hadn't moved from the address on the envelope, there was a chance we'd already triggered the proximity alert, starting the 15-minute countdown.

As the bus slowed to a stop, I thought back to one other thing Dr. Esso had told me, which I'd not shared with Olivia. It was about my real father, and in hindsight, it was something I should have told her a long time ago. Just as I was getting ready to confess, she yanked my sleeve, her impatience dragging us both off the bus a stop early.

Out on the pavement, a cold wind slapped my face, pinching a cold tear from my eye.

"Did you feel that?" Olivia asked, both of us stopping to stare up at the sky. Before I could say no, a pair of tiny stones landed at my feet.

Hail? Within seconds, the night sky was filled with white polka dots, a few of the missiles big enough to leave a bruise.

Olivia pointed to the apex of a tower block in the distance. "It's over there!"

We burst into a sprint, and a siren scream nearby forced us to move even faster. I was quietly praying it was just paramedics, because one scan from a police car would abort our mission before it even started.

As we entered the block, a man covered in wrinkles and wrapped in a filthy patchwork blanket wolf-howled in our direction. To our left, by the fenced-off playground were a group of boys against the wall, each in that number 4–shaped stance, one foot down and the other raised against the brick. Each couldn't have been more than thirteen, but they wore matching tattoos on their knuckles—Bloodshed insignia. The tallest one patted his pocket, letting us know it didn't matter how harmless we looked—two strangers pulling up without a G-pass at this time of night was a situation he wouldn't be caught slipping in.

We reached the ground-floor entrance, which meant we'd be facing Dr. Esso's door in less than a minute. As we turned toward the stairs, a drone swept down in front of us. Olivia and I stopped dead in the hail, letting the drone slice a line a meter from our noses before flying out of sight again. It was a reminder anything could happen now.

I grabbed her arm, just before we reached the bottom step. "Listen, there's one more thing I never told you. And I don't want you to find out up there." The hail was forcing me to shout. "It's about my dad. I didn't know how to process it when Dr. Esso told me."

"Listen, if you wanna do this another time," she said, looking up at the clouds, "when it's not dark and hailing, I'll get some cash off Poppy and come down the first weekend I can."

I followed Olivia's gaze to another Bloodshed boy floating toward us on a hoverboard. Thunder and lightning clapped as we stared, and I had to tuck my chin as another cold gust flew past.

"But if we still wanna see him tonight," she continued, "we have to do it *now*."

She grimaced as another hailstone scraped her ear. Behind her, the leaves were shivering in the wind.

We both turned to look up at the red door four floors above us. I didn't need to squint at the number; I knew it was his—I could feel it. And I knew my plan was either insanely genius or just plain insane.

"You're right," I replied, facing the stairs. "Let's fucking do this."

28

ESSO

LIGHTNING FIRED UP the sky, followed by another sonic boom of thunder. What had begun as a couple small hailstones pelting us every few seconds had turned into a storm of jagged-edged missiles. The weakly lit, trash-filled path wasn't made for cars, but I couldn't help wondering if an ambulance would be able to squeeze in if needed.

At one end of the alley—just meters behind D and his brother—was Peckham Hill Street, with crispy fried wind blowing in from Katie's. The other end—which Nadia and I were getting backed into—opened into an abandoned tower block, with all its gates and exits closed off.

As D towered over me, with Bloodshed also closing in, I reminded myself to stay calm.

D was wearing the same white shirt from school, a few specks of blood still staining the collar. He had a bandage on his cheek, but his blown-out eye and top lip were on naked display. The denting and bruising only made him look harder, and I wondered if anything could calm him down . . . or *bring* him down, if that was what this might come to. He didn't say a word, but his chest was heaving up and down and he might as well have been screaming, *I am going to kill you.*

Bloodshed licked his lips as his running mate finally entered the alley. And Vex's first move after checking in was to hold his knees and wait for breath.

My jaw clenched, the rest of my body already on maximum tense. The plan I'd come up with in the pub was our only escape, and I still believed in it. But I knew it had enough cracks that one bad breeze could bring the whole ting down.

"Don't hurt him, D." Nadia forced me out the way with surprising strength. "Please, it's not . . ." She stared at the ground, eyes closed, shaking her head. Never in my life had I seen Nadia stuck for words, and of all times, while giving what should have been a simple speech on why D shouldn't murder me.

"You're the last person I want to hear from right now," D shot back. "This is between me and the bredda here. So fuck off." He was talking to Nadia, but kept his eyes on me throughout, meaning I caught the spit flying from his mouth.

"You ain't gotta talk to her like that, D." I stretched my spine an inch to better match him and the height of my own words. "This is between you and me."

Bloodshed, who looked like he was done waiting, ordered: "Move her out the way, Vex."

An instant later, Vex swept in, lifting Nadia off her feet,

then dumping her, back first, on the concrete a few meters to the side. She fought to get up, emptying a rubbish lorry of swear words on Vex in the process. I couldn't make out what Vex whispered to her next, but I gathered, by the way she went quiet and sat back down, that it must have been dark.

"Listen," I said, facing D and ready with my speech. "What I'm about to say is gonna sound crazy—"

"Why you even letting man speak right now?" Bloodshed butted in, his face scrunched like a paper bag.

D replied by reaching for his pouch. Bloodshed and Vex already had their hands on theirs. Everything was moving way too fast for my plan.

Think, think, think! I had no choice but to get to the point, the thing that had created the mess in the first place.

"I can time-travel!" I screamed.

D stopped midzip, while everyone else froze up. The statement was so mental that even though they'd already run out of patience and pity, they had to pause to manage the confusion.

"Even this moment, the one we're all standing in right now . . . I lived it already today. *Twice.*" I counted a total of four baffled faces glaring back at me. At least they were all listening. "I figured out how to travel through time with my mind. I can see the future." I'd only seen and understood a fraction of what the Upper World could do, so my next sentence rested entirely on faith. "And I'm pretty sure I can go back to the past as well."

D shook his head and this time, got his pouch three-quarters open, the flat edge of his weapon handle already peeking through.

"No, no, no, please!" I rushed out. "Listen, man—I'm being serious!" I was bent at the knees, reaching out with both hands—my body's way of making me look too small and out of reach to bother with.

I thought back to the future I'd seen and what it might mean . . . not just for me, but for him. "D, I know for a *fact* that deep down you don't want to be doing this right now. I *know* the shit that's happened to you, to put you in this situation. I know what happened that night between your brother and your stepdad." His trigger hand slowly fell to his side, but I resisted the temptation to let up. "Bro, there's so much shit that's happened to all of us, that we've had to live with. And what I'm telling you is that I've figured out how to go back and make sure it never happens. We can use this power to change our pasts. Choose our futures."

Vex was first to dent the silence. "So what you're tellin' us, yeah—is that we can take today's lottery numbers, travel back in our minds to last week, and use the numbers to become millionaires?"

I looked over D's shoulder to respond. "What I'm saying is that once I figure out how to control this thing, we can win *every* lottery ever run from the start to the end of our lives."

D's eyes were shifting about in every direction but mine, but he seemed to be thinking about it. They all were. I bit my lip, getting fidgetier and fidgetier about the promises I'd made, wondering how on earth I would deliver. I'd effectively just written a trillion-pound check, hoping my day-old account had the cash and no one would ask for proof of funds. My only insurance, my only hope, was that with a bit more time alive, I'd figure out how to get back to the Upper World and keep everyone sweet.

I was dying to say sorry to D for getting him expelled and for setting him on a darker course than he'd started on. I was ready to tell him that I still remembered the ten-year-old D, the one whose portrait still lit up his mum's front room. And after going to the Upper World, I needed him to know that I'd seen, with my own eyes, the string that separated the holy from the hurt, and that every choice weaved together into a single garment of destiny connecting all of us. Because I'd been through so much in the past 24 hours, these truths had become obvious to me. And I'd assumed that by saying a few heartfelt sentences, I could make this obvious to them as well.

But the moment I heard Vex's acidic laughs slash through the air, I realized just how naïve I'd been.

Still cackling, he asked Bloodshed, "What you think, bruv? We go back in time and mash it up?"

Bloodshed stopped to stare at his tatted knuckles before replying. "Nah, fam." Then he turned to me with a sober face and said: "This is who I am."

That was when I realized he was right: that none of our futures would budge, and these might be the final seconds of my life. The jaws of fate had closed in on me. And even if I'd had time to explain every one of my thoughts on hope and love and second chances, it wouldn't have changed a goddamn thing.

D pulled the stick from his pouch, raising it so I could stare into the barrel's abyss. I'd seen a Baikal once before because Spark had one. They were cheap, crap, dodgy guns that feds used in Russia to fire tear gas at protesters. And apparently, with a few tweaks, you could upgrade them to fire bullets at kids like me in London.

"D, I'm begging you." I was banking on nothing but adrenaline and optimism now—substances not known for surviving contact with reality. The hail was crashing down hard. I wished I'd had more time to figure out how the Upper World worked. All I wanted was one more day to find them *proof* that it existed, instead of expecting them to trust my crazy claims.

I knew I couldn't give up. I had to make something happen—figure out one final trick, even if it was just a regular earthly one—to make sure we all left that alley without a scratch.

"Listen—I'm on your side."

"Is that right, bruv?" With his free hand, D pulled a sheet of paper out his jacket and whisked it open. Then he dropped Mr. Crutchley's snitch sheet to the ground, letting it melt into the wet concrete.

"I didn't snitch, man. I *promise*. You have to believe me." My hands were closed in prayer; I was shaking, stunned at how quickly things had gone from tit-for-tat to life-or-death.

Meanwhile, D's breathing seemed to get louder and shorter with each word that came out of my mouth.

Then the front doors of Peckham Library flung open, and I peeked around to see Kato and Rob flying out.

D stood thinking. Stalling, maybe. Or maybe he was just taking a few final seconds to psych himself up for his execution shot. I had no choice but to cling to the slight possibility that he was considering alternatives.

Bloodshed turned to his brother in frustration: "Slap that corn, fam. Or give man the stick and I'll do it myself."

D clicked the gun off safety, tilted his head to the side—his way, I guess, of giving me a moment to say my last words.

Desperation filled the tears racing down my face. I felt like I was drowning, like I had an anchor strapped to my ankle, and no matter how much I kicked out, it kept dragging me down.

Where was the Upper World now that I actually fucking needed it? I considered sprinting to the brick wall and banging my head on it in case another concussion would take me there. But if I made one flinch too many, D would shoot. Plus, there was the risk I'd just knock myself out . . . then get shot, leaving everyone behind to deal with my mess.

Think, Esso! Just because the Upper World couldn't save us didn't mean nothing could. But it was going to take something much, much more down-to-earth to convince D. Something he couldn't afford to ignore.

"Listen to me," I demanded. "Spark and all his guys are on their way here, *right* now. If you kill me, none of you lot are getting out of here alive," I added even more urgently. "I *promise* you I'm telling the truth, D. Please. I don't want you to die tonight. No one has to die tonight."

"You think I give a shit about my life? Or yours?" he shouted back. Any warmth or control left in his voice was gone. He cocked the gun and pressed it hard between my eyebrows. "I don't see one reason not to blow your brains out."

It was too late. *I* was too late. With my eyes shut, I waited for the bullet to arrive, hoping the end would be short and painless, but knowing death was probably worse than I could even imagine.

"Because I'm pregnant, D." The words came out gently. I snapped my eyes open and saw Nadia rising to her feet.

D turned to her, his right eye twitching in shock or fear—spasming up and down like a broken camera shutter. And in that instant, the puzzle snapped together in my mind. Odd-shaped fragments colliding neatly together and sending my head spinning.

Nadia throwing D's phone out the window in class.

The nasty look she gave him on Monday when he made the joke about Gideon.

The nasty looks she always *gives him.*

That kiss he blew back.

The reason she was always fighting D was that she actually *gave* a shit about him.

She liked him. Maybe even loved him?

And she'd held back at first when I'd kissed her, hadn't she?

She'd always held back.

I looked over at Nadia, tears streaming from her eyes, which were locked with D's.

That rumor that had gone round a couple of years ago, the one about D being out with a "chick" the night Bloodshed had shanked their stepdad . . . Had that been Nadia then?

Earlier, at lunch, the way she'd rubbed her belly each time she laughed . . . every time D's name came up. It was all so obvious now.

I thought about how, for as long as I'd known her, Nadia had talked about her mum working two jobs to make sure Nadia and her siblings had better options than she'd had. I thought about how Nadia must have felt when she found out she was pregnant at 16, the same age her mum had given birth to her. It made sense that she wouldn't have told D, or me, or anyone else.

Vex didn't bother stopping Nadia as she walked past him. Things had gotten too mad, even for him. Kato and Rob were standing at the far end of the alley, probably wondering what kind of ghetto episode of *EastEnders* they'd just walked into.

"The baby's yours, D," Nadia said. "If you pull that trigger, they'll lock you up. You won't get to raise your own child."

D stumbled backward, like Nadia's words were a gale-force wind. He stared at his hands, a gun shaking in one, the other a trembling fist. It was like he didn't recognize himself, like it had been someone else's finger on that trigger, ready to change all our lives forever.

D dropped the gun to the ground. And just as I was letting out a sigh so deep it made me dizzy, Bloodshed came back into view.

He pushed D out the way, reaching into his jacket to reveal the olive-green handle of a hunter's knife.

"Oi, Xavier, allow it," D said. But Bloodshed paid him no mind and kept walking toward me.

Vex slid behind me, squeezing my arms tight behind my back, so I had nowhere to move.

"I said, allow it!" D shouted again.

I wished I had a get-out-of-jail-free card. What was the point of all those visions if I was gonna go out like this? I squeezed my eyes shut, trying to transcend and transport myself back to the Upper World, where maybe, just maybe, I'd find a way to break free from the chains of time and save myself.

But when I opened my eyes, I was still in the alley by Peckham Library and hail was still thrashing the pavement.

And Bloodshed was in my face. Time was up.

"I guess, sometimes, when you wanna get something done," he said, pulling the blade out the sheath to reveal its jagged teeth, "you have to do it yourself."

29

RHIA · (15 YEARS LATER)

I CHEWED ON my pinkie nail as Olivia and I listened to the footsteps coming from inside Dr. Esso's flat. And as the door creaked open, a torrent of emotions flooded in. The strongest one, by far?

Hope.

If we got this right, I'd get my mum back, and he'd get his Nadia. The 15 years that he'd spent trawling through physics books, and that I'd wasted without her, would all be rewritten, renewed. I promised to make every second I got with her count. I'd make sure she knew how much I loved her. And I'd never leave her to suffer alone again.

Dr. Esso's confused face finally came into view.

"*Yes*, if you're selling cookies," he said, not knowing which stranger was knocking today. "*Hell no*, if you're shotting vacuum cleaners . . . or neon . . . or God."

It wasn't the magical opening line for our reunion that I'd imagined. But at least he was here.

Thank *fuck*. He was here.

"It's me," I said, watching his feet go rigid, just like they had the day we met. "It's Rhia."

He put his fist to his mouth, his eyes bulging and bloodshot. But on top of his obvious fatigue and shock was a look of gratitude. And on top of that, an expression that almost seemed . . . *expectant*.

I wasn't sure what to say next, and Olivia shoving me to hurry up wasn't helping. In the end, I dug deep, and told him exactly what I would have in more familiar times.

"You been working out?" He had on the same LBF T-shirt he'd worn in either our first or second lesson, and a rounder body inside it. "Your top's looking extra fitted now, that's all."

"Piss off, Rhia," he replied.

Olivia raised an eyebrow at our back-and-forth. "Are you two always this rude to each other?" she asked.

"Yep," we answered at the same time.

Dr. Esso smiled, and I couldn't help doing the same. I'd spent weeks building up to this moment, months if you counted from when we'd first met. And meanwhile, he'd waited half his life.

My phone vibrated in my pocket—a message from a coded number:

1133: A PROXIMITY ALERT HAS BEEN TRIGGERED. OFFICERS ARE ON THEIR WAY. STAY CALM AND ALERT.

"That was them, wasn't it?" Olivia pressed. "How long have we got?"

I watched the next two messages arrive in rapid fire and had to fight the urge to panic. "Six minutes."

"Quick," Dr. Esso said, flinging his door open. "Let's do this inside."

We rushed into his front room, where Dr. Esso waved at a couch barely wide enough for two toddlers. Olivia and I managed to squeeze into it with some painful compromises. I hadn't known what to expect in terms of living room decorations, but not much could have prepared me for the walls: reams of equations covering every patch, scribbled in this thick ink that had raised grooves he could feel to read. The place smelled loud, too, which probably had something to do with the weed burns on the carpet. Rings of shelves went around the room, one on top of the next, each one filled with books. *Emmy Noether's Theorem* was the title of one textbook, and the one next to it, called *Gravitation*, was massive enough to live what it was teaching. Partway along was a paperback with *Relativity* slapped on the spine—authored by Albert Einstein himself.

Dr. Esso crossed the short distance to his recliner, kicking two empty Red Bulls out of his path. He put his microwave meal on the table, while leaving his retro radio on his armrest.

"All right, sis," Olivia said. "You got this."

Five minutes was a third of the time I'd planned for, and we'd already wasted a chunk of it warming up at his door. The margin for error left was nil.

"I've waited awhile to hear this," Dr. Esso said, balancing

on the edge of his cushion. "But unfortunately, time's not on our side."

I sprang back to my feet. An ocean of nervous energy was rising in me. I could taste the urgency. I understood the stakes. But now I also understood something else.

"That's the thing," I said, correcting him. "Time *is* on our side."

30

ESSO

THE RAIN HAD stopped, and the police sirens, which had begun as an airy whisper minutes earlier, were now screaming off the walls of the alleyway.

Bloodshed was staring at the shank he'd just lodged inside me. He had this look in his eyes like he could feel what I was feeling in his own flesh, like my pain was flowing through the knife that connected us and back into him. A snarl spilled out of him, words I couldn't understand, as if he was speaking in tongues. Even his face didn't make sense anymore, so twisted with anger that he could have been a different person.

He must have needed to prove to himself that taking a second life wouldn't hurt as much as the first. Because he pulled the Rambo out of me, then stabbed me even deeper.

I barely felt it at first. When I did, it was different to how I'd always imagined it might feel. Each slash was like getting punched in the gut by someone with bony hands. Then the two craters in my stomach started radiating waves of pain outward, along with gushes of blood. And like at lunch, the pain demanded my attention jealously, not letting me divert any effort to crying, panicking, or even thinking. Everything went blurry, and I started going faint. Vex, who'd been restraining me, tried to let go, but I was the one holding on to him now, gripping his arm as tight as I could to stay upright.

"Let's dust, fam," Vex shouted. "Feds are coming!" He shrugged me off, swooping up D's gun as he and Bloodshed made a run for it.

But just as they reached the end of the alleyway leading to the deserted block, their path was blocked off by eight bodies entering from the same direction. It was Spark and his Peckham yutes, all in black, responding to the text I'd sent in the Penny Hill bathrooms that morning.

With nothing holding me up, I dropped to one knee and my hand sank into a pile of soggy leaflets wedged into the space where the tarmac met the wall. *Stay off the ground*, I said silently, using all my effort to obey my own orders, knowing that the closer I got to the ground, the nearer I got to death.

I was meant to be at home.

I imagined Mum alone on the couch with an uneaten plate of fish and chips steaming next to her. I pictured her wondering when I'd arrive, glancing at her phone every other second and rising to her feet each time the wind rustled the door knocker.

D was first to run to my side. Nadia, Kato, and Rob followed right after.

Vex and Bloodshed looked like they were thinking about

running back to the opposite end of the alleyway, but Spark's boys had cornered them on both sides.

Spark smiled as he pressed forward, probably not believing his luck that three T.A.S. boys had turned up with nothing more than a gun and a couple knives between them. But when Spark turned to me and saw the blood seeping through my school shirt, and the stained shank in Bloodshed's hands, his smile faded, and his focus turned to violence.

No words were spoken. No words were needed. Skengs just started coming up out of nowhere—three nine-millimeters, a snub-nosed shotgun, a couple of other semis. The other seven Peckham yutes kept their guns by their sides, but Spark lifted his at Bloodshed, who had the face of a man who'd just realized he'd brought a knife to a gunfight.

"I guess it's blood for blood. Right, Bloodshed?" Spark cocked the gun and leaned in. "You got my bro, so I gotta kill yours, innit."

Then, way too fast for any of us to react, Spark spun around to D, who was standing next to me. He walked forward until his stick was kissing D's forehead. Then he shot him point-blank in the face.

A red mist filled the air as D dropped to his knees. Where smooth skin should have been, a gaping hole now lived. He used his last seconds of life to gaze at Nadia, staring at her like he wanted to say something, but couldn't. A second later, he fell nose-flat to the concrete.

Nadia screamed, throwing herself to the ground next to him.

This can't be happening, I thought. I had no idea what to do with myself because I was too busy denying what I'd just seen. *Spark did* not *just shoot D in the head,* I told myself. *D is* not *dead.* I couldn't even entertain the idea of it.

And yet, I could. I *had.* I'd seen all of this coming. And I still hadn't been able to stop it.

Instead of words, a stream of vomit flew from my mouth.

Nadia started wailing hysterically, trying to flip D on his back. Maybe to try to breathe life back into him, maybe just to see his face. Kato and Rob, realizing how serious the mess they'd walked into was, started backing away from the narrowing circle of death in the alleyway.

A few wise words right then might have de-escalated the whole thing. It didn't have to end in total annihilation. One boy was dead, and only one other boy was hurt. The destiny part was over, which meant nothing else terrible had to happen. But with everyone now cocking and raising their weapons, no one dared say a thing.

Vex pointed his gun at Spark.

Spark's right-hand man, the same one who'd eyed me suspiciously in West End that Wednesday, pointed his snub-nosed shotgun at Vex.

Spark turned his stick over to Bloodshed.

Bloodshed was standing in the middle of it all and didn't seem to care. His big brother was dead. What else was there? He dropped his shank to the ground, staring zombielike at D's spiritless corpse.

The sirens grew louder, drowning out all my other senses,

and then a line of armed cops in Met SWAT gear swung around the corner from the main road shouting, "Police!" with their assault rifles trained on everything with a pulse. Red laser dots appeared on Nadia's, Rob's, and Kato's foreheads.

The first gun went off. And in that precise moment, a powerful jolt of déjà vu seized me. I'd experienced this all before. The feeling multiplied until it was like a thousand déjà vus springing on me all at once. And all the while, the words I'd read in my dad's notebook that morning, about the Upper World, were running through my head at the speed of light:

The WINDOW is a memory from the past or the future. A memory unique to each individual, often so severe or traumatic that our minds force us to forget it.

As my vision faded, the world around me dissolved into black nothingness. The violent *bang* of the bullet leaving the chamber had turned into a slow, winding drawl—as if the sound waves were rippling through tar to reach my ears. Even the silence between my heartbeats was widening. And so I waited, praying the next thump would arrive.

31

RHIA · (15 YEARS LATER)

OLIVIA AND DR. Esso were leaning in, waiting. We had three minutes left.

I lifted up Dr. Esso's microwave meal from the coffee table. "I'm holding your dinner in my hand right now, but I need you to imagine it's a Tesla."

"Done," Dr. Esso replied.

He couldn't see the prop—it was mostly for me, anyway. I needed to picture what I was thinking, say everything right. "Now, if you wanted to drive this car along a road, you'd obviously need some sort of energy source, right? Basically electricity or hydrogen to power the engine."

"Makes sense."

"It makes sense," I agreed, "because we all know that moving around every day in 3-dimensional *space* requires energy. Standard stuff. But, how about moving through *time*? We're all doing it right now, but where's *that* energy coming from? Where's the energy that's propelling all three of us, from the past to the present and into the future? The answer is, it's hidden." I lifted the lid off the tray to find some half-eaten bangers and mash buried inside. "Before, we had no way of touching or seeing this other kind of energy. Not until Einstein found a way to unleash it."

"$E = mc^2$," Dr. Esso whispered, sliding farther forward till he was barely clinging to his seat.

"Exactly!" I said, my confidence climbing. I could see something rising in him, too. I'd run out of tricks to keep calm so was rushing it all out instead. "In general, our everyday experiences tell us that the more mass something has, the more energy you need to drag it around. And that the faster you want to drag something along, the more energy you need as well. Einstein's equation is saying exactly that: the amount of Hidden Energy—E—that something needs to zoom through time is equal to its mass—m—multiplied by—"

"The speed of light, squared!" Olivia answered, now sounding the most impatient of all of us. I'd have kissed her on her long-ass forehead, but I couldn't afford to waste the five seconds it would take.

"Exactly, sis—which happens to be the speed we're all traveling through time right now." I doubled down. "And it can't be a coincidence that Einstein, the guy who came up with the maths for time travel, also discovered the equation for Hidden Energy a few months later. It's not luck that all the physicists after him found this same link between time and energy in their equations as well."

I looked down at my phone: one and a half minutes till the cops arrived.

"You've clearly read Noether's stuff," I said, looking at the book I'd spotted when we first arrived. "She proved time and energy are symmetrically linked a century ago. And look at all the quantum maths: Schrödinger's equation; Heisenberg's uncertainty principle. In all of them, time and energy are basically *stapled* together."

I paused for a breath and Olivia chimed in, saying, "You proper earned that oxygen, sis." But I wouldn't breathe properly till we got my mum back.

"Time is also meant to be hidden from our eyes, Dr. Esso. But when you went to the Upper World that day, you saw it—your whole life from start to finish cast in a string of projections."

Thunder rumbled. But at the speed my brain was rolling, nothing could shift me off course.

"And now, with everything you know, if you went back there you could see Hidden Energy as well. You could lift mountains, light up a whole city if you needed to. You could change what happened that night to your friends. To my parents. To us."

Olivia came to my side, resting a hand on my shoulder. I'd gotten it all out—all we could do now was hope the impossible became real in the 45 seconds we had left before the feds arrived.

Dr. Esso sat with his hands clasped in front of his lips. He looked like he'd already gathered his thoughts but was hoping one last piece of inspiration would strike him.

"I'm gonna say this with all due respect," he began. "Because I massively respect the fact you're literally spitting uni-level physics right now. And that you learned it on your own." His palms slid up to his forehead until his face was sheltered behind them. "But everything you've said. All that stuff about Einstein and time and energy and how it's all connected—I already *know* all that. I learned it ages ago, Rhia. It didn't make a difference then, and it won't now."

My chin started trembling. I had nothing left to say. *Of course he already knew.* The very room we were standing in was fenced off with thousands of pages of this same maths—his own fucking shrine to it. He'd probably been studying this stuff since he was my age. And yet I'd somehow fooled myself into thinking I could top that in weeks. Worse, I'd convinced myself that my entire existence, and his, had been building up to this night— the stale moment that was now behind us.

I felt even smaller, even dumber, than when I'd stood in Tony's living room and had my dreams shattered. "I guess I just figured that if you went back—"

"That's the problem," he shouted. "I can't go back. I don't know how!" It was like listening to a mountain crumble and implode. "I haven't been back to the Upper World since that night. I don't even remember what happened."

BANG, BANG, BANG was the stiff beat on the door outside. That was 12 knocking—no two ways about it.

"We are done out 'ere," Dr. Esso said. Stones were cracking against the window so hard I wondered for a second if it was possible for hail to break glass.

"There's a staircase through the back door," he continued. "You lot need to get out before they burst in swingin'."

Before I could blink, Olivia grabbed my arm and pulled me into the corridor leading to the back exit. But not before I saw Dr. Esso's bag leaning against the wall. Not before I broke free from Olivia's hold and snatched his tattered notebook out of there.

As Olivia scurried toward the door, I hung a meter behind, flipping through the pages at lightning pace and doubling back each time I'd gone too fast to absorb what I was reading.

A cave . . . Prisoners lived in chains . . . The Upper World . . .

Next page.

. . . Language influences what we see . . .

Scroll down.

And yet our ability to tap into chronosthesia (mental time travel) was not destroyed.

Please let this be it, I begged.

Only unplugged. Locked inside a crevice of our minds called the WINDOW.

Dr. Esso had mumbled something about a "window" that night he'd come clean, said it was the part of the mind where you accessed the Upper World. *Maybe this is it*, I thought to myself. *What gets us back to Mum.* But if it was, how come he hadn't figured it out himself? He'd had the notebook all this time, so what piece was he missing that only I could give him?

"Police!" At the far end of the corridor came the next round of whacks. "Open up!"

A hard shoulder from Olivia later, the back door opened and the narrow fire exit stairs came into view. I reread the passage searching for a final clue, something practical.

Then I scanned it again. And again. Nothing was clicking.

"We've done all we can," Olivia yelled over the gale. "We have to leave! Now!" Behind her, a web of lightning dazzled across the thick violet sky, as if in some electromagnetic realm out there, a war was being waged.

I looked back one last time to the door leading to the front room, to Dr. Esso. I had nothing left to offer him, not with the few seconds we had left. Nothing.

Unless.

"No," I said, breaking Olivia's grip. "This isn't how this ends. I think it's how it begins."

"Rhia, don't—"

I ran back and smashed open the living room door. Dr. Esso was on his feet, and I lunged into him, wrapping my arms around his back in a desperate hug.

"I know," he said, his voice broken. "I'm sorry."

The world was caving in around us, and I had to let it. "I know you don't like talking about what happened to my parents that night. I know you blame yourself." I didn't bother sniffling back the tears. "And for a while, I blamed you, too." I let my head rest on his shoulder while finding my words. "But

I forgive you. And my mum, if she was half the woman you say she was, she'd forgive you, too. She'd have wanted me to tell you that it wasn't your fault; that you did your best. She'd have wanted you to know there's a future out there that's worth living for, that's worth fighting for."

"I'm trying," he said. "I just don't know how."

"But what if you do?" I replied. "What if, deep down, you've always known? What if you never forgot what happened that night, you just turned away from it? Sometimes you have to look back before you can move forward. So look back, Esso. Look back through your WINDOW."

"Rhia—I've memorized every word in that notebook. It ain't changed a thing."

"Yeah, but there's a difference between knowing it up there in your head"—I stood back, then pressed my hand to his heart—"and feeling it in here."

My words stood taller. "When you fully believe in something, it flows from your heart, soaks into your blood. It makes the unbelievable . . . real."

The moment I finished my sentence, the main window ripped clean off its hinges and went flying through the air. I ducked just in time, turning to see the square dent it left in the wall.

What the—

Another vicious wind soared in, sweeping the radio off his armrest. The one after lifted the sausages out of his meal tray, along with a folder filled with scrap paper, and hurled them into a manic swirl above our heads.

"It was there all along." His voice was an inch above a whisper. And shaking. "My mind just chose to forget it; it had to."

I turned my gaze to his ankles, saw them twitching. Then I looked up to see an unholy whirlwind of objects defying gravity above us. He was causing this.

"But I'm not afraid anymore." He gazed wide-eyed toward the ceiling, reciting from memory the same words I'd just read in his notebook:

"'The WINDOW is a memory from the past or the future. A memory unique to each individual that's often so severe or traumatic that our minds force us to forget it.'"

As he opened his mouth to speak again, the strings of spit lining his lips snapped one by one like cracked jail bars. "The WINDOW is where we see the Upper World." He paused, faced me. "But the why . . . the how . . . that's always been *you*."

I took another step back and watched his eyes widen farther. It was like he was looking through me, through everything, like he was staring into a world beyond.

"There's hail," he continued. "Lightning, bullets." I'd never seen so much pain on his face. I'd never seen him weep.

As he raised his voice, a crack ripped open in the wall, exposing the sparking copper lines running inside it. A sharp buzzing noise came from the power outlets, and without anyone touching the radio on the floor, it turned on and started pacing through the stations.

"Nadia's next to me," he added, "and Devontey's dead." It

was my first time hearing both of my parents' names in the same sentence, as one connected possibility. "We're all about to die."

Everything I was seeing was impossible. But "impossible" was just a word now, a matter of perspective, a trick of relativity.

"'Rhia will tell you,'" he said finally, recounting what Mum had predicted. "You did."

He raised his arms to the sky, and his T-shirt rode up, exposing a stomach lined with long, thick scars. The swirl was moving faster, and the living room became a blizzard of heat and static. I could hear Olivia screaming behind me, trying to drag me away as the feds smashed through the front door. But I couldn't take my eyes off Dr. Esso—his face steadier than a leaf crossing the surface of a placid lake, his eyes beautiful and clear.

32
ESSO (TIME UNDEFINED)

I WAKE UP with one aching knee resting on cracked dirt, the other knee raised forward. A straggly bolt of lightning lands dangerously close by, illuminating a single file of projections behind me and another row in front. I've traded the anarchy of the alleyway for the unruliness of the Upper World. But I don't dare get up. I'm still bleeding out—the agony even more peak now than it was when I lost sight of Katie's. Worse, I still have the memory of the red dot on Nadia's forehead, and the assault rifles trained on Rob and Kato. I can't forget the armed police, the dozen Peckham and T.A.S. boys pointing their guns at each other, or the exploding gunshot ringing in my ear. And in my thoughts, I can still see D lying on the ground dead. Dead, because of what I did, what I failed to do. I have to remember. For them.

Fifteen years have gone since I last ran my feet along the grooves of this sooty ground. But to say I'm glad to be back in the Upper World would be half lying.

I think about Rhia and Olivia, left panicking in my front room. I hope I make it out of here and back to them. But if I can't get through to him first, there'll be nowhere to go back to. In my head, I start to recite all the shit I've learned about time, and most important, energy.

I hear rubble scraping the ground in the distance. Footsteps?

Someone's definitely approaching. And bare-toed. He looks like . . . Nah, that can't be right.

I can hear him coughing on the thick air. I'm close.

Every step he takes forward is lit up by some red light seeping through the cracks in the dirt below. It's almost like there's a molten trail of energy bubbling up inside this place. Following him.

"Are you——?"

"Yeah," I reply. "I'm you. Well, I used to be you, anyway."

I take a deep breath, but can't quite inhale the craziness of what he's telling me. It doesn't help that he's staring past me as he tells me, rather than looking me in the eye. "Prove it," I tell him. "Prove you're me."

"Well, I know you had that weird dream again two days ago." I give him a few seconds to stop me. "You know . . . the one where Nadia's holding the giant ice cubes and wearing those night-vision goggles and——"

"Okay, that's enough. I believe you." I've seen so much madness over my day that my ability to properly doubt is worn-out. "Tell me one thing, though."

"Go on."

"How'd you let my hairline slip that far back, bruv? Your forehead is running tings now." My laugh turns into a cough. Specks of blood dot my hands.

"You don't need to make light of this, Esso." I'd forgotten how much of a dickhead I used to be.

"I know how that knife felt going in. And I know you're scared to die. I know you just left a scene where a bullet's headed for Nadia, and a lot more are aimed at your mates.

"I know, because I remember."

As much as I'm terrified, I feel exhausted. What I'd love most is to just lie down and sleep. But I can still see their faces. Every time I consider letting go, I see them. Still loud in my mind is the clap of Spark's gun, the red mist filling the air around Devontey.

"D?" I ask, voice shaking.

"You can't save him."

"What d'you *mean* I can't save him?"

"The moment he got shot, it's already passed. Not just for me, but for you as well. And you can't change something you've already lived and seen."

"Nah, that's rubbish. We have to try, innit. We can't just let him die."

"I'm sorry. I don't think it's possible to be sorrier than I am.

"Listen—I've done the maths a hundred different ways, and it can't be changed." I keep my voice as steady as possible. Him panicking will only make things worse. "Life, the universe, God—whatever you wanna call it—doesn't let us change the past. It's the only way to prevent the carnage and contradictions we'd cause if we could. I've spent the last 15 years pretending I didn't know that, trying to deny the obvious, so I wouldn't have to face the truth."

I can tell from his sniffling and the breaks in his breathing that he knows I'm right. He's seeing what he's been blind to all day, what only the Upper World can show him: D was never his enemy. "Enemy" is the label we give to someone whose past and future we haven't seen yet, someone whose story hasn't been told. Everyone is better than their worst act. D was redeemable, because in time, we all are.

"You can do something about the present, though," I say down to him. "In fact, you have to or everyone dies. You, our friends, Nadia . . .

"Rhia will never be born. She'll never teach me what I needed to know to get here. It all comes undone unless you go back to your Now and fix it."

I scrape my nails through the rubble, before bringing the dust to my face. As much as I want him to disappear, as much as I want him to be wrong, I know he's here to help me. And I know everything he's saying is true. Even if he'd said nothing, I'd have known. 15 years are meant to separate us, but up here, he's in touching distance.

If I manage to "fix it" like he's demanding, there'll be more time to ask why all this happened, to find meaning, maybe even forgive myself. But for now, all I can do is make sure D's death doesn't lead to more death.

"So, what now?" I ask, dangerously close to vomiting again. "What am I meant to do?"

"Remember in Dad's notebook how he said that what you see in the Upper World reflects the language you understand?"

"Yeah."

"The maths you learned in school, plus the basic sense we all have for how time flows, is what's letting you see your world line in this place. That's also what let you interact with it when you came here after the car crash."

"World line?"

"Everything and everyone leaves a trail in 4-dimensional space-time. That's all a world line is—a trail of moments. Physicists draw them as squiggly lines on a chart. But up here—in this realer reality—your world line is a long line of projections starting from the day you were born and the last one being the moment you die. I'm guessing you can see a section of it behind you."

I wonder why he needs to "guess." The thing is ginormous and it's right there! It gets me questioning why he's still not facing me, and I land on a bleak conclusion.

"You can't see, can you?" He doesn't respond to my question, so I turn around to him and wave my hand. No reaction.

A future without sight. While I'm imagining it, I see a twitch in his face—so faint I wouldn't have noticed if it weren't my own twitch. He's holding something back.

"Listen, we both got here through our WINDOW—that moment when D got shot in the alleyway—a distant memory for me, but a fresh one for you.

"But the two head knocks you got—the car crash, and later, when D hit you—must have cracked our WINDOW open in some way, maybe even enhanced it. Because when you were laid out in that dining hall, you managed to somehow skip through time and tap into the Hidden Energy around you."

"But I can't control it."

"That's because it starts with you believing you can."

"Bro, I'm in an imaginary world right now, and if I'm not dead already, I'm minutes away from bleeding out. Please, please, give me something realer than that."

"You want real?" I step forward until there's no gap left between us.

"Remember when you asked about Pythagoras in class this week, and got called a neek for it?"

"Yeah."

"You remember what Mum said last night?

"'Bout how you'd end up dead . . . just like Dad?"

I don't respond.

I think back to other moments that made us.

"You remember in primary school, when Mrs. Ewu told you you'd be lucky if you ever learned to read? Or that one time in PE, when Mr. Aden told you your options were football, the wing, or the roads? D'you remember getting beaten up on your first day of secondary school, Esso?

And everyone telling you that you couldn't fight?"

"I remember," I say, knowing how long and hard I've tried to forget. "I remember all of it." I press my nose into the dirt.

"And each time, what did you do?"

"Just stop." I clutch my ribs.

"What did you do?!"

"I believed them."

We believed them. We knew no better, and so when they told us it was all true, we believed them. Then it started to define us, started to become real.

He's right. And the moment I accept it, there's a soft rumbling in the ground.

"Believing is seeing, Esso. Without belief, there's no hope. And without hope, there's just an alleyway full of teenagers who'll soon be hashtags on hoodies."

The red light tracing the cracks beneath him shines even brighter. It's like the surface of the sun is peeling away underneath us.

"Rhia helped me believe, and now all the stuff that's meant to be hidden, isn't anymore."

There is no time to explain everything I've learned about energy, but I can tell he already senses it. Believing is seeing, and that might be enough.

"Everything we need to do, everything we need to see and be, we have to start believing in right now. It doesn't mean that life and the laws of physics won't get in our way; it just means we won't be the ones in our way anymore.

"Now, stand up, Esso."

My school shoes are stained with my own blood, and my head is getting lighter by the second. If I'm gonna try, it has to be now. I already have one knee raised. All he's asking me to do is find the strength to push up and drag my trailing leg into place.

"Everything you need to be, you gotta believe right now."

"Come on," I yell to myself through gritted teeth. I smack my thighs a few times, trying to jolt them out of sleep.

But I only make it halfway before cracking down hard on my knees again.

It hurts to hear him grunt and crumble. Then try and fall all over again. But as much as I want to help him, I can't. He has to believe the way I do.

But I can also hear the fear fading from his voice, replaced with the kind of lethal focus I've not heard from myself in years. Rhia was right, I realize as he screams in exhaustion. I did do my best.

After minutes of groaning, I find myself wheezing, huddled over, but standing, finally, on two wobbly feet. "Tell me something." I'm panting between the words. "The future." I take another few seconds to gather breath. "It's worth all of this, right?"

He pauses for what feels like an eternity before answering.

"Yeah," I reply, a surge of heat rising from under my feet. "It's worth you fighting for. And it's worth me living for."

I nod. It's all I need to hear. Looking back at my day, my whole life, it was probably all I'd ever needed to hear.

"Only one of us can go back to that alleyway. And seeing as I can't see shit, and it's your 'now,' it's gotta be you."

He's already baffled enough, and if he survives, he'll forget everything I've said up here. But I have to say it anyway.

"One other thing—when it's your turn, I beg you, go back and help the next kid, yeah?"

"Safe, man. I reckon I can do that."

Lightning splashes light on the projection behind me. I should have flinched from the impact and flash, but I just stand there, staring. It's the image of me lying on the ground in my school uniform, cradling my gut. This is "now" in the world I just left.

I step into it.

When my eyes flutter open, he's gone, and so is everything else. I look up and the sky unfolds above me, spreading out into a sheet decorated with clouds and stars and night, until it engulfs the horizon in every direction. I'm back in the alleyway. Everyone's back. And a bullet is arcing through the air toward Nadia. *Déjà vu*, I think, knowing for the first time everything it means.

The shell is eating up the meters quicker than I can think, so I focus in on it, imagine I'm tugging on whatever it is that connects us. I feel a tension, like an invisible string between my mind and the metal casing.

But it's not budging. Even after a fourth and fifth pull, the bullet keeps running forward. And when I reach out to it with the hand that's not cradling my stomach, a sharp pain cuts across me.

I'm still human, I remember. Still proper close to bleeding out in this alleyway.

A fresh bullet spills forward from the barrel in Spark's hands. And then another from a rifle in the distance, this time aimed at Bloodshed. I think about running into the path of the nearest one, but there's no way I can get in front of it in time, let alone all the others.

There's nothing to hold on to. Nowhere to go. No one to help. There's only one place, I realize, left to look.

So I close my eyes and inhale deeply, giving myself space to think, to feel. Pain floods in with every breath, tearing the wounds farther apart. But I push through it. I have to.

Another two rounds go off—each explosion is an orange flash on the wet side of my eyelids. But this time, I give myself to the light and noise; I absorb the chaos instead of fighting it.

Believing is seeing, I tell myself, still not sure exactly what I'm meant to see.

I squeeze my focus tighter. This is the moment it's all been leading up to. *This.* I'm ready to see. I'm ready to fight.

The answer seeps into my flesh like sun on skin.

"Energy," I whisper.

When I open my eyes, I no longer see metal bullets; I see packets of fire crisscrossing the air, missiles of electric flame. Matter become energy.

I imagine being connected to every joule inside every bullet. I start trusting I can control it all, start believing I will.

I reach both arms forward—I'm not close enough to touch any of the shells, but I squeeze down hard anyway as if I'm wrapping my hands around each one. It burns, the way gripping a dozen hot coals would burn, but I press down harder, firming the waves of heat scalding my wrists.

There's an enormous amount of energy packed into every bullet; I can feel it ready to burst out. If I release it too fast, everything within a square mile goes up in smoke. But if I don't do something quick, the bullets hit their targets.

Just by thinking it, by willing it, I pierce into the bullets, splitting their fiery skins in two, letting heat and red light surge out. Watching it is like staring directly at the sun—15 suns, each only a few meters from my eyes. If I don't turn away now, I'll be blinded. *Just like he was*, I remember. But if I turn away or lose focus for a split second, they'll all die. From the corner of my eye, I see Kato and Rob turning away from the flash. All the others, including the men in SWAT gear, cover their eyes, too.

I'm folding. My fingers and calves cramp under the strain, and my eyes are drenched in crimson flashes. Blind spots start appearing. I go faint and lose my grip on the round heading for Nadia, and like unpausing a video, the bullet speeds up again. I've already converted most of its metal to light, but the remaining pellet would still cut a hole clean through her.

I ignore the pain, refocus, breathe slower. "Don't . . . fuck . . . this up," I cry to myself, pulling on the bullet—now an inch from Nadia's skull. And with everything I have left, I yank my arms back, releasing the final ounce of energy trapped inside, and a hot sphere of electromagnetic light floods the sky.

I'M LYING ON my back, melted hailstones connecting my spine to the concrete. I try to sit up and can't.

Sirens sing in the background, and people are shouting medical things. I grope my stomach to check if the stab wounds are still seeping. They are.

I did it.

I saved everyone I could. No fewer, no more.

The storm clouds have moved on. So has the blinding scarlet light that drowned the atmosphere seconds earlier, and I'm left with a star-specked sky to stare into, knowing that in a few minutes, my vision will get blurry, then spotty, then fade to blindness for the rest of my life. Soon, I'll forget almost everything I saw in the Upper World; the memories will give way to 15 years of static confusion. I'll forget that every moment of my life is still floating up there, waiting to be re-seen, to be relived. I'll forget it was all so worth it and the million reasons why.

But for now, while I remember, I smile.

Q.E.D.

The After-MATH
(Epilogue)

ESSO · (16.5 YEARS LATER)

JUDGING BY THE number of convertibles blasting neo-bashment in traffic, no one was taking the first sunny morning of summer for granted. With Peckham Library behind us, Rhia and I were standing where the alleyway opened up to the main road.

Eight months had passed since the night she and Olivia burst into my house, the night I finally went back to the Upper World. If it hadn't been for Rhia's therapist intervening on my behalf, I'd be in jail eating Pot Noodle out of an electric kettle right now, instead of enjoying a summer walk with Rhia. Anahera thought all the crazy stuff that had happened to us could be easily explained away by psychology and science (she was always careful to use the word "science" instead of "physics," since she didn't want to further "confuse" poor Rhia). Turns out, dissociative amnesia—where a traumatic event makes you forget the memories associated with it—is a surprisingly common medical condition that doesn't require an invisible world to explain. And when Rhia showed Anahera the CCTV foot-age, she responded that bullets go missing from crime scenes all the time, and that a freak power surge can put enough cur-rent through a streetlight to cause permanent eye damage in a grown man. Even Kato—who I'd told about seeing the Can-tor's headphones in the Upper World and who had literally been standing next to me when I bought their stock—doubted I'd ever seen the future. Just like everyone else.

But Rhia and I knew better.

"D'you reckon you'd do things differently if you could?" she asked. "You know . . . if you remembered what you saw each time you went up there and all."

"You know the mad part?" I replied, thinking about the 15 years I'd spent waiting to go back and change things, only to go back and cause what had already happened to happen. "I'm not sure I would."

I'd been so obsessed with getting to the Upper World to fix the past, I'd ignored how strict the rules of physics were, that our universe *was* that unchanging block of space-time Nadia had described.

But as rigid as the past and future might be, both eternities balanced themselves on a single point, a miracle axis we all live in: the present.

The here and now is the only place we're free to tilt our futures, where we can rediscover and remake our pasts. It's the only place I'll ever get to feel the sun's scorching touch . . . and Rhia's surprisingly suffocating hugs. The equations of relativity draw the same arcs whether you run them forward or backward—who's to say the present isn't where both ends of time flow from? Where we both experience and choose our fates? Sometimes we can't move forward till we look back. But when we do, Now is where we find that first step.

Rhia was doing her ting, too. After clearing her GCSEs, she took her Honors Exams a year early and smashed those as well. UCL offered her early admission to their physics program, and apparently, their football team already had an eye on her.

A car approached, carrying a group of men wolf-whistling out the windows.

"Oi! Peng ting!" came one husky echo down the alley. It actually took me a second to realize he was chatting to Rhia. We walked a bit farther in, pretending not to hear.

"Ting!" he shouted after her. "I said you're *PENG!*"

Judging from their laddish accents, they definitely weren't linked to a Bloodshed set (or "Uncle Bloodshed," as Rhia liked calling him for jokes, even though she'd still not managed to meet him). After another round of whistles, the car screeched off, leaving smoky fumes behind for us to choke on.

For the waste sergeants in that car, this was just Saturday-morning banter. I wondered how often Rhia had to deal with that kind of nonsense, and thinking back, how often I'd been the mandem in the car, or the silent pedestrian walking past with his head down.

"You know what?" I said, turning to her. "Don't have it."

"What do you mean?" Her voice was shaky, probably as angry

at me for what I was suggesting as she was at the men driving off. "You want me to run after them? Pick a fight with all four?"

"Nah," I replied. "Do it the other way." While she was considering it, I used my finger to draw an arrow from street level to the sky. "The roof . . . as far up as you can get it. You'll need to hurry up, though."

I heard her skip over to the pavement edge, probably to get a clearer view of the whip.

"I can walk you through the memory again," I offered.

After Rhia's trip to St. Jude's, I'd shared more details about my last meetup with Nadia, and in the process, turned Rhia's faintest and most painful memory into one that shined with love. The way I remembered it, baby Rhia was chillin' happily on the grass when I took the photo of Nadia on that bench. But Nadia had been so anxious about letting her baby go that as soon as I pressed the shutter, she leapt up and grabbed Rhia, smiling as she hummed a sleepy lullaby into her ear.

"Nah, it's light," Rhia replied, as a gust of noisy wind entered the alley. "I got it this time."

"Remember: gravity is an illusion," I said anyway, imagining her already opening her WINDOW. She'd read up about how Einstein—after figuring out space, time, and energy—spent another decade in a hole scribbling equations, then came out realizing we'd been seeing gravity the wrong way round as well. She'd derived the maths herself, even taught me a thing or two about Riemannian manifolds. The next line was all me, though.

"And remember: when an apple breaks from a branch, it doesn't actually fall to the ground—"

"I know, I know," she replied. "The apple stays still. It's the ground that accelerates up to meet it."

There was a harsh groan—twisting metal and the sound of bolts popping out of their sockets. Then came a loud *SNAP!*—the roof tearing clean off the chassis, and finally, the soft whistle of an unidentified car part leaving the atmosphere.

Thanks to Rhia, a roofless Vauxhall was now riding around Peckham, with four terrified dudes screaming inside it. What made it even more hilarious, poetic almost, was that the universe felt like a lighter, breezier place because of it.

We both laughed so hard we had to slump down where the concrete met the brick wall in the alleyway.

"Don't go bussin' up your lungs," Rhia said, after seeing I was still neck-deep in it. "You're all the fam I got right now."

I found myself choking up, and tried to create some distance between us so she wouldn't notice. I was getting softer by the week.

"Anyway, I told you I had something important to tell you," she reminded me.

"Yeah, go on, then." I was still blinking faster than I wanted.

"So, I might have . . . sort of . . . asked an old friend to download Mum's records from a deleted St. Jude's database."

After copping a judging stare from me, she added, "Look, it *is* about Mum, but it's not what you think."

"I don't know, Rhi. I've finally—just about—turned the corner on this whole acceptance thing. Was assuming you were trying to do that, too."

"I am. And I mostly have. I mean, don't get me wrong—I

still wish I had my parents around, the same way I wish the guys who just drove past us weren't all pricks. But I'm not waiting for anyone to come along and fix me anymore. I feel like I'm whole already."

This time I had to take a really deep breath to fight the tears. We couldn't save Nadia and D, but we'd at least managed to save each other.

"So, you wanna know what I found or not?"

"Of course I bloody do."

"Well," she said, taking a long pause. "It turns out Mum kept a notebook while she was there."

"And?"

"And . . . you were definitely right about her not being insane." She took another painful break. "I think it's the Upper World that's madder than we thought." That part didn't surprise me—whenever your circle of knowledge expands, the wall of ignorance that surrounds it does, too.

"And," she added, almost whispering now, "your dad . . . wasn't the only one who knew about it."

APPENDIX I: PYTHAGORAS PROOF

(FROM ESSO ADENON'S SCHOOL NOTEBOOK)

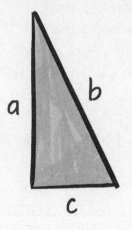

Apparently, Pythagoras took four identical triangles (like the one above) and arranged them on a square white plate—the first time making the pattern on the left (below) and the second time making the pattern on the right.

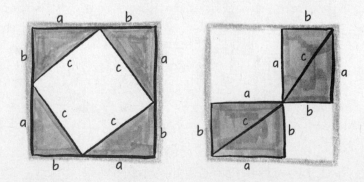

The left plate has got an empty white square in the middle. Since the sides of it have a length of c, the white square has an area of c^2 (since the area of a square is length times width).

But the right plate has <u>two</u> empty white squares on it. Using the same logic as before, we find that the white one at the top has an area of a^2, and the other one has an area of b^2.

Here's the clever bit: In both the left and right arrangements, none of the triangles have changed size and the plate underneath hasn't changed size either. Which means the total uncovered white space must be the same for both patterns . . . which means the combined area of the two white squares on the right must equal the area of the big solo square on the left.

Or in maths speak, $a^2 + b^2 = c^2$.

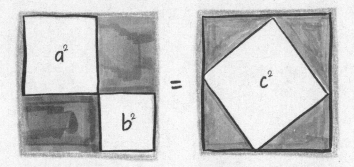

Like a page from God's sketchbook . . .

APPENDIX II: SPEED OF LIGHT DERIVATION
(FROM RHIA'S NOTEBOOK)

Maxwell's equation for calculating speed of
electromagnetic induction:

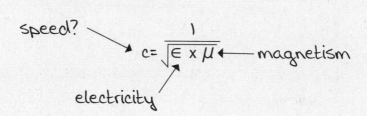

From my textbook, I plug in the numbers for the
two symbols to the right of the equals sign and
get:

$$c = \frac{1}{\sqrt{0.0000012566370\underline{6} \times 0.000000000000885\underline{41878}}}$$

Punching that into my phone calculator gets me:
c = 299,792,458
Or, rounding up...
c = 300,000,000
(the exact speed of light in meters per second)

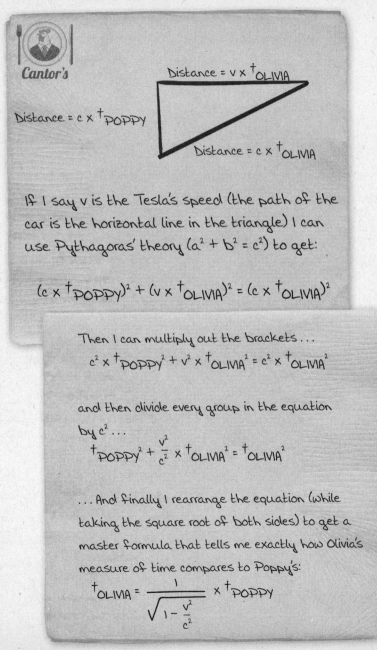

Cantor's

Distance = $v \times t_{OLIVIA}$

Distance = $c \times t_{POPPY}$

Distance = $c \times t_{OLIVIA}$

If I say v is the Tesla's speed (the path of the car is the horizontal line in the triangle) I can use Pythagoras' theory ($a^2 + b^2 = c^2$) to get:

$$(c \times t_{POPPY})^2 + (v \times t_{OLIVIA})^2 = (c \times t_{OLIVIA})^2$$

Then I can multiply out the brackets…

$$c^2 \times t_{POPPY}^2 + v^2 \times t_{OLIVIA}^2 = c^2 \times t_{OLIVIA}^2$$

and then divide every group in the equation by c^2…

$$t_{POPPY}^2 + \frac{v^2}{c^2} \times t_{OLIVIA}^2 = t_{OLIVIA}^2$$

…And finally I rearrange the equation (while taking the square root of both sides) to get a master formula that tells me exactly how Olivia's measure of time compares to Poppy's:

$$t_{OLIVIA} = \frac{1}{\sqrt{1 - \frac{v^2}{c^2}}} \times t_{POPPY}$$

APPENDIX IV:

FROM RHIA BLACK'S SCRAPBOOK

Starting with the same triangle as last time, I get the following equation (using Pythagoras).

$$(cT_{OLIVIA})^2 = (vT_{OLIVIA})^2 + (cT_{POPPY})^2$$

I can also break out the car's speed, v in the equation, into its components across all three dimensions of space (again using Pythagoras).

$$v = \frac{\sqrt{x^2 + y^2 + z^2}}{T_{OLIVIA}}$$

Then substitute this version of v back into the first equation.

$$(cT_{OLIVIA})^2 = \left(\frac{\sqrt{x^2 + y^2 + z^2}}{T_{OLIVIA}}\right)^2 (T_{OLIVIA})^2 + (cT_{POPPY})^2$$

$$(cT_{OLIVIA})^2 = x^2 + y^2 + z^2 + c^2 T_{POPPY}^2$$

If I divide all terms on both sides of the equation by T_{OLIVIA}^2 I then get:

$$c = \sqrt{\left(\frac{x}{T_{OLIVIA}}\right)^2 + \left(\frac{y}{T_{OLIVIA}}\right)^2 + \left(\frac{z}{T_{OLIVIA}}\right)^2 + \left(c\frac{T_{POPPY}}{T_{OLIVIA}}\right)^2}$$

If an object/person is traveling through space at the speed of light, the three gray terms on the left equal c2 (again because of Pythagoras) and the time-travel term on the right is zero (ie, travel through time stops). If an object/person is stationary in space, the three gray terms on the left are equal to zero and the time-travel term on the right is equal to the speed of light.

APPENDIX V:

FROM RHIA BLACK'S CLOUD ACCOUNT

Kinetic energy

$L_{\triangledown} = \int_0^s \text{Force} \times ds$

... Looked up equation for Force, $F = \left(\frac{dp}{dt}\right)$ and threw it here.

$= \int_0^s \left(\frac{dp}{dt}\right) \times ds$

... Then swapped the ds and dp, before fleshing out dp ....

$= \int_0^p \left(\frac{ds}{dt}\right) \times dp$

... momentum is mass times velocity

$p = m \times v\text{-space}$

... and velocity is distance over time

$= m \times \dfrac{distance}{\frac{t}{Esso}}$

... I'll then use the chain rule to expand the equation ...

$= m \times \dfrac{distance}{{}^t Chaperone} \times \dfrac{{}^t Chaperone}{{}^t Esso}$

... so it's in a form where I can substitute in the time-dilation equation that I wrote out on that old Cantor's napkin.

$= m \times \dfrac{distance}{{}^t Chaperone} \times \dfrac{1}{\sqrt{1 - \frac{v\text{-space}^2}{c^2}}}$

$= m \times v\text{-space} \times \dfrac{1}{\sqrt{1 - \frac{v\text{-space}^2}{c^2}}}$

After fleshing out dp, I put it back into the main equation, then updated the integral limits to be in terms of v-space (instead of p). Then took out the m and put it in front of the equation (since it doesn't vary based on speed or any of the other variables) ... I know that ds/dt is equal to velocity, v-space, so made that replacement also.

Kinetic energy

$L_{\triangledown} = \int_0^v \left(\frac{ds}{dt}\right) \times d \left(m \times v\text{-space} \times \dfrac{1}{\sqrt{1 - \frac{v\text{-space}^2}{c^2}}} \right)$

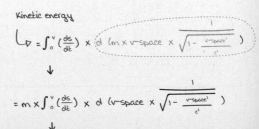

$= m \times \int_0^v \left(\frac{ds}{dt}\right) \times d \left(v\text{-space} \times \sqrt{1 - \frac{v\text{-space}^2}{c^2}} \right)$

Then took out the new bundle in gray
so I could work that out separately...

$\downarrow$

$$= m \times \int_0^{} \text{v-space} \times d \left(\text{v-space} \times \frac{1}{\sqrt{1 - \frac{\text{v-space}^2}{c^2}}} \right)$$

$$d \left(\text{v-space} \times \frac{1}{\sqrt{1 - \frac{\text{v-space}^2}{c^2}}} \right) = \text{v-space} \times d \left(\frac{1}{\sqrt{1 - \frac{\text{v-space}^2}{c^2}}} \right) + d \left(\frac{1}{\sqrt{1 - \frac{\text{v-space}^2}{c^2}}} \right) \times dv$$

I'll use 'differentiation' (calculus) to solve the
equation, then simplify it

$$= \left(\frac{1}{\sqrt{1 - \frac{\text{v-space}^2}{c^2}}} \right)^3 dv$$

After fleshing out the grey bundle,
I put it back into the main equation.
Then used "u-substitute" calculus method
(where $u = 1 - \frac{\text{v-space}^2}{c^2}$) to get the equation
in a form I could solve (...took two days,
but I got it).

... Then I worked out the top limit (v-space
= v-space) and bottom limit (v-space = 0)
of the integral equation...

...to get to this equation, which basically
says kinetic energy equals the total energy
(the complicated term in the middle), minus
the other almost "hidden" form of energy
on RHS of equation, which for some reason
doesn't have v-space at all in it, and is
therefore positive even if the object's not
moving

Taking that thing on the right out on
its own gets me...

Kinetic energy

$$\hookrightarrow \quad = m \times \int_0^{} \text{v-space} \times \left(\frac{1}{\sqrt{1 - \frac{\text{v-space}^2}{c^2}}} \right)^3 dv$$

$\downarrow$

$$= m \times c^2 \times \frac{1}{\sqrt{1 - \frac{\text{v-space}^2}{c^2}}} \Big|_0^v$$

Kinetic energy

$$\hookrightarrow \quad = \frac{1}{\sqrt{1 - \frac{\text{v-space}^2}{c^2}}} mc^2 - mc^2$$

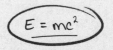

$$E = mc^2$$

(The formula for Hidden Energy)

ACKNOWLEDGMENTS

Thank you, **Afkera**—my soulmate, homie, and (not so) secret weapon. Thanks, **Mum** and **Dad**, for the love and imagination that allowed me and this story to exist. Cheers, **Jumy**, **Modupeola**, **Bose**, and **Femi B**—the Greatest Siblings in the World™. Thanks also to my wider fam: the **Unstoppable Adepojus**, the **Unmatchable Falades** and the **Everlasting Emiolas** (special thanks for the roof, **Aunty Tayo**, and "boardroom" chats, **Tosin**). Thanks, **John**, my earliest and most unexpected physics teacher.

Hold tight **Abim**, **Sam**, **Bishup**, **Kate**, **Jasmine**, **Ella**, **Loquacity**, and **C.S.** for helping to make this dream real. And to all my early reviewers—**Kura**, **Viki**, **Matt**, **Tunuka**, **Pete**, **Kwasi**, **Linda**, and **Tobi**—your time and wisdom made a difference.

Love to my MEF team (**Denice** and **Asmeret**) for steering this ship beautifully. Thanks to my peerless agent, **Claire** (for being Claire); the **Penguin Random House UK** and **HarperCollins US** teams for taking a bet on me; and my sick trio of editors—**Emma**, **Stephanie**, and **Asmaa**—for getting this thing right on both sides of the pond.

Tom, **Weruche**, **James**, and **Lazzro**—you guys dripped all over the audiobook. I praise God for your drip. And love to **Daniel**, **Eric**, **Tendo**, and **Michelle** for giving this story a second life off the page.